Wakefield Press

# Troop Train

Elizabeth Hutchins, former teacher and executive officer of the Australian Association for the Teaching of English, is author of a dozen books, as well as prize-winning travel and environmental articles and many short stories. She lives in Adelaide with her husband and her constant companion Millie, an RSPCA rescue cat.

This moving and uplifting family saga was inspired by the stories of those who lived through the war in the Adelaide Hills. It is based on well-known author Elizabeth Hutchins' careful research studying newspaper articles, books, memoirs and historical collections – and talking to those who were there.

# Troop Train

### Elizabeth Hutchins

**Wakefield
Press**

Wakefield Press
16 Rose Street
Mile End
South Australia 5031
www.wakefieldpress.com.au

First published 2021

Cover designed by Stacey Zass
Edited by Julia Beaven, Wakefield Press
Typeset by Michael Deves, Wakefield Press

ISBN 978 1 74305 854 1

A catalogue record for this
book is available from the
National Library of Australia

Wakefield Press thanks
Coriole Vineyards for
continued support

*Our women shall walk in honour*
*Our children shall know no chain,*
*This land that is ours forever*
*The invader shall strike at in vain ...*

*And we swear by the dead who bore us,*
*By the heroes who blazed the trail,*
*No foe shall gather our harvest,*
*Or sit on our stockyard rail.*

From 'No Foe Shall Gather Our Harvest'
Mary Gilmore, 1940

# I

Today we hung heavy black curtains at every window. Now we can hide like mice in a hole.

That's a better start! I've already torn the first two pages out, because everything I started writing sounded so boring. 'My grandmother has given me this diary.' It's a pity the flyleaf came loose too, because Grandma has such perfect handwriting, and I loved her message. I must stick it back in:

*With love to Rosemary*
*on your fourteenth birthday,*
*15.2.1942.*

*May all your stories have happy endings.*

So here begins my story – a not-so-happy beginning. It's been a bad week because a few days ago came the news that the Japanese have overrun Singapore, and we know that's where Father's ship was heading. It should have reached there a week or so ago. To think Heather and I were quite excited when he finished his leave, with our whole Lister family waving him off at the station as if he was going on a holiday. (Except for Mother, who was wiping away tears.) We just managed to push through the throng of troops brandishing slouch hats, and families with fluttering handkerchiefs or flags, to get close to his window as the train pulled out.

'I'll bring you home some Chinese silk to make evening dresses,' he shouted.

Heather screamed back, 'Make mine pink with gold thread!' He wouldn't have heard me call out that I'd rather have blue – cobalt blue – with silver embroidery. I can't imagine anyone else in Adelaide having a ball gown as beautiful as the night sky. When I'm old enough to go to balls, of course.

Now we don't know if Father is alive or dead, still fighting or a prisoner.

My insides have been all twisted up ever since I heard about Singapore. We've been glued to the wireless day and night, desperate to hear any mention of the Eighth Division – Father's a Lieutenant in the 2/15th Field Regiment – but of course the public are never told any real details. Security is so tight that we weren't even told the name of the ship his unit went on, but we did hear that from Singapore they were going up to Malaya. All we can do is pray that he is all right.

Even though we know Father is there, the war has been dream-like until now, something that's happening to other people – almost an adventure story. We were warned when Australia declared war on Japan before Christmas that this was the gravest hour of our history, but Singapore and Malaya still seemed worlds away, especially from here down south.

As for Hitler and the struggle for Europe and Africa, Australia has been so remote from it over the last couple of years. The only times I've been knocked right off my feet by the reality of war were when someone I knew died. First we were all heartbroken when Uncle Brian, Mother's brother-in-law, was killed in the Middle East. Then last November my best friend Janet's cousin Terrence went down with the HMAS *Sydney* when it was sunk by the German raider *Kormoran* off Western Australia. Everyone was terribly upset about that disaster, as the *Sydney* was our most famous warship. It's so hard to believe that 645 men could disappear without trace. The wreck still hasn't been located. Before Terry left he gave Janet a silver serviette ring with the ship's badge on it, and when she brought it to school I cried over it, even though I'd only met him once.

Last night the war leapt a whole lot closer. This is today's headline: DARWIN BOMBED. The mainland of Australia has never come under enemy attack before! The Prime Minister was right when he told us that the fall of Singapore opens the Battle of Australia.

I never thought I'd be interested in wars or politics. We're not that sort of family – normally.

Anyway, with these developments, I listened and took in all I could when Mother and I walked to Mr Forbes the draper's round at the Dulwich shops for a bolt of heavy black lining material this morning. I don't often tag along with her like a six-year-old, but somehow I needed company today. And it did lift our spirits, joining in with the jokes and banter.

We grabbed the last bolt of the black serge then lined up to pay, watching Mrs Marryat who moved in two doors away a few weeks ago. The family has come down from Darwin. Mrs Marryat was scrapping with our shared neighbour, haughty old Miss Browning, each snatching at the next best thing to block out the light – a length of dark brown woollen dress material. Miss Browning won the war of words as well as the tussle, naturally, and poor Mrs Marryat trudged off with Billy and Alec in tow and little Betty in her pusher, to get some brown paper that she could paint black on one side. I'll bet the boys will be pestering to help her! Perhaps I'll go and give her a hand tomorrow after church; I've been doing a few things for her since our family met hers there, because she doesn't always seem to manage very well, and sometimes I'm at a loose end.

It was while we were waiting to be served that I got the idea that we will be like mice in holes. Though an unsuspecting mouse has one advantage: it doesn't know the cat is about to pounce.

*Rosemary's come with me today, Les. It'll take her mind off things, mine too.*

Sylvia Lister shifted her weight from one foot to the other as the queue inched forward. Sighing, she resumed the one-sided conversation to her absent husband that she carried on almost constantly in her head.

*We waste so much time because of this war, doing useless things while you are up there fighting for our freedom. Standing in queues to see officials or buy essential goods. Mending old clothes, growing all our vegies like we did in the Depression. Lucky you dug the air-raid shelter in the fowl yard last time you were home, or we'd be doing that too. Although soon …*

Beside her, Rosemary seemed to be lost in a daydream. Was the girl thinking of her missing father? If so, she said little. The only signs that the current situation was affecting her were that she niggled her older sister even more than usual, and could often be found scrounging every scrap of war news from the paper.

*It's usually hard to know what she's thinking. She's deeper than Heather, that one, isn't she, Les? And clever like you. Always hiding away with a book, or busy writing something. I forgot to tell you she had to give up her penfriends in England and France, because the Government thinks it's a danger to national security to have children writing overseas. I ask you! So now she's started pouring her heart out into the great doorstep of a diary that my mum gave her*

*for her birthday. Good present. Take her ten years to fill it,
I reckon!*

As Sylvia finally reached the counter to pay, the chatter all round her was starting to filter into her consciousness. She finished quickly:

*Anyway, Les, I'm dreading having to tell her of my big decision, but I know I can't put it off for much longer.*

Outside, Mr Harrison was wobbling down the street on his ancient pushbike, as he did every morning. You could set your clock by him. He was heading to the butcher's, followed by his scruffy brindled bitzer dog, to get a chop or a sausage for his tea and a bone for old Rover. Mr Clay the baker sometimes gave him yesterday's bread too. Living alone, he obviously hadn't caught up with the latest news, because today he stopped to see what had brought this little crowd together.

One of his neighbours explained the new blackout law to him in a patronising tone: 'The Government says there's to be no lights seen from the houses, and hardly any street lamps lit, you understand.'

Her companion added, 'They'll cover the signposts too, and we're supposed to tear up our maps. Mustn't let those Japs get an idea of the layout of the city.'

Mr Forbes had popped his head out to greet his old mate. Deftly tying Sylvia's brown paper parcel with string, he imitated the women's tones: 'You'll have to get a hood over your bike light if you go out at night you know, Harry,' he joked.

'Reckon I'll make it 'ome before dark if I 'urry,' the old man replied with a gap-toothed grin. 'Though I might get lost. I'll be just as befuddled as the enemy, without street names!'

Mr Forbes kept the good mood going as he produced a loop with a final flourish and handed Sylvia's purchase to Rosemary. 'If a Japanese pilot looked down and saw a pitiful specimen like you, Harry, he'd think this place wasn't worth capturing.'

'Might want me dog though. They reckon the Japs eat dogs and cats,' was Mr Harrison's reply. And while those round him shuddered and exchanged looks (was he *serious?*) he gathered the folds of the frayed grey gabardine coat that he wore in all weathers, revealing skinny, white legs and knobbly knees where his khaki shorts ended, and creakily remounted his bike. After hanging his tatty string bag on a handlebar he steadied himself, pedalling off with surprising strength.

By now the queue of perspiring women, some waving makeshift fans, extended out on to the footpath. A group of neighbours moved on from their inevitable grumblings about the weather ('Nearly as bad as the '39 heatwave, don't you think, Connie?') to discuss digging air-raid shelters in their backyards, and burying their jewellery or silver and crystal. Miss Browning stalked off without a word of farewell as a large woman announced in a belligerent tone, 'If they want to get my money, they'll have to get me first.'

'Where are you going to hide it?' asked Rosemary.

Her smile exposed the gums of her dentures as she patted her buxom chest. 'In my corset, dear,' she said.

*SATURDAY 21 FEBRUARY CONTINUED*
Back to those curtains. Grandma, Mother, Heather and I measured and cut, with some laughter and the occasional exasperated sigh as we got all tangled up in swathes of the cheap, scratchy cloth. A melancholic business (today's new word) – reminded me of when Mother made us black frocks years ago for Grandpa Lister's funeral. Thank goodness serious mourning clothes are going out of fashion, for children at least.

Next we took turns sewing the long seams on our new Singer. I've been doing straight seams on things such as tea towels since I was eight, and now that we have pensioned off the old treadle machine I zip along at a great rate. With the room getting stuffier by the hour, I was glad when the phone rang as I brought in glasses of lemon cordial and some meringues for everyone. But since it was Aunty Joyce the doldrums set in immediately. Aunty Joyce has that effect on us.

I suppose you can't blame poor Aunty for being so bitter and panicky. Uncle Brian died fighting in Libya in the North African desert in August last year. He had rushed in to enlist the minute the upper age limit was raised from thirty to forty – that's what Father did too – then headed off from Perth straight after his training finished. He survived the whole long five-month siege defending a place called Tobruk, only to be killed just as the very last Australian troops were withdrawing. Aunty is burning up with resentment that he could leave her and the boys the way he did. Since then she has been struggling to look after their farm in the Hills, as well as bringing up Johnny and Bob on her own.

All I could hear from our end was my mother tut-tutting: 'Now, Joyce, you mustn't overreact. Getting in a tizzy won't help, you know.' Then, after a silence she added, 'Never mind; you'll have more help soon.' Don't you hate hearing one side of a conversation?

Must ask what help she meant.

After she had hung up Mother muttered something about how morose her sister was, but obviously wasn't going to say more, at least not while I was there. There were questioning looks followed by sideways glances at me, so I obligingly left the room, and then – naturally – lingered behind the door to listen. 'Poor Joyce is nearly out of her mind. She says if we're invaded she'll put her own children to sleep before she lets the enemy get to them!' I heard Mother exclaim in horror. I felt my skin go all prickly. Then, when a floorboard creaked near the door, I ducked into the bathroom.

On my return they were fitting the first curtain, which is where I started my tale of this awful war. Of course, the blackout curtains only have to be drawn at dusk, but we needed to try them out. We peered at each other through the deep gloom in the sitting room after we hung them on top of the lovely old ivory nets whose hems are weighted down with gold beads. Spooky!

When Grandma murmured, 'The Prime Minister was right; this is our darkest hour,' I had to stifle a giggle. She was talking about Australia being at war of course, while here we were literally experiencing darkness in the middle of a glaring February heatwave. She must have mistaken my gurgle for a sob, because she put her arm around me and patted my shoulder.

'I'm sorry; I shouldn't be so pessimistic, my dears. Mr Curtin isn't. He says Darwin has been bombed but not conquered.'

Heather sighed dramatically and said that in the right company this could be quite romantic. Typical of my big sister; she's been out with a few boringly polite and mostly nervous-looking boys, but now she's eighteen she's just waiting to be swept off her feet by someone (tall, dark and handsome, naturally). Then my mother brought us back to reality. She said that it might be funny if it wasn't so serious. If we weren't practically looking into the barrels of enemy rifles.

We were all quiet for a minute; Mother had put the fear we felt into words at last.

It was Heather who broke the silence. 'That was *so* claustrophobic!' she exclaimed when daylight flooded the room again; and Grandma was impressed that she has such a big vocabulary. I think Heather is Grandma's favourite.

# 2

Sylvia wiped her floury hands on her apron. She had steeled herself to tell Rosemary about the family's plans that afternoon. To that end she would have a batch of rock buns just about ready to come out of the oven at 4.10 – strategically timed to keep the two of them chatting in the kitchen. But ten minutes later her younger daughter bounced in from school in such a light-hearted mood that she held off once again. Apparently a new security code for schools had been drawn up, and Rosemary was laughing about the air-raid drill they had just had. She spoke as if it was fun when, with the siren blaring endlessly, all the classes had to take turns sprinting to the big trench along the end of the oval and crouching down in it; and some elderly teacher had tripped on the edge and fallen in, arms and legs flailing. Sometimes Rosemary was such a child still. Why, the day before she had even been playing games with the little children in the corner house, all of them parading round in their gas masks, and wearing their yellow blood group discs like necklaces, instead of tucking the ribbons in under their singlets.

Perhaps all that was just bravado though. You never knew with teenagers, did you? The next second her daughter was talking seriously about how things had changed. 'You know, last year our teachers did everything they could to keep us from worrying about the war. Miss James gave one of her long talks at assembly, all about how much Australians have to be grateful for. Like people who hadn't had jobs through all the Depression years finding work in factories in the last year or so, or joining the Army.'

'Nice to hear that the war has a good side then,' Sylvia replied. The sarcasm was lost on Rosemary.

'Yes, Heather has done well out of it too. Look how she was taken from her job and sent to an essential service. She only used to get fifteen shillings a week as an office junior.' Sylvia smiled.

*Well that's about the only benefit I can see for any of us, Les.*

*Trust a youngster to look on the bright side.*

'And Miss James said there were men who had tramped the country for years and years through the Depression. Families living in shacks or caves in the riverbanks too, who had homes now, thanks to the war. Home's such a nice word, isn't it?' Rosemary's hand traced an arc round the unpretentious kitchen, from food safe to bread crock. 'Like a nest.'

'Mmm,' Sylvia mumbled distractedly.

*I can't put it off any longer, Les. She has to know.*

Her stomach lurched.

'But now,' Rosemary stuffed down the last of her rock bun, 'we could be hounded out of our homes by an invader. How can human beings *do* such terrible things to each other?'

'Yes, well – you'd better go and get your homework done. I want us all to have a good talk when Heather gets home. She's working till six.'

MONDAY 23 FEBRUARY

Mother has just announced that we're having a family meeting after tea. She looked serious, and that set me churning inside again. Wonder what it's all about?

I keep trying to sound cheerful, which means that I gabble on too much. But half the time she doesn't even seem to hear me.

I suppose I should try to learn my Latin vocabulary while I wait. As the first person in my family ever to learn foreign languages, I want to be good at them. I like Latin because I'm interested in words and where they came from. Same as Father. Last year I started to learn French and German, but the French mistress enlisted, along with a dozen other teachers, and everyone was so suspicious of Germans – even ones who were born here – that poor Herr Schneider lost his job. There's a rumour he's been interned as an alien. Then they sent a Latin teacher, who is just a student teacher helping out. She says, 'You should learn as much as you can while you have the chance – you know what language we'll all have to learn if Australia is conquered.' It won't be Latin! But did she have to make me feel quite queasy?

When Rosemary marched into the kitchen with a scowl, her mother whispered, 'Give me strength, Les,' while she went on draining water from the tray of the icebox. Sylvia talked inside her head the way people talk to God. She was reserving her opinion about God though; relations with Him would probably only be resumed if Les came home safely.

Rosemary's hostile gaze switched to Heather, who was toying with the plate of sloppy Irish stew and greyish cabbage that had just been put in front of her. Then on to Grandma, fiddling with teacups at the other end of the table. 'Well?' she questioned. 'What do we have to talk about?'

Her overture was ignored. Heather got up to close the window, since the gully wind that had sprung up was making the blackout curtain billow into the room. Grandma offered the girls a cup of tea. Rosemary waved Grandma's hand away from the pot impatiently. 'Come on! You all know something that I don't. So what is it?'

Everyone looked at Sylvia, who wiped her hands on her apron, sat down and took a deep breath. 'Um – there's no easy way to tell you this, Rosemary. You and I are going up to the farm to live – just while the war lasts – to help your Aunty Joyce.'

The blood was draining from Rosemary's face as the first shock wave washed over her. 'No, not me!' she gasped. 'You go if you like; I'm staying here with Grandma.'

'I'm afraid you can't stay here. We're going to let the house. Grandma –'

'*Let* it!' Rosemary almost screeched. 'Who to?'

('To whom!' Heather mouthed primly.)

'Oh, there'll be a growing family that needs a bigger place.' The speech that Sylvia had been rehearsing was evaporating – a mist blown away by her younger daughter's hot words. She tried again, speaking more strongly. 'Grandma is going up north to live with Uncle Keith and his family at Whyalla. She'll help look after your other cousins so that Aunty Nell can get a job at the shipyard canteen.'

Rosemary turned to her sister suspiciously. 'And what about you, Heather?'

Heather gave her that calm mouth-closed smile that never failed to infuriate her. 'I'm moving into a boarding house. It's over Kilburn way – so that I can walk to work. I'll be sharing with Violet.'

When Rosemary stared at her, open-mouthed, she added, 'We're best friends. We'll look after each other.'

'With *Violet!* You can't be serious! That's *not fair!*' spluttered Rosemary, anger fast replacing shock.

Sylvia tried to placate her. 'Violet's parents will keep a good eye on them both, and I'm told the landlady's very strict. They won't be allowed to carry on with any nonsense.'

'Then I could board with them too.'

Sylvia and Grandma told her then, in their different ways but both in firm tones, that she had no choice. She was too young. Going to help on the farm was her contribution to the war effort. If they didn't come and lend a hand, Joyce would have to sell up. And how else would our troops be fed if the farms didn't keep producing? Didn't she want to help save her country from invasion – so that it would be a free land for her father to return to?

Since she had no answer to this barrage of blackmail, Rosemary gathered herself up with a shrug, glared at her sister who was sitting there so complacently, and ran from the room before they could see the tears welling in her eyes.

*LATER*
*Catastrophe!!!* It was worse news than I ever imagined. We're leaving Adelaide and going to the country to live, until the war is over, or Father comes home.

Mother and I are going to move in with Aunty Joyce and the little boys – brats – on her farm in the Hills, up Nairne way, to help run it. Imagine us as farmhands! Poor Grandma has to go and live in Whyalla with Uncle Keith and Aunty Nell. It's the end of the earth up there, and I'll be lucky to see her once a year.

And Grown Up Heather gets to board with her best friend Violet, where she'll be closer to the Islington Railway Works. She's so uppity about the importance of helping make parts for Beaufort bombers. She and Violet will be able to kick up their heels and go to dances and parties! All the girls are dying to meet American soldiers when they are in camp here; you should have seen the goofy look on Heather's face in town the other day when one asked her where the City Hall was.

That Violet is frivolous and unreliable, with no ambition except to have a good time. She's everything that Heather isn't: dark, pretty and vivacious, with sparkling blue eyes and a cheeky smile. She'll be such a bad influence on Heather. Though, come to think of it, she might wake up my steady, stuffy sister. Even so, it's unfair.

Everyone knew some of this except me, of course. And naturally, no one consulted me, did they? My head's spinning with questions I didn't think to ask.

Which school will I go to?

If it's a school in the Hills, how often can I come down to town to see my friends?

Will I still be able to play netball?

Where will I get library books?

I forgot to say it's a dairy farm. No one in the world works harder than dairy farmers. All that cow dung ... And the only time I tried to milk a cow, it swished its tail in my face and half blinded me.

Too tired to write any more. Upset, I mean.

# 3

*TUESDAY 24 FEBRUARY*

All evening my memories kept taking flight from whatever I was doing, only to crash land in a soggy paddock on Aunty Joyce's farm. Ugh! All those great lumbering cows to be milked morning and night – then in the hours between there are a thousand chores to be done. I know; I've stayed up there for 'holidays'.

I cried myself to sleep last night, thinking about leaving this house, which is crammed with reminders of when we were a real family, complete with a father. Now there's just a bunch of narky women who preach at me.

When I sat down in class this morning it struck me how much I'm going to miss my friends and school. Even teachers like Mrs Pearson, who has come back from retirement. Every woman who doesn't have young children and isn't too old is expected to try to get a job. Mrs P. is short-sighted, dithery and hopeless at controlling us. But I discovered today that she has a kind side.

In Algebra I shut out the racket and found myself listing some of the things I'm so used to doing, like going to Saturday matinees down the street at the Melba. (Heather and I saw Judy Garland and Mickey Rooney in *Babes on Broadway* last week). Or coming home from the beach on a stinking hot summer's night, and sleeping on the front lawn till the mozzies drove us inside or we were woken by the milkman's horse and cart. Even calling in to Mrs Martin's little shop for a twopenny ice cream on the way home from school on pocket money day. What if I'm grown up when we get back and I never get to do any of those things again?

Then there were birthday treats … I sighed and must have smiled.

'I asked you what $x$ minus twenty-seven times three equals. Are you going to share your thoughts with us, girl?'

Suddenly I was back in algebra lesson, with every head turned in my direction. Red-faced, I stuttered something. Someone giggled, but fortunately the recess bell put an end to my embarrassment. Everyone piled noisily out of the room.

'So,' Mrs Pearson still hovered over my desk, 'why did you sigh so contentedly?'

'I was remembering my birthday – it was on the fourteenth,' I told her. 'My mother always takes me to the Quality Inn for afternoon tea on my birthday; it's a family tradition.' I tried to explain how special and grown up the outing always made me feel, even if I still liked sucking up raspberry malted milks, not sipping tea. Oh, and squashing cream puffs so they squirted. To my surprise Mrs Pearson's face lit up as she recalled the downstairs café with its starched tablecloths and vases of real flowers.

'There's even a pianist playing in the background,' I agreed. Then she sent me out to recess, after smiling rather sadly and thanking me for sharing my happiness. I nearly told her that I'm far from happy. Angry too. But I couldn't get the words out. I suppose we all have something to be sad or angry about, with our lives so threatened.

Out in the yard my friends were standing round, some of them knitting Army socks while they chatted. As usual they had placed themselves near the boys' school fence. You never know who might have his eye on you … Janet left them to bail me up. She was amazed that I could dream my way through one of Mrs P's shambolic lessons. But I can't face telling anyone yet that I'm leaving. I might cry again. So I couldn't explain to Janet why I'm acting so strangely.

I don't even want to think what it will be like sharing Aunty Joyce's big old farmhouse. We won't be going for a week or two yet, but Mother is already talking about what we will take and which parts of our lives will have to be packed up in boxes and stored in our friend Mr Bolton's shed till we get back. She's refusing to answer my question about school. 'We'll see. I'm making enquiries,' is all she will say.

Sometimes I want to throttle her.

It was a relief that after her initial outburst Rosemary had taken the news so well, Sylvia mused. Children were so adaptable. Although a good shouting and kicking session might have been better for her than bottling it all up.

*She spends half her waking hours scribbling away in that new diary of hers, Les. I'm not sure now whether Martha should have given her that. Though she says she's writing it so that she'll remember things to tell you when you come back. I suppose you'd approve of that, wouldn't you?*

The girl had become far too serious. She was scouring the daily paper even more thoroughly than before, too; even cutting out articles at times. And still hovering around the wireless whenever they turned it on. The whole country was puzzled by the fact that no news at all was coming out of Singapore – only they had to get used to that. Some wives or mothers went into the Red Cross every day without fail, but there was nothing to find out. Secrecy was part and parcel of war, or so all the old folk who had lived through the Great War said.

There hadn't been much war news from anywhere in the last few days, just a brief report that another enemy plane was seen flying over Darwin. And now tonight as the four of them gathered in the sitting room to listen, heads bent over their mending, knitting or hemming, Prime Minister Curtin was reminding Australians that their country had been struck 'a severe blow' because with the bombing of the north, nowhere was safe. 'We too, in every other city, can face these assaults,' he said, adding that they must act gallantly, and face this onset with fortitude. It was their duty to fight grimly and victoriously.

All the needles were still as the four cast sideways glances, each waiting for the others to react. Sylvia got up and switched the wireless off.

*We're all wondering if you're fighting grimly up there in*
*Singapore, Les. Personally, I reckon you'd never give in.*

'"Facing this onset." Sounds a bit like the way Father talked to his football team when he was coaching the Norwood Under 15s,' Heather ventured at last, with a nervous titter.

'We can't all fight,' said Grandma, 'but each of us is doing our bit for the war effort. Even Rosemary, with her knitting.'

'That's charitable of you,' Rosemary forced a grin as she waved the lopsided sock she was trying to knit for some unlucky soldier. She was exceptionally bad at knitting, being left-handed.

Heather said, 'You should stop at one sock, and send it for a one-legged soldier.' Sylvia reprimanded her for making a joke in very poor taste and Grandma tut-tutted, but Rosemary, still feeling shaken by this latest reminder of their situation, could only give her sister a filthy look.

They went on to talk about more important matters, like why the Japanese were setting their sights on Australia. It was all about Japan wanting to control the oil supplies, Sylvia tried to explain; but, as usually happened in these discussions, the details were beyond them all.

'Well,' Grandma summed up, 'since we can't understand where the world is going, we may as well keep working at little things that can make a difference.'

'Like misshapen socks,' agreed Heather.

Rosemary had the last word before flouncing out of the room. 'Then we can all pretend that life is going on as usual – even if *our* lives are about to be turned upside down.'

# 4

The war situation sounds more serious than ever, yet I seem to be the only one in my family who really feels the gravity of it. I wish I could scream and throw a chair or two around. (But I couldn't bear Grandma's disappointed look.) You should have seen them all sitting calmly round the wireless last night while Mr Curtin talked about remembering that we are Australians, whatever the future holds, and about fighting to the death. Heather even made a bad joke.

Father's friend Councillor Bolton, who has been helping us a lot since we've been on our own, has found a family with five young children to rent our house. We'll be leaving on Monday week, the ninth. My Uncle Keith has managed to borrow a small truck, and all the family have saved up their petrol coupons so that he can take Mother and me and our mountain of possessions up to Aunty Joyce's. Not the furniture though. Then he will load up Grandma's belongings, even her precious ornaments, and head back to Whyalla with her. Heather has been taking a case of her stuff to Violet's on a tram followed by a train every few days, ready for the move to the boarding house. You wouldn't believe how many clothes she has! Of course, I mainly get her hand-me-downs, a few of which have been flung my way this week, along with some junky jewellery. Mother says I'd better scrounge all I can, since there's a new regulation prohibiting the manufacture of luxury goods – unless I happen to want a wedding ring. Very funny.

I'm going to miss Grandma so much. Everyone says I mustn't be selfish, and that it's my cousins' turn to see something of her. But I know where Grandma would prefer to live, and it seems a shame she has to be uprooted again at her age. She's had to go from one family to another ever since Grandpa died and his house was sold to pay for his funeral and his debts.

Uprooted … That's how I felt this afternoon when Mr Bolton came round to help Mother draw up a lease agreement. He's a great organiser, and said it was a pity I couldn't be one of a thousand local 'runners' that he's recruiting for the Emergency Communications people. He needs boys and girls from fourteen to eighteen in our Burnside area who will be summoned to take messages to the community on bicycles if telephones and public transport are put out of action. They will be trusted to use their initiative – to get the message through to someone, and see that it is acted on. I'd love to do that! I felt so disappointed.

*LATER*

I was wrong in thinking no one else feels as concerned about the war as I do. Tonight I asked Grandma why we're taking so many precautions right down here in almost the very south of the country. After all, we're about two thousand miles from the north coast that has been bombed.

She simply said, 'Because we're afraid.'

'Afraid,' I repeated stupidly.

So she explained. 'You see, if the Japanese invade the North, they won't head across the desert to the bigger cities – they'll just march to the railhead and take trains straight down to Adelaide.'

Sylvia was cradling a secret, for, anxious as she was about her missing husband, she wasn't dreading this move back to the country life of her childhood at all. On the contrary, she was looking forward to it. It was a feeling that wouldn't go away and one that she wasn't sharing, even with Les.

The house was so quiet tonight that Sylvia found it almost unnerving. Heather was out saying goodbye to some old school-friends and would be brought home by an obliging father, while Rosemary and her grandmother had huddled over cups of cocoa on the back verandah, talking about goodness knows what, before both headed to their bedrooms at about eight.

The battered photo album that surfaced as she packed up the jumble in the bottom of her wardrobe had taken Sylvia back in one leap to her carefree teenage years in the little river town where her father had helped build the first lock on the Murray. Picnics on the riverbank, her old dog Patch, childhood friends, socials in the church hall – and Ted. Young as she was, she and her first boyfriend had made plans to buy land downstream, a fruit orchard perhaps; but the Great War meant their dreams would never come to anything. Ted had been gripped by the frenzied fervour to serve King and country (the chance for adventure too), and everyone knew the result of that. Sixty thousand young men dead and over 150,000 wounded.

She shook herself, straightened her shoulders and jammed down the lid of the suitcase.

*FRIDAY 27 FEBRUARY*

Today I told my class that I'll be leaving in a week, and they were all very sympathetic, though one or two couldn't help teasing me by saying, 'Oooh! You'll fall in love with the first boy you see up there and end up a farmer's wife.' Not worth a reply.

I still don't know which school I'll be going to, but I'm sure I'll hate it. I'm counting off the days with dread, not excitement, and trying to imprint the details of my everyday life in my memory. For instance, tomorrow I'm going to the pictures for the last time with Janet and a few other friends. I'm not sure what we're going to see. We wanted to see *Affectionately Yours* at the Regent in town. Merle Oberon and Rita Hayworth are in that. But when Mother saw the advertisement for it in the paper that said 'He had to choose between these lovely wildcats', she got cross and said that I was too young for such trashy romances. I'll bet Heather will go to it – probably hanging on to the arm of a dashing soldier.

The next day I will take Billy and Alec to Sunday school for Mrs Marryat, just as I used to be taken by Heather. The boys love splashing in puddles or dragging their feet through the dust on the way. Not me; I used to try so hard to keep my black patent-leather shoes dry and shiny, or my white sandals and socks from getting dusty. Oh dear, I am getting nostalgic again. I'm even remembering my frilly blue organdie party dress with the puffed sleeves and Peter Pan collar. 'Snap out of it!' I say to myself.

Mother's calling me. 'Rosemary, I need to talk to you.' She's sounding serious. Not bad news about Father, I hope.

'I'm sorry Rosemary – I'm doing my best for you, and I've looked into all the possibilities, but there is just no way to get you to town to school each day.'

'So, where will I go?'

'Nowhere. Unless you're prepared to do Grade Seven again and go to the local school with Johnny and Bob.'

Rosemary stared at her in disbelief for a second, before exploding. 'As if I'd do that! I'm a *high* school student!'

'They might let you be a monitor, if they still have them – Aunty Florence did that once – and then a junior teacher.'

'A century ago. *I* know! I can go to boarding school.'

Sylvia gave a wry smile. 'If you knew how little we're surviving on. And Aunty Joyce has even less, now that she's a widow.'

'Well, I'll get the train. They go past the end paddock at the farm, you know. There's that old siding. I can – '

'We can't rely on trains for civilian travel any more. You know that. The lines are filled with troop trains taking people off to war, and bringing them home on leave. Or wounded.' She added a bit about petrol rationing, about needing Rosemary's help on the farm.

'Anyway, you've reached school leaving age now that you're fourteen, so *that's that*,' she finished. Better to be brutal and cut off Rosemary's last lines of appeal.

*I know I sounded harsh, Les, but the sooner the child accepts the facts the sooner she'll get over her disappointment. And I think it worked, because she just looked at me blankly and she's gone quietly off to her bedroom.*

A slamming door down the passage forced her to qualify her last observation.

*SUNDAY 1 MARCH*

First chance I've had to write again, with Mother obsessed about leaving the house spotless and even the garden weeded. Her news was shattering, though I'm sure it would please some of my classmates if it happened to them. I'll be leaving school!

There's no high school in Nairne, and nobody has enough petrol to drive to the city regularly, with the limit set at a thousand miles a year for a family, I've done my sums. At nearly fifty miles each way, Aunty Joyce would use that up in a few weeks, even with a gas producer on her car, and counting in the miles saved by turning off the engine when going downhill. Come to think of it, you only get to buy a little petrol at a time, and if you use too much one week, you're grounded until it's ration day again.

Next there is the time the journeys would take. Finally, we don't have enough money to send me to town to board, but I reckon I'd hate that anyway, despite all the jolly tales I've read of boarding school life.

I said I'd come down by train. One of my strongest memories of holidays at the farm is of standing by the southern fence, and watching passenger and goods trains puffing by. Usually passengers would wave at us, and once a lady threw some Minties out of the window for me. But of course trains are used now to shift troops in their thousands – sometimes even in cattle trucks – and regular train travel is impossible in wartime too. There are signs at every station that ask, 'Is your journey really necessary?' If you do get a ticket and set off, your train is likely to be shunted into a siding while troop trains hog the line.

Mother says she's doing her best for me, but she just doesn't understand how I feel about school. She never even went past primary school because she lived up the river at Blanchetown. It's a hundred miles from Adelaide and worlds away from a high school. And when Heather turned fourteen she couldn't wait to leave and get a job. I remember her borrowing Mother's Fair Isle cardigan and putting it over her school uniform, then plastering on some crimson lipstick to go to the interview.

As for university, there's no point even trying to explain how much I want to get a degree when I leave school – or at least go to teachers' college. But Father would have understood. Even though he didn't get there himself – no one in my family ever has, and especially not a girl – he is clever, and says you should never stop learning. He wouldn't have let this happen to me.

One minute I'm furious with life in general and Mother in particular. (I'm making a bit of a habit of slamming doors.) Then the next minute I feel guilty about the way I've been carrying on. Like a pork chop, Heather says. I suppose it's not easy for her either.

And who knows what Father is going through? That's if he is still alive. It was hard to write that. I don't want to face the thought of him being dead. In fact, I'm always going to assume that he's alive from now on when I write.

Our chief hope is that he may have escaped, but it seems that the Japanese have sunk lots of ships, even hospital ships with Red Cross flags flying.

Mr Marryat, who is a teacher, explained when I delivered Billy and Alec home from Sunday school that it would be very difficult to make one's way to safety by land. When the Japanese headed south they captured the narrow causeway across the Straits of Johore, above Singapore. Then apparently thousands of them simply took bicycles from the local people and rode in on them. He said they had already taken Malaya and invaded countries to the north, so Father's regiment wouldn't have got far. I looked up my school atlas before lunch and I can see what he means. Singapore is a tiny island on the tip of a narrow peninsula, and apparently all its big guns were set in concrete to face out to sea! No one thought an attack would come by land: that the enemy would in fact come in by the back door. The troops are completely trapped there.

If Father hasn't got away, the next best – I mean least bad – thing is to hope that he may be a prisoner of war. Surely the Red Cross will start to put out lists of survivors and wounded soon?

Grandma knew why Rosemary was so miserable, even if she didn't condone grumbling.

The two of them were shelling peas at the kitchen table, her dejected granddaughter working with nimble fingers but unwillingly. 'I may as well get used to drudgery,' Rosemary sighed. 'There'll be plenty of it soon. Farm life is so *primitive.*'

'The farm may not be a nice brick bungalow like this. But a stone house with electricity – even if it's a cranky generator that relies on wind power – is not primitive, young lady!'

'I didn't mean – ' Rosemary tried to explain; but Grandma was in full flow.

'Now, when I got married our little hut in the Mallee *was* primitive. We had dirt floors, and newspapers lining the walls, and we had to cart water. I cooked outdoors too at first, and there were only kerosene boxes to sit on.'

'That's not what I mean! It's so – isolated!'

'No one's isolated these days. You'll have the wireless to listen to, and Brian even had the telephone put on for Joyce before he went away.' But then Grandma's voice grew softer.

'It's leaving school that's worrying you most, isn't it?'

Rosemary could only nod, as tears streamed down her cheeks.

'You mustn't give up your dreams, sweetheart,' she told her. 'I've been through it all before, and this war won't last forever, even if it seems as if it might.'

'I might be too *old* for school by the time it ends. And I don't want just any old job.'

'You might have to show a bit of grit then. Keep reading and writing and learning while you're at Joyce's. Go to night school later to catch up, perhaps. You've always been the one with plenty of spirit, haven't you?'

Rosemary nodded, but doubtfully.

'And so quick on the uptake. My dear, you've got the brains to be anything you choose. I hope I live long enough – your father too – for us to be proud of you one day.'

They both had a good cry then, the sort of cry that left them feeling a lot better.

Grandma was so nice to me once she finally understood why I'm so upset, but Heather is very short-tempered and hard to get on with. She and I seem to argue about little things all the time. Like who will take the fine china dressing table set that we share, and whether Angus, the teddy bear with the tartan ribbon, is hers because she had him first, or mine because I kept playing with him for years after she grew out of him. Tonight I ended up hurling him at her across our partly dismantled room, and said that since she was having all the luck she might as well win that point too.

'Luck!' She flung Angus back at me. I hung on to him and chucked my half-knitted Army sock in her face instead, needles and all.

'*You're* the lucky one,' she shouted. 'You get to stay with Mother.'

I just gaped at her. 'You're scared about leaving home!'

Her face went red and she shrugged – and then she was crying the way Grandma and I had, and I ran out of the room because I didn't know how to comfort her. How can I help other people when I'm so devastated by all of this myself?

# 5

*THURSDAY 5 MARCH*

Just a few days to go. I still can't imagine not living in Adelaide, and especially Dulwich. I've just been to the baker's and the butcher's, perhaps for the last time. Past Miss Browning's single-fronted cottage. (I used to be sure that a witch lived there, and I would creep along beneath the overhang of its massive, dark cypress hedge, holding my breath in fear.) Next the Marryats, then round the corner, along to the picture theatre, and over the road to my favourite shops.

Here I go again – writing about my past, in case I don't have a future ...

At least I've got past the crying stage. This afternoon for old times' sake I meandered home, picking the soft, warm middle out of the high-top loaf that Mr Clay had broken in half for me. When I was five or six it was my job to collect the bread, and it always used to be a good day when I got the fat half (I can hear Mrs Pearson saying, 'Call it convex, girl.') so I could have a nibble on the way home. At our house we always have to finish off a stale loaf before we start another; which means I hardly ever get really fresh bread. Anyway, Mother eventually became suspicious that we always seemed to be given the concave half! Today when Mr Clay broke a loaf and gave me the hollow portion, I boldly asked if I could have the other one. He raised his eyebrows but obliged happily enough.

I called in to see the Marryats on the way home, and read Betty some *Bib and Bub* and *Ginger Meggs* cartoons that have been cut from the newspapers and pasted in a scrapbook. It's hard to get children's books. That let Mrs Marryat concentrate on cutting the boys' hair. We could see Miss Browning peering in the direction of the kitchen window through her side one and we began chatting about her. Mrs Marryat says Miss Browning has given up struggling to make her own blackout curtains, and ordered some new-fangled metal blackout shades from Moores. And apparently she always carries a packet of pepper in her handbag, ready to throw in the face of the enemy if there's an invasion. I laughed, but that did make me feel a bit jittery.

When Mr Marryat got home from his school just as I was leaving, I told him how I have to leave school. He agreed that it was a pity, but tried to convince me how much I would learn, living on a farm. Typical teacher! I looked at him in disbelief. He laughed and said that a few weeks ago some of the children in his new class hadn't even known that milk comes from cows. (So when they hang a billy can out by their front gate, what do they think will be going into it?) When Mr Marryat started talking about the current milk shortage, a girl had asked, 'Why don't they just make more then?' As if it was made in a factory like a brew of lemonade! I can imagine his rather pompous voice explaining how the shortage is due to the very dry season and difficulties in getting farmhands. He even gave me a lecture about how so many dairy cows are being slaughtered that it's hard to supply Adelaide with all the milk it needs each week. I think he said 150,000 gallons; and the cheese factories are closing down.

Guess who agreed to write Mr Marryat a letter about dairy farming after I've settled in, so that he can share it with his class?

The news took a back seat in this last week of packing and farewells. Anyway Sylvia had taken to hiding the papers from Rosemary; sometimes the less you knew the better. And yet always the war intruded. Which was understandable, because just about everyone had relations who were involved in some way. Every heart gave a jolt when the telegram delivery boy rode up the street, in case he was bringing news of a family death. They'd all seen one of those telegrams. They usually began, 'It is with very great regret ...' If the delivery boy propped his bike against someone else's fence, that was nearly as bad, because they all knew each other, and each other's business. Dulwich was like a village really. It had been the turn of the Johnstons at number six on Monday, when they heard their only son, Ross, had died in Malta. Their blinds were drawn and no one had seen them all week, poor things.

*We don't want that to be us one day, Les. You hang on up there, won't you?*

Sylvia shrugged off her dark thoughts and went out to water the vegetables. She'd been lucky to get seeds, what with every man and his dog planting frantically like they were expecting a famine. The paper had even given helpful hints to housewives on how to grow vegetables; as if most of them wouldn't have seen their husbands do it! She was doing the right thing, and had even pulled out the love-in-the-mist and ageratum (but no, not the roses) in the front garden to plant broad beans. A pity to leave such a fine young crop for the new tenants, but then life was all about give and take, wasn't it?

*FRIDAY 6 MARCH*

My last day at school. I found Hilda, the captain of my Heathpool netball team, and told her I won't be playing this winter. I didn't say many goodbyes though, trying to pretend to most people that I'll be back in a few weeks when Father comes home.

There's not much chance of the war finishing soon, unfortunately.

I was reading the paper just now – I found it hidden under a cushion for some strange reason – and it was all doom and gloom. First there was an interview with refugees from Darwin, with a photo of bedraggled women and children on a railway platform in Sydney, clutching little bundles of belongings. One of the wounded who arrived on an ambulance train said the raids were like an ugly dream, with black smoke everywhere, thunderous noise – and then apparently he choked up and couldn't say any more. Or perhaps they cut him off because they don't want us to know too much. There was news of another raid in Darwin too, and it said there are also some casualties reported from Broome. (I'll admit I didn't know where Broome is, so I quickly got out my atlas again to make sure it's a long way from Adelaide. It is.) Another article said that if Java falls to the Japanese, an invasion of Australia is likely. Then when I turned the page I was confronted with plans for making an air-raid shelter – under the stairs. Bad luck most of us don't have posh two-storey houses.

But the worst thing of all has been helping Mother put all Father's clothes and his sporting gear into my great-grandfather's big sea chest that has 'Edwin Hurtle Lister' painted on it. As if we were stowing Father away too. I just feel numb inside.

The only bright spot in the week came out of my last visit to the Children's Library. Miss Morley, who has seen me borrowing a book almost every afternoon after school for years, must have heard the wobble in my voice when I handed in my *Girls' Own Annual* and told her why I couldn't get another book.

'Ah,' she pondered, 'I'll write you a note for Miss Whyte.' I had never heard of Miss Whyte, but I watched and took in as much as I could read upside down, as Miss Morley penned a neat letter about me. The bit that sticks in my mind is '… one of our most avid borrowers; it would be a pity if she were deprived of reading matter. Can you do anything for her?'.

Then she took me over to the front door and pointed down the lane. 'See that wooden building? That's the Country Lending Service. I know they've been planning to get books to isolated children. Tell them I sent you.'

Well, I object to being labelled a child these days, and isolated is not a cheerful word, but I held my tongue.

Miss Whyte, who was very young and quite pretty in a strong sort of way, thought for a minute, and checked a list on her desk. Then she shook her head and said, 'We can't deliver to individuals yet, though we wish we could. Sending books to Army camps is overloading the library's resources at the moment – not to mention all the research that librarians are doing for the munitions factories.' She must have seen my disappointed look, because she went on: 'However, we supply country schools. Nairne? Oh! We send boxes of books to Nairne School every month. Can you get in there sometimes?'

'Yes! That's where my little cousins go.'

'Well, it's a bit irregular, but I'll earmark some books for you each time, and ask the school to let you know when they come in. What types of books do you read?'

'Oh, just about anything – except cowboy and Indian stories or how to play cricket!'

'I hope you will keep studying,' she said, and I told her I want to go to university one day. Then she admitted that she has only just left school, and has started studying part time for an Arts degree. She has had to leave her family who live up in the bush in order to do it.

'You can do anything, you know, if you set your mind to it,' she said. 'You're like me: from a family of battlers. Generations of us.'

She is the second person to believe in me. So now I've promised both her and Grandma that I'll try to keep my mind alive for when I go back to school. And to make Father proud.

Pretending I'm doing weekend essays when I write in this diary is a good start.

◁■▷

Tensions had been affecting the family in different ways. But their spirits lifted once they reached their last afternoon in the Cleland Avenue house, and were enveloped by a crowd of relations, friends and neighbours who had come to say goodbye. Everyone kept telling them brightly that with each day that passed without news of Les, there was more chance that he was not among the dead. It was a theory that didn't bear close examination, but the well-meaning platitudes brought comfort anyway.

Sylvia found moments in between welcoming guests to keep Les up to date.

*Lucky we put in those glass doors to open up the sitting room into the dining room. Such a nice crowd of young ones here too – so many of them that they've spilled out on to the front verandah. Makes me realise that we've done well bringing up our girls. You do remember little Violet, don't you, Les? The one Heather has known since they met at Brownies when they were eight. She's looking very pretty and grown-up now, and mixes so well. I think she'll keep Heather from fretting for us.*

Aunt Agnes was in a flutter.

'You just sit here, Aunt Agnes. Heather will bring out your butterfly cakes in a minute. No, dear, this is Rosemary, not Heather. Yes, she *is* a big girl – she's fourteen now.'

*The aunts never change, do they? Although dear old Agnes has gone downhill quite a lot. She's away with the pixies half the time. And then there's Florence ... There has to be someone in every crowd who spreads misery like the rest of us spread Vegemite.*

34

Aunty Florence had been going on and on about how last week's air-raid test had shown that many people were still not observing the blackout properly. Why, the little bride next door to her had even gone out one night and put her front light on as she left.

Sylvia was ignoring Florence.

'Sylvia, I hope you'll be joining the Red Cross up there at Nairne. Sylvia?'

*And now the tedious woman is insisting on telling us all about the Red Cross's plans to treat people for bomb shock. Can't you just hear her? 'We must never assume that anyone is all right. Someone may appear normal for a day or two, but ...'*

At least the neighbours were being positive. They kept saying how much the family would be missed. The Marryats lamented, 'How will we manage without you, Rosemary? You can come and stay with us any time, you know.' Even the reclusive Miss Browning turned up, with a plate of Anzac biscuits. She said she had enjoyed watching the girls grow up, and they must let her know if she could ever help in any way.

'Well!' Heather exclaimed when she, Rosemary and their mother were pouring tea in the kitchen. 'There's no doubt about her spying on us but – '

Rosemary broke in: 'You can't walk by without her curtain twitching, can you?'

' – but I certainly haven't ever noticed her joy!'

'I call her haughty.'

'You're being hard on her,' said Sylvia. 'You don't see Miss Browning much because I think she is actually shy and lonely. We should be honoured that she has come today.'

When the girls looked at her blankly Sylvia added, 'She's had a sad life.'

'Why? What do you mean?' Rosemary always pricked up her

ears at the hint of a story. But Sylvia had already headed off with a loaded tray and the opportunity passed.

Contentment was dispensed with the cups and saucers. There was nothing like a good cup of tea to cheer you up, they all agreed.

*SUNDAY 8 MARCH*

A last quick note. We're all exhausted after having our relations, friends and neighbours in for a farewell afternoon tea. I made two bottles of lemon cordial, and it's all gone. The ladies all brought a plate so that we wouldn't have to bake. My schoolfriends kept saying how much they'd miss me, but I think most of them will soon forget me – except Janet, perhaps. Most of the oldies said such nice things about us. I was terribly polite in return, though it was hard to agree with Father's Aunt Agnes, who kept telling me what fun I will have, living on a farm. As if I'm going for a lovely holiday, and will be gambolling with the little lambs, making daisy chains and jumping off haystacks.

Then there was Mother's aunt, Aunty Florence, who is still sharp as a tack but even more difficult to have a conversation with. Nothing flowery about her! She bailed me up to give me a long list of all the countries being overrun by the Japanese: Philippines, Malaya, Borneo, Burma … And now Port Moresby in New Guinea bombed.

Heather came in for her share of advice too; and rightly so, since everyone could see Violet flirting outrageously with Janet's big brother, and hear her shrill peals of laughter.

I'm waiting to get in the bath, when my sister stops wallowing like a whale in the shallows. That's it for now, until we're settled at the farm.

# 6

The farmhouse was plenty big enough for them all. You left your gumboots by the back door and came into the porch, where the cream separator and the butter churn took pride of place. Then on to the big kitchen with its vast wood stove and battered-looking dark dresser and cupboards. The worn old table would seat a dozen, but these days there was a cloth just at one end, where the five of them, and usually Grandpa Jack from over the creek, sat in a bunch. This was where Grandpa Jack had brought up Brian, Norm and a quartet of robust girls, adding rooms as needed. But he had patched up the pioneer homestead and moved back there after the girls became farmers' wives, the boys took on much of the management, and his wife died.

Sylvia and Rosemary had two rooms at the old end of the house, separated from the others by the seldom-used entrance hall and the big sitting room, with its comfy ancient couch and armchairs, and a gigantic fireplace that could burn just about half a tree. They'd need fires soon, as it was so much colder at night up in the Hills. Although they would probably all crowd round the kitchen range most nights, since there wasn't much formal entertaining these days. The bedrooms overlooked undulating paddocks, which young Johnny said were like messy fair hair when the grasses dried off. Not to be outdone, little Bob informed them they would be as green as peas in winter.

Sylvia, in her saggy feather bed, lay sleepless – as, no doubt, did a million other abandoned women all round the world. She visualised the golden days and solitary nights that comprised her new life, trying to paint them for Les.

*Never thought I'd be living here! You remember what Scott's farm is like, don't you, Les? There's little huddles of honey-brown cows – so docile – resting under big gum trees, and the sky's cornflour blue and empty. It's like an idyllic, peaceful landscape painting, but of course the country's so alive, and quite noisy at times. You wake up to the lowing of the cows, the bleating of Lamb Chop – that's the boys' pet lamb – and the cawing of crows. Not to mention the darned rooster. And then you can hear trains chuffing through the darkness on and off all night. Uphill, downhill … They blow their whistles as they clatter in or out of the little cutting near our boundary, and I think of when one will bring you back to us. We might not be up here for long, you know.*

As she had expected, Sylvia was already relishing country life. It was a pity Ted had taken to the drink after his bad experiences in the Great War … *Not that I haven't been more than happy with you, Les,* she hastened to add. As if he could be listening.

She would have said their move had gone very well, except that Rosemary was still as scratchy as a wild kitten. One day she would lose her temper over nothing at all; the next she would be quiet and moody. Sylvia had had to ask Joyce to be a bit lenient with her niece for a few more days, in the hope she would settle in. If not, she would need a good talking to. She'd simply have to get over this nonsense about missing her school and friends and grandmother. She was probably missing her sister too, but you'd never expect her to admit that. They had always been chalk and cheese, those two; never close and sisterly. A bit like her and Joyce, in fact.

*She looked at her schoolbooks for a while yesterday, but her heart's not in it. I suppose I can't expect her to grow up overnight, can I? And life shouldn't be all work when you're only fourteen. I'll ask her if she wants to take up a hobby, or start some embroidery or something. No, you're right Les, not embroidery …*

Talking to Les and composing his replies always did her good. It called up the good times for her, when they had chatted dozily after turning off the light. A final sigh, and Sylvia was asleep in an instant.

## THURSDAY 12 MARCH

What an exhausting business moving is! And farm life is so different. I can see it won't be a daily task keeping up my diary, or easy finding time to write to Grandma as I've promised. As for Heather, well, I suppose she'll bother to contact us one day. I'm a world away from the city – and it's a world I'd give anything to escape from.

It's funny how you write in a diary as if someone is going to read it. At least, I wouldn't be stupid enough to pour out my innermost thoughts and desires in this one; what if the boys came snooping and found it? I'd better find a good hiding place for it in any case. Can you imagine if I put down 'I caught another glimpse of Ian from the next door farm today, and my heart started fluttering' – and then Johnny found it? He would quote me in the kitchen, at church, at school and even at the grocer's shop in Nairne when he went in to buy a bag of broken biscuits with his pocket money.

So who is going to read my ramblings? Maybe I'll have children one day who will ask what I did in the war, and I'll dig it out again, to help me remember. What a weird thought! Perhaps, as I said to Mother, it will just remind me of things to tell Father when he comes back.

Still no word of Father. I'm forcing myself not to think too much about him. In fact, there is no news at all out of Singapore, and there has only been one small casualty list from Malaya. The paper today was listing all the reasons for the 'dispiriting' defeat in Singapore: no natural protection, no dynamic leadership, lack of help from the local people, complacency ... I can't believe the last one; I'm sure our soldiers would have cared a great deal and would have fought if they could.

I pick up the paper down at our front gate after I've taken the boys to school, and try to get a quick look at it while Mother and Aunty are still busy in the milking shed. They both specialise in glaring at me and telling me there's work to be done whenever they see me reading. In fact, Aunty Joyce says we should stop getting the paper, as it's expensive and no one has time to read it. But luckily Mother has talked her out of that for now by insisting that she will pay for the papers from the 7/- extra a week she gets from the Army for having me as a dependant.

Mother seems to want me to get a new interest, so last night I let her help me make a big scrapbook out of brown paper, sewn together with strong cotton. (No one can get white paper; the boys are not allowed to waste a single line in their exercise books.) We made flour paste too. Mother thinks I'm going to put a collection of drawings in the scrapbook – suggested I could practise fashion drawing, or try sketching landscapes. But of course I'll use it to collect cuttings of the most important war news to add to the notes I'll keep in here, and anything else that may interest Father one day when he wants to catch up on the time he's lost.

I suppose I can't put off writing my impressions of the farm any longer. As for Aunty Joyce's first impressions of me ... I'll get to that.

My very first reaction on stepping out of the truck was 'Ugh!! I can smell cow dung!' Mother dug me in the ribs and hissed that I'd soon get used to it.

My new home, which has been called Scott's farm for several generations, is quite familiar to me of course, because we sometimes used to visit Aunty and Uncle on Sunday drives. And I spent two or three holidays here before the war. Johnny was quite small and Bob just a toddler the last time I stayed, and now they are eight and five, with their own little jobs to do each day. They are so pleased to have what they call a new sister that they hardly ever leave me alone, unfortunately; but I must admit they're not brats.

Mother gives them a lot of attention, because we agree that they have had a pretty rotten time, only half understanding why their father will never come back, and stuck here with a gloomy, tearful mother. When I'm not slaving away I've been doing a few little things with them, like drawing faces on their boiled eggs, or keeping a dipper full of the foam from the Lux flakes when we've done the washing, and helping Bob make a snowman out of them. Yesterday I played marbles with Johnny (and lost deliberately).

We've – see, even though I don't want to be here, I sound as if I belong already! – got sixteen milking cows (jerseys) and seven young heifers who haven't calved yet, so they're not in milk. They are in different paddocks according to age and they lead a very tranquil life. Then there's an old unpruned orchard, a neglected vegetable garden and a yard full of assorted poultry. Not a very big farm, but that's because Grandpa Jack's property was carved up when his sons grew up. Each generation has built another house. Grandpa Jack is back in the tiny original cottage, while Uncle Brian and Aunty Joyce stayed here in the big farmhouse, and his brother Norm and sister-in-law Ivy have built a new one on their portion. It's on our northern boundary, out by the Kanmantoo road. (I love that name!) They grow wheat and keep a few sheep. They have three girls, none of them living at home, as well as Ian, the boy I mentioned before. I only wrote about him to make a point of course. I'm not madly in love with him; although he's seventeen and not bad looking.

Uncle Norm can't help Aunty Joyce much because he was once injured really badly when his tractor rolled and pinned him under it. He drags one foot out sideways as he walks, and he can only work for an hour or two at a time, other than keeping the accounts etc. So, with all the farmhands enlisting, Ian pretty much runs their place for them now. He's got an old Ford buckboard and a tractor, which he shares with Aunty Joyce.

Uncle Norm reminds me a bit of Father, even though they are not blood relations. It's something about his eyes, thoughtful and watchful. Aunty Ivy is all right, just brown haired and dumpy. Not dismal like Aunty Joyce. Not much to say. Ordinary.

Grandpa Jack, who thinks he still runs both properties, stamps around yelling at everyone and telling them what to do. I must say he's a very unpleasant old man, skinny as a scarecrow, and with a twisted, twitchy face that makes him look even more fierce than he is. But Mother says we have to be nice to him, because he was shell-shocked after the Great War. Badly affected by gas too. And after all, he has lived here all his life, so he cares a lot about the land that his parents settled. She says he's not all that old either, but I don't believe her. He's one of those people who can't possibly have ever been young – any more than you could imagine that Hitler was once a baby …

Blast! Why did I mention that name?

Several other farmers in the district have been hopping in to help Aunty Joyce; but she really hasn't been coping well. The whole place is looking run down. That's why Mother and I are here – and you may well ask how much we can do.

To my surprise, Mother is very good with farm animals. She has admitted that she once had a boyfriend on a farm who taught her to milk a cow, harness a horse and look after poultry. (*Note*: must find out why she gave him up for Father.) So she has commandeered Uncle Brian's overalls, with the legs rolled up, and is willing to turn her hand to anything. She's quite strong. She looks more contented up here than she did in town. I suppose she thinks of Father a lot though, even more than I do.

*LATER*
Had to stop for a while, and help with the washing, as Aunty Joyce says I'm not doing my fair share. 'Snap to it!' she ordered after telling me to heave the clothes prop *up* so that the sheets wouldn't flap down into the dirt. That time I just managed to swallow the quite nasty reply that was sitting right on the tip of my tongue. *Grrrr!!!*

I wonder if I'll fit in at all. Aunty looked me up and down on our first night, and said in her usual blunt voice that I didn't look very big and strong for my age. 'Most of the girls round here drive tractors by the time they're twelve or thirteen,' she said. 'You're tall enough, but you're so skinny that Ian's cranky Massey Harris would run you straight down into the dam. You could round up the cows on one of Norm's horses, though.'

I went numb from head to toe. Uncle Norm is spelling his massive Clydesdales on our land now that his harvest is over and his sheep are eating the stubble. The thought of those dinner plate feet mashing my dainty ones to pulp is terrifying.

'Don't let a horse loose near me!' I squealed.

'Well,' she said, 'you'd better stick to the housework and the poultry until we get a bit of condition on you.'

Of course, my heart sank to my shoes. Chores and chooks. (I never could stand squabbling hens and bossy roosters.) I started to stammer that I wanted to pull my weight with the dairy work like everyone else, at which Mother interrupted and tried to tell me that we all have different contributions to make, and each of us is a valuable member of the team. But I didn't hear her out. She sounded so much like the netball coach I had last year that I'm afraid I was very rude to her and to Aunty before I dashed down the passage and slammed my bedroom door.

When nobody came near me, I decided after half an hour or so of sulking that this was not what I wanted at all. Eventually I swallowed my pride, apologised to Mother and Aunty Joyce, took a couple of deep breaths and tried to untie the knot in my gut enough to eat some leftover casserole.

# 7

No real war news. Just a first list of Australians still alive in Hong Kong. Why can't we get one from Singapore???

Despite the shaky start that I made I must admit our first week here hasn't been too bad. I'm so lucky not to have to go out in the dark every morning to get the cows in and start milking. Even stoic Aunty Joyce admits that it's a rotten, finger-freezing job in winter. No matter if it's pelting rain or blowing a gale, someone has to go out with a torch to search for the cows, which apparently know every little hollow and thicket to hide in. Mother's getting good at seeing the tiny glint that means her torch beam has picked up the eye of a cow. Imagine blundering into one in the dark! Eventually the big beasties all line up in the holding yard – in the same order every day. I'm told it's very important to keep them in a routine. Then the process is repeated before tea, except that this time the cows come in by themselves to be milked again. They feel uncomfortable when their udders are heavy with milk.

I'm learning to do real cooking, not just the cherry macaroon biscuits and scrambled eggs that I was already good at. My first challenge was to get used to the finicky wood oven, which has a mind of its own. Mother helps quite a lot, so being kitchen hand is not too dreadful. Everything has to be made in big slabs or heavy pots, so I'm finding out how you plan meals using the ingredients that are on hand. There's no corner shop to run to if you choose to make a currant cake, weigh the flour, butter and sugar and find there are no currants. That one turned into a rather strange raisin cake with a layer of heavy, soggy fruit at the bottom. (Johnny started making rude jokes about soggy bottoms until Aunty stopped him.) Tomorrow I'll try the old family apple cake recipe since we have lots of windfall Granny Smiths. Even I should be able to slice apples on to the cake mixture and sprinkle spice and sugar on top.

As I predicted, the worst bit of my new life is looking after the chooks. They peck, they flap in your face, they lay their eggs under prickly bushes then go broody, and you have to chase after them to shut them all in at night. They don't love you the way a good pet does – they only like you for the food you bring them. At home Heather was always the one who would muck around talking to ours. I'll swear they talked back – '*Ook*dookdook'. She even used to tame them, and would often be seen walking round with a hen on her shoulder. And then she'd break her heart when they had to be killed. It's definitely not a good idea to give a name to a pretty speckled hen or get fond of a clutch of fluffy yellow chickens – because they will turn up on your dinner table one day. And most likely you'll have already held them while someone chopped their heads off, helped pluck their feathers and cleaned out their gizzards. Sticking your hand into a dead chook's slimy innards is truly the most disgusting job in the world.

It's worse on a farm, because the same goes for all the livestock. There's not much that manages to stay a pet on a farm. Even the old dogs that are past their best at their work get shot, and surplus kittens are drowned; not that Aunty Joyce has a single cat or dog on her property. The Sunday roast lamb isn't quite as appealing as it used to be now that I've seen a carcass hanging to bleed over at Uncle Norm's. No, not Lamb Chop, he's a pet. Though I don't know how long he'll survive, since Aunty Joyce is furious every time he starts munching the garden. As for tripe with parsley sauce, or lamb's fry (that's liver) and bacon …

I haven't worked out yet what happens to all the calves.

⊪⊪

The neighbours from a mile around came in one by one to greet the new arrivals and invite Sylvia to go with Joyce to church or the CWA, to bake for some auxiliary group's fundraiser, or help the Mothers' Union in writing to lonely servicemen overseas.

'Oh, and there's sure to be a dance for young people soon,' they usually added as an afterthought when they looked at Rosemary's pale, downcast face.

Young Mrs Gurner from down the road was there tonight, having come to tell them about some special Red Cross meeting with a visiting speaker. She and Joyce were outside in the dusk checking to see the chooks were all in the run for the night, because on her way in she had seen a fox slinking along near their shared boundary.

'It's nice of them to ask Aunty to all these meetings and socials and so on, but I don't see how you'd ever run a farm if you went to everything,' said Rosemary while she and Sylvia were alone for a minute, finishing the dishes.

'Well,' Sylvia was thinking aloud, 'all these groups are working in some way for the war effort. And anyway, it's such a raw wound that poor Joyce is still carrying. Seeing other people is probably the only thing keeping her sane. You have to believe that getting her to meetings is helping her.'

'They'd better try even harder then. There's no one more sour than Aunty Joyce.'

'She did forget herself and have a laugh yesterday, you must admit,' smiled Sylvia.

Rosemary blushed. 'Oh yes – my apple cake!' She had thought

she was sprinkling some mixed spice on top of the apples, but it turned out to be allspice. Allspice, she was informed as Joyce, Sylvia, and the boys all screwed up their noses and tried to keep straight faces, was used in stews and pickles. It was such a change to see Joyce laughing that Rosemary decided to take it in good grace, joking that they were lucky she hadn't mistaken cinnamon for pepper. At which Joyce opened up a little further and said that when she was first married she served up custard to her parents-in-law flavoured with salt instead of sugar.

'I'll bet Grandpa Jack was rude about that!'

Tonight Joyce looked as grim as usual when she and her neighbour came back in.

'We found the big black hen roosting in the cherry tree,' she told Rosemary pointedly.

As always the children had been put to bed before the nightly news. Everyone settled down round the wireless to hear the war report, chatting about how the country's thinking had shifted since the disasters in Singapore and Darwin. Sylvia said it was good to have heard Curtin demanding that all Australian troops be sent back from the Middle East immediately.

Rosemary knew all about it. 'I read that Mr Curtin is furious because Mr Churchill still wants to keep using most of our troops in Europe and the Middle East. But they say the tide is turning in Europe, now that the Russians – '

'I heard Curtin,' Joyce interrupted. 'He says our primary obligation is to save Australia, and he's quite right.'

Mrs Gurner, who had grown up in London, eventually got a word in. 'But that's so *selfish*! Why – '

'*Shhh*! It's starting,' said Joyce, in the same way that she would *shoosh* the boys if they ever appeared at this important hour.

The American General, Douglas MacArthur, was Australia's new hero. He had come all the way down from the north to Adelaide by train the previous week, and now tonight he and Mr Curtin were announcing a partnership between their two countries. When MacArthur said, 'I pledge you all the resources of all the mighty power of my country and all the blood of my countrymen', Joyce surprised them all by cheering, and Sylvia clapped too.

'It's just as well Australia is turning its back on England at last,' stated Joyce, the news report abandoned. 'The Motherland is only interested in saving itself. It has let us down badly.'

That really got Mrs Gurner's hackles up. 'Surely you know how *terribly* the English are suffering compared with us!' she exclaimed. 'Whole cities bombed …'

Sylvia looked uncomfortable, but Joyce was not to be swayed, coming back with, 'And doesn't England have *any* idea of what Australia is going through?'

'You can't compare what the Japanese are doing with the evil unleashed by that monster Hitler!' was the angry reply.

'Well, the only reason I'm staying alive is to keep bread on the table for *my children* and preserve their heritage here,' said Joyce. 'I can't take on the whole world's problems.'

The discussion was starting to turn nasty when there was a sudden diversion – a terrible commotion outside. They all scrambled out to glimpse the dim shape of a fox disappearing, with the black hen in its jaws.

'That chook would have been safer up the cherry tree,' Rosemary observed. But Joyce retorted that it would have been safest of all if Rosemary had noticed the hole in the wire netting. She proceeded to do some quick repairs in the fading twilight, announcing she was going to keep watch for the fox.

'You may as well go home,' she told Mrs Gurner. 'And you others can go to bed. I won't need company.'

Sylvia saw their neighbour on her way. 'Don't take too much notice of Joyce,' she urged. 'It's not that we're anti-British. We just know that we can't win this war without America's backing.'

As she turned from the gate, she observed Joyce settling down with Brian's overcoat on, her rifle at the ready and an intense look on her face as if she was waiting to kill a human invader. 'It won't be back tonight,' Sylvia told her; but Joyce chose to ignore her. She obviously looked forward to waging her own little war.

*WEDNESDAY 18 MARCH*

Not everyone likes the idea of the United States ordering our forces around, but I think it's comforting to know that the Americans are bringing so many troops and ships our way. The Japanese are spreading down through the islands to our north, and we could never stop them on our own. Listening to their General MacArthur tonight was really inspiring; he sounded so confident and capable.

I've just had an interesting thought! We were starting to get lots of American troops here before – but now there will be thousands of them based in all our cities, and swarming around on leave, looking for a good time. The few that I saw before I left town were mostly scrumptious looking – tall and very polite and cheerful. I don't think our men will like having competition; but then, most of our young men are away, aren't they?

Heather is probably already going to dances where she'll meet Americans. They say the troops are pretty lonesome and at a loose end, so one of them might even be desperate enough to want to take her out. I'm really missing doing things with my friends. I wish I was Heather's age. I wish I ...

But to get serious again: I reckon the authorities are keeping the worst of the facts from us, because they don't want us to panic. For example, no one talks any more about the terrible defeat that the English and their allies have suffered in Singapore and Malaya, even though there were so many thousands of troops in the region. The fighting in Singapore simply stopped. What has happened to all the servicemen from different countries who were stationed there? About 50,000 of them, I read somewhere. The Japs couldn't possibly have killed them all. I wish I could find out more. Are they in prison, or hiding in the countryside?

*Where is my father?*

It's the same with Darwin. The papers just make vague statements like 'Some casualties, but damage slight'. However Uncle Norm's neighbour has a cousin home from the Top End on sick leave from the Air Force, and when I was delivering eggs the other day I overheard the three of them talking. The cousin was saying that the air raids are still going on, and that you wouldn't believe how many people have been killed up there. Hundreds and hundreds, he said, not just the fifteen killed and twenty-four wounded the Prime Minister announced. And that was without counting the number of Aborigines because they couldn't. In other towns as well as Darwin too. Then he clammed up, and told them to forget he'd said that, because they had been ordered not to spread rumours in case ordinary people panicked.

Thank goodness the Marryats got away when they did, although it would be awful to have to leave your home with just a suitcase each. Some people even had to set off walking down south. I wonder what I would take. Mrs Marryat said the worst thing was leaving behind the lovely crêpe evening dress she'd just had made for a ball, but had never worn. She had to take out her best clothes to fit in Betty's nappies. And Mr Marryat was most upset about leaving the intricately carved wooden sofa that he had imported from some island up north.

Anyway, I'm going to drop them a line tomorrow. I'll tell Mr Marryat a bit about how the cows are milked so that he can read it out to his class. Not that I do any milking, but I've picked up a fair bit about the process. The children will like the bit about the cows getting soothing music from a wireless to keep them calm and happy while they are being milked! And I'll explain about the Moo Bar (some people call it a Calfeteria) that's ready for when we have young calves to rear in the spring. It's a board that has teats attached. You pour a bucket of their special formula into a trough at the back, and they suck it up through tubes. I could also describe how a heifer is trained, before she has her first calf at the age of two, to take herself through the little lattice gate into the holding yard and stand in her special place in the line. Ten or twelve feed bins filled with a few bales of hay are ready to entice the cows in there. Then in the milking bail each cow gets a gallon tin full of chaff and a few oats – it has to be just enough to keep her occupied so that she doesn't get restless before she's finished giving her milk. So there's a lot of work involved apart from the actual milking. And everything has to be washed down afterwards.

P.S. It's six days since I slammed a door!

# 8

I'm only going to say one thing about the war today. Yesterday's main headline said, 'MacArthur's Appointment Regarded as a Masterpiece'. That's the American General. I agree.

Describing the cows being milked for Mr Marryat made me realise that it's high time I wrote a bit more about life here. Since I don't do English compositions every weekend now, this sort of reporting might keep me from getting rusty.

One of my jobs each weekday is to take Johnny and Bob to school. Johnny is old enough to go on his own (some quite young children walk miles on their own, or ride horses) but he can't be trusted yet to look after his brother as well. Bob would probably want to head down to the creek and find frogs!

It's nearly two miles into Nairne, and some children have even further to go, because lots of the smallest schools have closed since the war started. Johnny used to walk with Uncle Norm's youngest, Marjorie, until she finished Grade Seven at the end of last year. She's gone to board at St Peter's Girls' School. I haven't ever got to know her much, but I'm told I'll meet her in a couple of weeks when it's Easter. Lucky thing, at least she's still at school.

So now I get to take the boys most days, and pick them up again when school finishes, unless anyone is driving into Nairne for something. They don't do that often, on their sixteen miles' worth of petrol a week. I call in and collect the Gurners' two giggly little girls, Pam and Janie, too. Of course Johnny usually runs ahead of us, but Bob drags his feet a lot. He only started this year. Frankly, I'm starting to get bored with all their demands; but little Bob looks so sweet and innocent when he has his clean clothes on, socks pulled up, fair hair smoothed down and darkened with hair oil and, with the new leather schoolbag Grandma somehow managed to get him slung over his shoulder, I sometimes feel like mothering him.

It's another matter in the afternoon, when he's bedraggled, dirty, hot, tired and grizzly. Today when he whined he couldn't walk any further, I threatened to get out the old wicker pram from the shed and wheel him in it. He sat down on the dusty roadside, and I was about to lose patience with him when luckily Ian came by in the buckboard and picked us up. The boys hopped on the back with the dog and the girls squeezed into the cabin after me. Ian apologised that he was greasy and smelly from dipping sheep, but I didn't mind that I had to squash against him! He's got dark wavy hair and an attractive smile.

I'm off to bed. You wouldn't believe how tired we all get by 8.00 – but I get up at dawn. By then Aunty and Mother have already got the cows in for milking, while I have to feed the pathetic poultry, light the stove, prepare breakfast, cut lunches and get the boys ready for school. (Yes, I can make porridge that's not too lumpy.) And of course the seven miles that I walk most days, doing the school delivery and collection, finishes wearing me out. I'm still skinny! When there's a spare hour between the cooking and the housework, I help with separating the cream. That includes washing every single part of the cream separator – every day. It has dozens of little cups for collecting the cream, and they all have to be scrubbed individually.

In summary: slave labour.

Heather's so lucky not to be trapped up here. She should be

ringing us on Sunday, because Mother made her promise she'd ring every week. I wonder how she's liking her new freedom? It must be such fun to be in a boarding house, with all your meals just put in front of you, no family to bother you, and no one to tell you what to do.

◀━▶

Heather and Violet sat impatiently at the dining-room table with their fellow boarders, a pair of stodgy, podgy sisters called Marlene and Carlene, under the watchful eye of Mrs Jones. No one was allowed to leave until they had all finished, folded their serviettes and put them in their serviette rings. They all had different rings, so the serviettes wouldn't get mixed up; if you spilled gravy down yours on Monday, you had to put up with it for the week. Then the table was cleared, and the two rostered for dishes got to work.

'By rights she should be paying us as servants,' said Heather softly, balancing a pile of sweets dishes when the boarders were at last allowed to leave the table.

'Paying us to eat her ghastly food too. I'm *sick* of spinach and rhubarb! Anyway, lucky it's the others washing up tonight,' Violet whispered back. 'We might catch the 6.43 if we run.'

To be truthful, Heather had been hoping for a quiet night home for once. There was something a bit empty about this carefree lifestyle, where you headed to town nearly every night to meet others like yourself in a café, at the pictures, or simply walking along the street. At best you might get taken by a soldier to the Cheer Up Hut down by the river, where there was always dancing or singing round the piano. Of course, it was the visiting American troops who had made things 'swing', as they liked to put it. The city was making a real effort to entertain all those homesick young men.

So she obligingly hurried into her new floral dress, searched in crammed drawers for her black cardigan, put more bobby pins into her curly fair hair and lent Violet her second pair of stockings in return for a smear of Michèle lipstick.

'I'll be needing those stockings back. You'll have to paint that false tan stuff on your legs and draw lines down the back if you can't buy any,' she said as they left the house.

'Or get chummy with a sailor who can find me some!' laughed her friend.

Mrs Jones's strident voice cut through the growing distance behind them. 'You be careful out there in the dark, you girls! Did you know that *twenty-five* people were taken to hospital after motor accidents last weekend because of the blackout?'

'We're going on a train, aren't we?' Violet called back cheekily.

'Well, mind you behave like young ladies. It's a week night, remember. Don't be late.'

'No, Mrs Jones! We'll be in by ten,' they chorused, breaking into a most unladylike gallop on hearing their train toot in the distance.

*SUNDAY 22 MARCH*

Sunday is a good day to catch up on writing – i.e. my homework! – since we only do the essential farm work. But even today we had to bottle a batch of late peaches that were getting a bit too ripe, before we headed off to church. Not a mouthful of food gets wasted. At least preserving is one job even city dwellers are good at. Grandma always said I was her best helper in that department, because I could put my small hand right into the tall thin no. 27 bottles, and pack the fruit more tightly and neatly than anyone else. 'Pity we're not in the country,' she used to say. 'We'd win a prize in a show with these.' Well, now I'm here with all my skills, but I don't think they are even running shows these days.

It's a nice change to get dressed up for church. I've taken over Heather's green shantung dress with the lace collar – perfect for the warm dry days we are still having. It's not my favourite colour, but as Grandma always says, beggars can't be choosers. Heather didn't grow out of it, because she's really slim, but she said it made her look too young. My old school hat with a new band of green ribbon goes with it quite well, but my gloves have so many holes that they are now past darning, and Mr Forbes couldn't get any more in stock before we left town. So, having lost an argument with Mother about not needing gloves at all ('For goodness sake Rosemary, *nobody* goes to church without a hat and gloves!'), I had to borrow some pink ones from her. How embarrassing! I tried to hide my hands behind my prayer book, hoping that my poor dress sense wouldn't be noted by anyone who mattered.

Which reminds me – Ian was there. I don't think he even saw me. The teenage boys all sit up the back in a bunch, and afterwards they get together in a mob outside, laughing raucously.

The sermon was entitled 'What are your gifts?'. I quickly decided I only have one gift – no, it's not packing fruit into jars! Some of the middle-sized children thought hopefully of Easter eggs, but of course the minister was thinking of talents. It's from the Bible: we have all been given different gifts, so 'Let us use them'. I won't find it at all hard to use my gift; I've hardly made inroads into my massive diary.

Okay, I won't get too cocky. I think there was a mention of humility in the sermon. As long as humble doesn't mean servile …

Another thing. Aunty says she's not going to church again if they insist on singing 'Eternal Father, strong to save'. I can understand that the words upset her; but doesn't she know how we feel too when everyone chants, 'Oh hear us when we cry to Thee/For those in peril on the sea' in a mournful minor key? Aunty Ivy, who called in to borrow some potatoes, reminded us of something else the minister said today: 'Prayer has always wrought miracles and will do so again.' But Grandpa Jack agreed with Aunty that we'll all have to perform our own miracles if we want to survive this war.

When Heather rang tonight as arranged the line was bad, and she ran out of pennies before I could get a turn talking to her. Just as well, maybe, because before she was cut off she apparently told Mother, 'Give my love to Chook-face.' That's me. Mother wasn't going to pass on that message, but Johnny overheard her laughing about it to his mother.

On the whole Aunty's mood seems to have improved since we had a nice afternoon tea with Mrs Gurner, who must have been trying to make up for the hot words exchanged the other night. I think we're all learning that we have to make allowances for each other. The exception is sisters who call you names.

What should I call Heather next time she rings? Warmonger? After all, she's making planes to carry weapons. She says she's helping to protect our country, but the fact is, she chose to work at Islington because she earns a pound a week more than she used to get before. At least she's not filling rifle cases with cordite. That's what Violet does at her factory at Hendon. I'd hate to make bullets; I'd keep wondering who might be killed by them. And Violet says that breathing in the gunpowder as you work on the assembly line makes some of the girls vomit. Ugh!

Anyway, Mother told me that Heather is okay. Naturally my big sis didn't let slip any of the things I want to know, such as whether she has a boyfriend yet. That's the first thing you do when you leave home, isn't it?

'Hi there, my name's Charles. Charles Dwayne Payard Junior. But call me Chuck, why don't you?'

An American. Heather and Violet smiled, politely but with fluttering stomachs, at the sociable stranger who had edged his way over to their booth, which they shared with a strange couple who had eyes only for each other. The Squirrel Café was unbelievably crowded.

'And what are y'all called?' he went on. But although Heather told him her name she might as well not have bothered, for this Chuck was staring straight at her friend. Violet bloomed under his gaze. With sparkling eyes she shook her unruly black curls as she pushed further along the seat and squeezed Heather in against the wall, saying, 'Come and join us; there's plenty of room.' Followed by the predictable, 'Where do you come from, Chuck?'

Heather had to hunch up in her corner, holding in her elbows. This man's brash exuberance didn't appeal to her. As for calling himself Junior – he had to be thirty if he was a day. He already had the beginnings of a middle-aged spread.

In his southern drawl he told them about his home town in Louisiana, and how much he was missing his two sisters, Doreen and Lavine – the only ones left of his family. He said that he was a sergeant, based in the 32nd Division's camp up at Sandy Creek, and employed in training raw young privates. Soon his arm had crept round Violet's shoulder.

Heather stopped listening to them, longing only to escape. There wasn't even anywhere to look without seeming to pry on the pair at the opposite side of the narrow table. Ten minutes later, when Violet and Chuck's relationship had already leapt into a new stage of intimacy, she interrupted with, 'Um, do you think I could get out, Violet? I need to go to – '

'We-ell,' drawled Chuck, 'I was just saying to Violet, it's too darned crowded here. Would you mind if the two of us went off up to the Covent Garden Restaurant for an hour?'

Violet's eyes beseeched her to say yes. 'I can meet you at the station in time for the 9.35 train. Promise!' Heather could read her unspoken plea: *I've always dreamed of going to a really posh restaurant.*

'All right, but if you're not there I'm getting on without you,' she warned. 'Think about walking along that street in the pitch dark.' Violet was already at the door. 'And think about facing Mrs Jones's wrath if you're late!' she called after her.

Left alone, she felt very conspicuous. Wondering how to fill in the next hour, she got herself another malted milk. Covent Garden indeed! That was the one round the corner in King William Street next to Balfours, with the pretty window boxes and 'The House of Food Treasures' emblazoned on its front wall. The café was not so expensive, but upstairs in the restaurant, with its silver service and starched serviettes, food and drinks cost the earth …

'Excuse me – '

The young man addressing her nervously was unmistakably Australian – and not even a soldier. So she gave him a shy smile.

'I couldn't help seeing how you've been deserted,' he said. 'And my mates haven't turned up. Would you mind if I just sat with you for a while?'

She beamed at him, a load lifting from her shoulders. 'That would be lovely,' she said.

His name was Jim. Plain old Jim Smith, with wavy brown hair and freckles. By the time he delivered her to her platform, they had arranged to meet on Saturday night to go to the pictures.

# 9

'Step on it there, girl – we're all starvin' to death out 'ere,' Grandpa Jack called to Rosemary in his gravelly voice as she strolled down, swinging her basket, to where he, Joyce and Sylvia were mending the fence by the railway line.

*Wish you would die of something!* she muttered under her breath, refusing to pick up her pace. As instructed that morning, she had brought them some lamb sandwiches with lots of salt and mustard pickles, a large thermos of tea and dark-fleshed plums straight from their orchard.

'These are doorsteps!' laughed Sylvia, stretching her jaws to get her teeth into her sandwich.

Grandpa Jack held out his chipped enamel pannikin for some tea. 'That's the way a sandwich should be,' he said. He looked at Rosemary as if for the first time. 'We'll make a country girl of you yet. Like to be a farmer's wife one day, eh?'

Rosemary caught Sylvia's warning glance, which was fierce enough to make her tone down her intended reply to 'Oh – I'm not sure about that'.

Grandpa Jack left soon after, saying he had to see a man about a dog. They all relaxed, even Joyce taking a few moments to lie back on the bank in the warm dry grass. It was so peaceful in the paddocks, until trains went by and the earth trembled. Luckily there was little wind today, but still their smoke swirled round and steam spurted out as they emerged from the cutting.

They made them sad, these trains. Waving at the cheery soldiers setting off for goodness knows where was not so bad; perhaps they were just going to training camp. But when you saw the crowded carriages full of men coming home you couldn't help scanning each window, trying to focus on the shadowy khaki-clad figures inside in case you picked out someone you knew. It would never be Uncle Brian, and logic told them it couldn't be Les – not yet, anyway – as they would have had warning. They were always quiet with their own thoughts after a troop train passed.

The arrival of Ian today cheered Rosemary up though. He said he'd just dropped off a present for her by their back door.

'Present?' quavered Rosemary, blushing.

'Well, it was my father's idea to lend you an old bike we've had in the shed for donkeys' years. It's got a little cart wired on to it – made out of an old crate – so we thought you could ride to the school with Bob in the back.'

Rosemary hurried back to try it, and agreed it was going to be a godsend, even if it didn't look very elegant. Elegance was something that hadn't been worrying her much lately.

*SUNDAY 29 MARCH*

Out of the blue Heather got a ride up on Friday night with her boss, who was going to the South East on business, and who dropped her off just as we were getting ready to turn in. We all got quite excited, though why I should have welcomed a sister who calls me Chook-face, I don't know. We made another pot of tea and sat round the kitchen table talking till late.

Finally she admitted – she has got a boyfriend already! She says it's nothing serious, but you can see from her shining eyes that she's in love. His name is Jim Smith and, no, he's not American. So far she's just been out with him once, to see *This Thing Called Love* at West's Theatre. (I've checked the paper, and it's billed as

62

'the sauciest show of the year'. Wonder if Mother knows that?)

'Where does he come from?' was Mother's first question. Of course she kept probing until she found out all about him and his family. When she worked out that his Uncle Gerald had once lived down the road from her at Blanchetown she gave her cautious seal of approval. 'But you promise me you'll be sensible, my girl,' she demanded. 'Don't you let your standards slip for the first young man who tells you you're special.'

Heather protested, 'I've only just met him, Mother!'

Aunty Joyce hopped in to say, 'And of course, Sylvia, you were the most sensible girl in the world when you were courting, weren't you? Didn't rush into things. Stopped to consider everyone else's feelings.' Then it was Mother's turn to look uncomfortable. Fascinating! I'll have to see if I can find out more about Mother's past.

I thought it was funny seeing my mother being baited by her sister just the way Heather and I carry on sometimes. If you're jealous of someone, or want to stop being the underdog, does that last right through your life? Will Heather and I be calling each other names when we are thirty-four and thirty-eight? Will we still fight over Angus the teddy? Will I still think she's so lucky to be the older one?

Back to Heather's visit. This Jim is a butcher's apprentice. She's scared he will enlist, as his best friend is in the RAAF and has told him how exciting the training is. Anyway, there's talk of conscription, so he may be drafted. I'm glad I'm a girl, and too young to be sent to fight. I think I'd declare myself a pacifist.

(Question: what happens to pacifists?)

Heather said the city streets are absolutely crammed with troops, and naturally everyone seems to love men in uniform. When I asked her about the American soldiers, she said girls have gone particularly crazy over them. Yank happy, Aunty says. Everyone loves their accents, their wonderful manners (they usually call you Miss or Ma'am or Sir when they address you) and especially their wealth. Violet has fallen madly in love with an officer called Chuck (!) even though he seems much too old for her. Apparently they are paid nearly double what our soldiers earn, and they seem to be able to get items like nylon stockings that we can never buy here. Violet got some from Chuck.

The conversation turned to stockings. Mother and Heather boil up odd-coloured stockings until they turn into approximately the same shade, while Aunty soaks hers in cold tea. Heather said that these days most working girls simply wear ankle socks and stout shoes, except for best.

'Well, if you're my age you just wear heavy old lisle stockings,' said Sylvia.

'And of course it's not a problem for you,' Heather turned to me with that infuriating smile. 'You don't need to wear stockings at your age.' I stuck my tongue out at her. If she thinks I'm a child I'll act like one.

I was reminded again that I'm just the kid sister when we both went to a farm down the valley with Ian last night, to meet some of the other teenagers in the district. I'm the one who needs friends up here, but I was years younger than anyone else. I was left quietly sitting by the piano listening to a girl playing songs from the new American stage show, *Pal Joey*. (I've been humming 'Bewitched, Bothered and Bewildered' under my breath all day. Wish someone would bewitch me.)

Meanwhile Ian introduced Heather to all his friends. She was popular because she had met some Americans. Soon she was telling everyone about the old piano at the Cheer Up Hut. Its cracked veneer has been covered in cream paint, and if you pay 1/- to the Fighting Forces' Comfort Fund, you can write your name on it in ink – which she and Violet have done, of course. Chuck too. He put 'USA' after his name. The Cheer Up Society has already raised £410 doing this; I'm too lazy to work out how many signatures that is.

When they all started talking about dancing, Heather said the Hut became so crowded that they're having dances at the Palais Royal now. The girls oohed and aahed at the thought of dancing under the big crystal ball that revolves above the dance floor, casting iridescent shards of light. Then the rug was rolled back in the sitting room and everyone started dancing. Except me. I helped the mother make curried egg sandwiches and ice a chocolate cake for supper. I've realised you can be quite alone in a crowd.

Heather looks more at home here at Aunty Joyce's than I was when we arrived. She's naturally good with animals, just like Mother is, and seems to really like the cows. So she is let in to help in the dairy during milking. Unfortunately Aunty overheard me complaining that Heather was the favourite as usual. She told me in no uncertain terms that I'm too moody and changeable to work with cows, because they react to your frame of mind, and she couldn't afford to lose gallons of milk every time I put on a face that would turn cream sour. Well! I was about to disgrace myself by telling her that she was the queen of bad moods, but she stopped me. She must have read my mind.

'Yes, I know what you're going to say. But I never take out my feelings on the livestock. If I did, this farm would have failed long ago.' I'll admit I'm starting to admire Aunty's grit.

Johnny and Bob deserted me while Heather was here, spending most of the weekend trying to impress her by showing her every last toy and treasure they own, and even their secret cubbyhouse behind the old stable, which they think I don't know about. I do, of course, because Lamb Chop, who follows them everywhere (unless Aunty has shoved him back in his paddock) makes it quite obvious where they are hiding! And she never once let them see they bored her. At least, I assume she was bored; I must say she's got more patience than I'll ever have. Okay, I'm envious of her again. And she had a weekend's holiday while I cooked for her.

But she's gone now, toting a pound of butter and a big jar of cream for her landlady; she hates boarding-house food. Just when we were starting to think she'd have to stand on the roadside and hitch a ride to town (I'm joking – young ladies would never do that!), Ian found someone who could take her right home. He smiled at her so charmingly when she thanked him, that now I'm really jealous ...

# IO

Wednesday was the Red Cross meeting, where a Miss Dorothy Marshall spoke to the women about how she was trying to get the Government to form a Women's Land Army like they had in England. She had already organised groups of girls to help harvest pea crops somewhere because the growers were desperate for more pairs of hands. And up in the Riverland, she said, fruit picking had been a disaster. Everyone agreed it would be a good idea to have Land Army girls come up their way too, with labour so scarce even though most of the men's work was being done by women anyway. But it was disappointing that girls already on the land wouldn't be eligible to earn a living from their work. Sylvia smiled and commented to her absent husband.

*Come to think of it, Les, Rosemary and I are Land Army girls already! The difference is no one pays us. Still, helping keeps up our morale.*

When Joyce said she'd take on a girl if the scheme got going, Miss Marshall told her she would be given top priority, considering her circumstances. But when Grandpa Jack heard that he ranted, 'A woman's place is in the kitchen! We don't need any more useless creatures on this farm.'

'And what do you think Joyce and I do all day? Who do you think *really* runs this place?' Sylvia confronted him in fury.

Unabashed, Grandpa Jack added, 'What we need round here is a good strong man.'

Joyce burst into tears. 'You're a narrow-minded, insulting old pig!' she shouted at him. 'You know as well as I do that *my* good strong man left because you pushed him into it.'

Grandpa Jack looked quite taken aback for once, stumping off home without another word. Maybe, Sylvia told Rosemary later, it did Joyce good to let down her guard at last.

'I wish I could have shouted at him too,' said Rosemary.

*WEDNESDAY 1 APRIL*

I've finished my jobs early tonight, and I'm not tired for once, since Aunty collected the boys from school after her Red Cross meeting this afternoon. (I sent along my first pair of Army socks, for the Fighting Forces' Comfort Fund, with a little card for the soldier who will receive them. I should have put a false name and address as one of them is darned already, where I dropped a stitch or three.)

After a war news drought we've now heard that our General Blamey is back from the Middle East. Let's hope he and General MacArthur can hurry along the campaign to stop the Japanese advance. Perhaps he'll help do something about our missing troops too. About my father ...

At Uncle Norm's today I talked to that Air Force pilot who is on leave because he is wounded. He flies Catalina flying boats, and was shot in the leg by anti-aircraft fire while dropping mines over Japanese-held territory. He says it's easy to get hit because their planes are so heavy and slow. Dozens have been lost already, yet he can't wait to get back ...

I got a nice letter back from Mrs Marryat, telling me about the children (Alec has nasty boils), and thanking me from Mr Marryat for my information about milking. He has asked me to write lots more – an informal essay, he says – about what happens on a dairy farm. I obediently got straight on with it; so much for trying to become grown up and independent. I've made a carbon copy:

# DAIRY CATTLE AND DAIRY PRODUCE

By Rosemary Lister    1.4.42

Dairy farms differ greatly in size, in the types of cows kept, and in what is done with the milk produced. We're Jersey people here on my Aunty Joyce's farm near Nairne in the Adelaide Hills.

Jerseys are small-boned light-brown-coloured cows with pretty faces and gorgeous eyes like deep pools of melted chocolate. They don't eat as much as big cows, so they are good for our little farm. They are gentle and quite nice, as far as cows go. You get used to their deep mooing. I'm still a bit scared of them, but not as petrified as I'd be of big rangy beef cattle. They all have names like Daisy, Buttercup or Jessie, and after a while they are quite easy to tell apart. (Some have white patches, for example.)

We still milk by hand, because when my uncle went away to the war, my aunt could not afford to buy the diesel motor he had ordered so that she could switch over to machine milking.

Jersey cows only give about three gallons of milk each per day, compared to a big Holstein which produces about seven. But their cream is more than twice as rich in fat – from 6% to 7% – so the return on them is very good.

I was surprised to find that after the cream is separated out of the milk, that is all we keep for the market. The skim milk is mixed with bran and pollard to make mash for the chooks, or fed to pigs in what they call a slurry – or even thrown away. The Gurners next door take most of ours in return for things like vegetables we don't have. (That's where my cousins' pet lamb, called Lamb Chop, came from; they sent him along one week when there was nothing else we needed.) When whole milk is poured into our separator, which has a vacuum bucket that holds three gallons, the barrel whirs round at a great speed, and centrifugal force (which I don't quite understand!) sends the cream to the top, where it is scooped up by fifty-two little cups, called patty pans, and collected into a bowl.

Then the cream is kept in five-gallon cans, with each day's new supply added over a whole week. Our pickup day is Tuesday. When that was explained to me I said, 'Imagine if it all went sour in a heatwave!' Grandpa Jack, who helps run the farm, growled at me that that's exactly what can happen, and if it was totally off then it would all have to be thrown out.

'And if it's just a bit pongy?' I asked.

'Then you get paid according to how bad it is,' he replied, with a snort that made it clear he thought I was stupid not to work that out.

We are getting a good price for cream because a lot of dairy farms have been forced out of business due to shortage of labour.

Some farms have Coolgardie safes with wet bags on the sides, or coolrooms with concrete floors to keep the cream fresh, but we have something better – an underground 'well' lined with cement. Its concrete lid is six inches thick, which is fortunate, or my young cousins would be trying to open it to play down there. That could be terribly dangerous, as it has no ventilation once the lid is shut.

To finish the cream story, the milkmaids and farmer have to be careful to keep everything clean at each stage of the milking and storage process. If the cream was contaminated by dust, grass or germs – or if anyone added water – it would get a poor grading when it was tested at the factory, and wouldn't be worth much. What's worse, poor hygiene might make the cows get infected udders (that's called mastitis) and sometimes the infection goes right through their bodies and kills them.

So all the cans have to be sterilised when they are emptied. We've got an ingenious cleaning machine that my Uncle Brian made years ago from two ten-gallon coppers, one upturned on top of the other, and a fire underneath to make steam. After a can is scrubbed by hand, inside and out, it gets upended on to a steam jet on this hissing, spitting contraption.

Luckily I don't have to sterilise cans. But we make our own butter. Everyone has a go at turning the handle on the butter churn, even little Bob. And then there are all the bits of the churn and separator to be washed – again and again and again ...

I would like to assure the pupils who read my account that if they had to do this sort of work, without a day off *ever* (because you can't tell a cow to have a holiday) they would never complain again about any of their schoolwork being hard or boring. The thought of reciting French or Latin verbs in class seems very attractive to me these days.

## THE END

That last sentence reminds me I was going to learn some more vocabulary tonight. I've made my way to Chapter 10 in the Latin book; it helps keep my brain from getting rusty.

*THURSDAY 2 APRIL*
You wouldn't think that writing about keeping cream fresh could give you a nightmare. But I had a horrifying one last night, after describing the underground well where we store the cream cans. You see, I didn't put the whole of what Grandpa Jack said into my essay. He muttered this story about a local farmer in financial trouble who got so depressed that he shut the lid of his coolroom down on himself, and wasn't found for days. Aunty Joyce *shooshed* Jack just at the crucial moment, and I never found out whether the man suffocated. But the story gave me the creeps, all the same.

Then in my dream the Japs were pouring down over the hill with their rifles raised – and Aunty Joyce was trying to stuff Johnny and Bob down the hole and force the lid down on them. Bob still had a hand sticking out, and the boys were both screaming ...

Only, I was the one screaming. Mother shook me awake, then

held me tight, and asked me what was wrong. I couldn't explain, except to say that it was a bad dream.

'Well,' she said, 'we all have them.' And she sounded terribly sad. I felt guilty about adding to her worries, but after we had a whispered talk I think we both felt a bit calmer. It's the first time she has let on how she feels too.

I did have one laugh today – a quiet chuckle anyway. When Aunty went to light the fire under the copper to boil up the sheets and white towels, there was no kindling wood cut up. Now, it's one of Grandpa Jack's regular tasks to keep up the wood supply, and he was nowhere to be seen. So Aunty stormed out to the wood shed, shouldering the axe like a rifle, and dragged out some old fruit cases to chop up. A bit later we spotted Grandpa Jack in the distance working in his own yard, but he kept his back turned. So he's not sick. It took a few hours for us all to agree that he has gone on strike! I reckon he's trying to teach us 'useless creatures' a lesson. Mother said she thought he's waiting for an apology, to which Aunty Joyce replied, 'Well, he'll be waiting a long time, won't he?' And she and Mother set about hosing out the dairy.

'You haven't laid a place for Jack,' Joyce observed as she passed through the kitchen, her arms filled with clean linen.

'Well, we haven't seen him all day. Do you really expect him?' Sylvia replied.

'Mark my words, he won't sulk for long. His empty stomach will lead him here. And when he comes, he'll want to pick a fight, but I'm not going to react. That'll really rile him.'

Sure enough, right on six o'clock, they heard the scrape of the back screen door. Grandpa Jack came in with a snort and plonked himself down – but in Bob's place, not his usual spot. Joyce and Sylvia went on serving up.

Next Joyce went to the back door and rang the handbell she kept there to summon anyone who was still outside. When the boys came running into the kitchen, Bob stopped in surprise. 'That's where I sit!' he told his grandfather.

'Hmm,' grunted Grandpa Jack. After a moment he added, 'The ladies seem to reckon they're the bosses here, so I thought one of them better sit at the head of the table.'

'Please yourself,' said Joyce.

*Hey, Les, you should see what's brewing here!*

Sylvia had been keeping Les in touch with this stand-off.

It was Bob who saved the day. 'A *man* has to be at the top of the table, Grandpa Jack. And if it can't be my Daddy, I want it to be you.'

He looked as if he might cry at any moment. But in the nick of time, Grandpa Jack reached out and ruffled his grandson's hair, then shifted himself around.

'You're right, you know. Got to keep up traditions. Been eatin' at this table since I was knee high to a grasshopper. Now when I was a lad we couldn't start until our old man had picked up his knife and fork. An' we weren't allowed to speak unless one of our parents started the conversation neither.'

*Well, that's broken the ice! They're going hammer and tongs, arguing whether the good old days were really good.*

A truce had been called – for now. Just as well, thought Sylvia. Heaven knows there were enough unpleasant jobs to be done, without taking on the mucking out of the milking shed, or digging drains, or – heaven forbid – burying carcasses. Though woodchopping was another matter. Any farmer's wife worth her salt should be able to do that. Now, if she'd married Ted …

73

*FRIDAY 3 APRIL*

It's Good Friday, and Heather's coming up on Sunday. Mother can't work out why she isn't here for the whole weekend, but I'll bet it's because of lover boy. We've already got her a ride back on Easter Monday with a commercial traveller coming through from Murray Bridge who is also picking up Uncle Norm and Aunty Ivy's Marjorie, so I will see someone in my age group at last. Hope she'll be friendly.

We will be meeting all of Uncle Brian's family from far and wide on Easter Day, at a big lunch over at Uncle Norm's. They have one every year between harvest and seeding. We'll have to cook for that tomorrow. Our contribution is a tray of lamingtons and two blackberry tarts (with cream, of course). Since I cooked a passable batch of pastry last week, I'll get to make the tarts after I've taken the boys blackberrying down by the creek.

Johnny and Bob are excited about getting an Easter egg each on Sunday, even though Aunty Joyce, who is still really crotchety with them sometimes, has warned them that in these hard times the Easter Bunny often only brings painted hard-boiled hens' eggs. They are planning to leave a carrot outside their bedroom door so he will know where to find the little nest they have already made from leaves and ferns.

The boys and I made a lovely card to send Grandma for Easter, because it's her birthday too. We decorated it with silver paper from a cigarette packet, cut into the shape of an egg. I wish ... Well, I won't finish that sentence. I can hear Grandma saying, 'If wishes were horses, beggars would ride.'

Bob asked, 'How old is Grandma?' and I smiled before making a vague reply. Grandma used to say, 'As old as my tongue and a little older than my teeth' – at which Heather and I would groan.

Today, since it's the most solemn day in the Christian calendar, we're not supposed to do anything except go to church. Mother says that when she was a child every Sunday was like this. I think I would have rebelled. Anyway, thank goodness for my first batch of books from the Country Lending Service at last. I've been trying to read some of my school textbooks, but it's hard on my own. As well as an annual that I've read before, my bundle includes a novel, along with *How to Build Your Own Puppet Theatre, A Traveller's Guide to India* and *Getting to Know Moths* (!). I'll read them all, but it's the stories I love most. The main characters in a good book almost seem like friends, especially now I don't have many.

It was Miss Selby, the Grade Seven teacher, who had the books for me, and called me into her classroom when I was collecting the children yesterday. She's nice – young – and Johnny told me she lives on a farm the other side of the bald hill that you can see from the kitchen window. The interesting thing about the meeting, though, was that a boy not too much older than me was sitting ever so quietly, sort of slumped over as if he was ill, at the side of her desk. I caught him casting a sideways glance at me and he gave me a half smile, which I returned. He was unusual looking, with a mop of very fair hair, a pale complexion and attractive green eyes. Afterwards when I asked Johnny who he was, he just shrugged and said, 'I dunno.' But Janie Gurner thinks he's the teacher's cousin – and Bob thinks he's her husband! I wonder what he was doing, just hanging around there?

Aunty Joyce got the fox last night. The sound of the rifle nearly gave me a heart attack. I think Aunty's very brave. Today the poor animal's skin is hanging on a fence to be admired; it was a vixen. We're not supposed to have sympathy for them because they are not native to Australia, but there's something beautiful about its reddish fur and brushy tail, and it probably has young ones starving in its den.

I'm going to curl up now with *Dorothy's First Term*. Lucky Dorothy. I'll bet her biggest worry is the rich girl in fifth form who flaunts her pocket money. I don't think she'll be much of a friend.

*EASTER MORNING*

A quick note to record that the Easter Bunny did find his way to Johnny's and Bob's bedroom, and left them each a sugar egg decorated with pretty flowers made from icing. Funny, I saw some very similar eggs at the stall raising money for the Returned Soldiers' Relief Fund. Ah, I wish I was still a little child.

But then Aunty spoiled the happy mood by smacking Bob because he took a bite out of the end of his egg before breakfast, when she had said they must keep them on the mantelpiece for later. He's such a little boy, and it was a shame to see him sent to his room crying. Mother and I exchanged looks, but it's not our place to interfere with his upbringing. Aunty seems to have more patience with Johnny; I think she favours him because he looks so much like Uncle Brian.

I've made a resolution not to have a favourite when I have children.

Have to get ready for the big lunch now, and Ian will be picking up Heather in the town soon. Oh, I nearly forgot to add that Grandpa Jack is back to normal, even though Aunty Joyce hasn't apologised to him. For the first time I'm thinking that maybe there's a nice side to him, because he was kind to Bob yesterday; though he wouldn't want you to work that out.

My head is still buzzing with meeting new people and my system is overloaded with far too much delicious country food. That rabbit pie! Aunty will soon get her wish – I'll be as fat as a pig that's headed for market if I keep trying everything on the table at social gatherings. Actually, I think Aunty meant she wanted me to gain muscles, not fat.

Heather thought it was an amazing spread too. Do you know that Mrs Jones didn't give her boarders any of the dairy food we sent home last time she came?

Anyway, enough about food; it's just about all we talk about these days. Producing it, eating it, selling it. Considering my sluggish state, I'll confine my impressions of the people I met yesterday to Aunty Ivy and Uncle Norm's girls. The older women there were friendly enough, but a bit nosy.

I'll start with Marjorie. I hope she'll become my friend now that we're part-time neighbours. She seems used to getting her own way; she announced that we'll do things in the holidays. (But do I get holidays?) I'm eighteen months older than she is, so she doesn't tease me too much when I show my ignorance about farm life. She is not tall and lean, like Ian, but takes after Aunty Ivy. That is, she's rather stocky and has a mane of long brown hair. Mane is an appropriate word for her, because she's mad about horses, and was looking smart in jodhpurs, a white shirt and riding boots. When she said she'd teach me to ride, I decided not to tell her yet that I'm pretty frightened of horses. That's silly, I know, but one reared up in front of me when I was little. I don't need to envy her, because she misses home terribly, especially for Millie her skewbald pony, and she absolutely detests boarding school. Since she hates schoolwork too, French in particular, and almost boasts that she's bottom of her class, we don't have a lot in common. She chatters away non-stop though, and is a change from mothers, aunts and small children.

Of course, Ian's company would be better, but he hardly ever left the safety of his little bunch of friends all day. Though they spent a bit of time looking across from near the shed to where we women and girls sat under the big walnut tree, I observed. That very fair boy was there for a while too. He looks nice. I didn't notice him at first, because he was sitting down, with the other boys standing round him. Then after lunch a buckboard driven by a middle-aged man, with Miss Selby in the front too, came and picked him up. I heard someone joke about him going home for his beauty sleep. It's funny, that's the third time I've seen him, but I still haven't been introduced to him. While we were down the creek getting blackberries yesterday I noticed him in the distance, alone, walking very slowly along a dirt track winding up over the hill. Johnny and Bob, who had got tired of finding berries, were playing with the skulls of two sheep washed down by last winter's flood, and didn't see him. He was bent over a bit; I'm wondering if he's had infantile paralysis. Marjorie doesn't know who he is either, and you'd think she would know everyone around here; so I'm calling him the mystery boy. I could ask Ian about him.

All of that is a diversion from describing the family but, then, it's my diary and I can write whatever I want.

Next – Janice, Marjorie's oldest sister. I can dismiss her in a sentence, because she's stodgy like Aunty Ivy, has a big red-headed husband who hardly ever says a word, a bald baby that would be the spitting image of him if it had hair, and which everyone drooled over, plus conversation that's strictly limited to the baby's feeds, sleeps and poos – which they call Number Twos. They live on a wheat farm in the Mallee. Oops, that's two sentences.

Valerie, the other sister, is a different kettle of fish altogether, to use one of Grandma's favourite terms. She looks more like Ian. She surprised me by having an opinion about everything; in fact she seemed keen to pick an argument with anyone who would take her on. Her chief complaint is that women don't have the same rights as men to fight for their country. Apparently when the war started everyone kept telling her that if she was all that keen to help she could become a nurse, like that nice girl Verna from down the road who had trained at Murray Bridge hospital. Verna left for Egypt on the *Queen Elizabeth* last November when things started getting tough for our troops over there. (Her mother, who was present, made sure we all knew that.)

Anyway, nurses are the only women directly involved with the active armed forces. Marjorie says Valerie finally yelled that she didn't want to be a nurse, she wanted to fight for her country. So the following week she gave up her job at Chapman's (the smallgoods factory), packed her bags, left home and joined the Women's Air Training Corps. It's only a voluntary organisation, but it made her feel more useful. Now, she's a WAAAF; that's the Women's Auxiliary Australian Air Force. They get paid, though it's less than the men get, and since Australia has become fully mobilised she's hoping she may end up overseas. Marjorie and I sneaked into her bedroom and had a peep at her smart blue uniform and peaked cap.

Over lunch when I asked about auxiliary groups, she said these women still don't go into the front lines, but they do real jobs in the Force that free the men to go into battle; so I suppose that's one step closer. Nurses are wonderful but I don't think I'm cut out to be one. So maybe if I ever get called up in a war, this would be another way to avoid killing people.

'Janice and Valerie are so different, aren't they?' one of the women in the big circle remarked as the afternoon wore on. Ivy had to agree, smiling fondly at Janice, who was rocking her baby in its pram under the back verandah. At the same time, Valerie's voice could be heard coming from the knot of boys over by the tractor shed. She alone had been bold enough to enter their ranks, and she was telling them how WAAAFs even flew new aircraft to the war zones. They were often in real danger.

'And what do the rest of you girls want to do when you grow up?' asked the mother of that 'nice girl' Verna.

Heather replied she was already doing more than enough for her country, since she was in military manufacturing, and if the war went on for long enough she'd probably be married by the time it ended.

'Talk about Miss Prim and Proper!' Rosemary whispered to Marjorie in disgust. But to her surprise, Marjorie also said bluntly that she just wanted to keep living in the Hills and get married and have babies.

Unfortunately for Marjorie, Valerie came over to sit down at that precise moment. She exploded: 'Don't *any* of you realise that things are never going to be the same after this war? Women aren't going to stop wanting proper jobs. I'm amazed you have so little ambition.'

'Won't be much point in ambitions if we become an outpost of Japan,' said Joyce grimly. 'Little yellow men will be living in our houses and we'll be sleeping in the sheds and be their slaves.'

There were shocked looks. 'We would *never* give in to them!' someone declared.

Aunty Ivy agreed. 'Where's your spirit, Joyce? You sound like that Gilmore woman – the poet. Did you read those verses she wrote in the *Women's Weekly* the other day?'

'Shame on her,' someone else agreed, and Rosemary made a mental note to find out what poem they were talking about.

Valerie broke the uncomfortable silence by asking Rosemary what she wanted to do when the war was over. And Sylvia answered for her, saying she should go to night school and learn domestic arts, because she was really getting quite good at cooking.

Rosemary's stomach knotted with anger, but she just managed to keep her calm. 'I want to go to university eventually,' she stated as firmly as she could. At which almost the whole circle of women stared at her, bemused. Except for Valerie, who smiled and nodded.

'What course would you do? Teaching?' asked Ivy.

'I – I'd like to do something with languages – words,' she stuttered.

The older women were still looking nonplussed. Only Valerie responded enthusiastically. 'What a pity you're too young to join up! We need interpreters so badly, you know.'

Later, when she was cleaning Bob's hands and face in the washhouse, Rosemary overheard Ivy telling Valerie that she shouldn't have encouraged Joyce's poor little niece in that way, since she wasn't even going to finish high school. And a light flashed in her brain as she remembered what Grandma and Miss Whyte said about her doing anything she set her mind to. I *will* have a real career one day, she told herself as she headed back with her family for milking.

# 12

I've been neglecting my diary, but I have the whole evening to myself for once. To be honest, the days and weeks are starting to merge into each other, and I feel as if I left school a year ago, not just a month. It's all beautiful, autumn-leafy mellowness up here.

So, what has happened? Not much. (But the weekend will be better; I'll get to that eventually.) I turned down an offer to join a netball team because I hope we won't be here for the whole winter. And there was a barn dance at one of the churches – quite enjoyable now that I'm getting better at dances like the Military Two Step and even the Gay Gordons. If you're not sure of a move your partner just swings you around. Strip the Willow, which always ends the evening, is pretty complicated though.

I met a girl there who's about two years older than me, called Wendy. I already knew her slightly because she used to board with her aunt and uncle in town and go to my school. Only her brother is missing, presumed dead, from when the HMAS *Perth* went down somewhere up north of Australia called the Sunda Strait – the week before we moved up here – and her parents have taken her back home. That's what happens; families gather everyone close, like lions with cubs, as if they are afraid they might lose another one. I told her my father is missing too, and the next minute we were both blinking back tears. Wendy feels like she's in prison, she said, although she plans to try for an office job at the Littlehampton brickworks. Her farm is down that way. Too far away for us to visit each other, but I said I hoped I'd see her sometimes.

Talking to Wendy made me so aware again of how much I am missing Father. We keep scanning lists of dead and wounded in the papers but I don't think any of us expect bad or good news anymore. I've never mentioned that Mother writes a letter sometimes, and I add my love. But we can only send them to him care of the Army, with his details and 'AIF Abroad'. We only half believe they will get to him. Another thing: Mother sometimes says she has already told Father about some matter, and I know she hasn't. Does she write letters in her head, the way I start poems sometimes, and forget to put them on paper?

Back to the social ... (Just as well I don't have an English teacher marking this. She'd say, 'Rosemary, you write fluently and have a good vocabulary, but whatever happened to planning your work?') I kept watching to see if my mystery boy might turn up, because church socials are the event of the month in the country. Just about everyone I've ever seen round here who is under twenty-five was at the barn dance, even Miss Selby who might be his relation. But he seems to have disappeared. I've decided he's much better looking than Ian, and more suited to my age. (Now that I've been here a while I'm starting to just think of Ian as a sort of cousin.) I'd like to meet this boy one day! Only I've decided that if I ask the family who he was they'll all tease me, so I'll just be patient and hope he's not gone for good.

The air raids on Darwin are apparently continuing, and there were small raids on little towns called Katherine and Wyndham recently too. Since there seems to be a lot of censorship of stories about the Japanese attacks, most of the news comes from civilians returning south. It's passed on by word of mouth. For once we heard some good news in this way, because Uncle Norm's neighbour was told by his cousin that a week or so ago Australian troops shot down seven Japanese planes near Darwin.

Meanwhile I get what I can from the paper. But some of the stories from Europe are too bad to even think about. There's talk that Hitler's followers are rounding up Jews and putting them in concentration camps. I don't know much about Jews, but that's terrible!

I'm not going to write about even more ghastly things I'm hearing, just in case one of the children finds this. It's important to shield the little ones from the worst of the news. Johnny was leaning over my shoulder today, trying to pick out some words he knew in the paper, when I realised he was looking at what to do in the event of a gas attack, complete with a crude diagram of a house exploding when a bomb hit it. 'Making your shelter sp- splinter-proof,' he read out to me. So I quickly turned the page and pretended to read the market reports. Exciting stuff like 'Choice butter 1/3; eggs 1/5 a dozen'.

Suddenly Johnny was laughing. 'Cotton duck requ– requis –. What's a cotton duck, Rosemary?' he asked. 'Is it a baby's toy?'

The headline said 'Cotton Duck Requisitioned'. After scanning it swiftly I was laughing too. I told him that duck was very heavy cotton material, and that there was a new ruling that anyone who had stocks of it had to hand them over to the Government to make Army tents and suchlike! Ordinary cotton is very scarce too, as it's needed for uniforms. Aunty had to buy an artificial silky material called bemberg for 2/6 a yard last time she went to town, to make a blouse.

We're all having to make do, and there's even a campaign called 'Fashions for Victory', where the Government publishes hints for cutting down on the amount of material you use when sewing, while still producing smart garments. It's the same with knitting patterns. I read a Bulletin for Knitters, hints for working 'with speed and economy – ' (too late for my socks!) ' – without sacrifice to the appearance of the garment.' The result is plain, slim-fitting clothes.

How boring! Mother is getting one of Heather's pleated skirts ready for me, and we've lengthened the sleeves of my best twinset with contrasting stripes. The weather is getting colder although the drought hasn't shown any signs of breaking yet.

The reason for my new interest in clothes is that I'm about to go back to town for a couple of days! The Marryats rang Mother for a chat last week, and ended up asking if they could 'borrow' me to help with Billy's birthday party this Saturday. He'll be six. As it turns out, Aunty has an appointment about her nerves with a specialist at North Adelaide on Friday, so she will drop me in town. Mr Marryat is going to bring me all the way home on Sunday, with his family coming for the ride. I can't wait! (The Marryats don't have a car, and Mr Marryat rides his bike the few blocks to his school at Rose Park, dinkying Billy on the handlebars. But he has arranged to borrow a car from another teacher who doesn't use his much, and pay him for the petrol.)

The night before the party I'm going to help Mrs Marryat make crêpe-paper streamers and party hats cut out of coloured cardboard. Decorations are getting scarce, but Mother, who brought some sewing things with her, has unearthed a few sheets of yellow and green paper left over from the daffodil costume I wore in a school concert when I was little, and apparently a friend has donated a packet of silver glitter. We'll make crowns for the girls and sailors' hats for the boys. As well I've told her we always had party baskets made out of half a tea packet covered in crêpe-paper frills with cardboard handles.

I'm itching to see Janet while I'm in town, as we don't write to each other much now. Only with the blackouts it is harder to get around at night, so I don't know yet if it will be possible.

P.S. I checked out that poem in the *Women's Weekly*, and I can see why some of the women are upset about it. The poet, Mary Gilmore, is very well known. She says point blank that our soldiers in

Singapore and Malaya were cowards if they showed no resistance to the Japanese invaders. I know the reports suggested this, but I refuse to believe that someone like Father would be a coward, and I won't be ashamed of any of our troops. I'm not going to keep the poem with my other cuttings, because it makes me feel sick.

# 13

*MONDAY 20 APRIL*

Back again, after a weekend that did me so much good. (Except for one incident that left me furious – but I won't write about that until I've calmed down, if at all.)

It was a relief to get out of Aunty's car at the Beehive Corner in town, because she hardly spoke for the whole journey, even when I tried to get her talking. I knew she was going to pick Marjorie up later and take her home to Ivy and Norm for the weekend, so I asked why her niece seemed to hate school. Her reply was, 'Silly girl. One of the best schools, Saints.' And when I opened my mouth again she added, 'Just homesick. *Shoosh* – I have to concentrate.'

I had a quick lunch with Heather at Balfour's café. Luckily Heather offered to pay, to celebrate a pay rise to £2/10/- a week. So I stuffed down a Cornish pasty with sauce, one of their special green frog cakes and a banana milkshake.

Heather hoed in too, and when I commented that the lunch was a nice change from farm food, she laid it on about how dreadful boarding house food is. She said it was even worse than she had expected, due to shortages. Mrs Jones her landlady manages to put either sago or something called Mex barley kernels into almost every dish to add to its bulk. Then there are Mex oat petals, and even Mex vegetable flakes ... The only green vegetable is spinach from the garden, sometimes complete with grit or baby slugs.

'Okay,' I finally said, 'you've made me feel guilty!'

She added, 'And sweets are usually rhubarb and runny, lumpy custard.'

Heather normally only has half an hour for lunch, but she wangled an extra hour so she could get a train to town to meet me. Even so we had to talk nonstop. She said she goes out to cafés, the pictures and dances with Violet and others, but now that she's friendly with Jim, and can usually only see him at weekends, she sometimes feels as if she's just there to be a chaperone to get Violet home safely along the blacked-out streets. When Chuck is there, it's a case of 'two's company'. Oh – Violet has entered the Miss Munitions Quest between the Hendon and Finsbury munitions girls. It's already raised £1000 for the war effort. Heather said she's glad the Islington girls aren't part of it, because she would hate to have to parade in public, and for once I agree with her. I think Violet must be going a bit wild.

I asked how long this Chuck would be around, and Heather thinks he'll be here for the rest of the war, as he's involved in running training courses. So Violet may be in luck with him – if that's what she wants.

I've just realised that Heather and I met as equals, and never teased each other once. Wouldn't Mother be pleased if I told her that? We were giggling as we made vacuum cleaner noises into our glasses to drain every last drop of syrupy milk. She listened to my stories of farm life and she didn't mind telling me about Jim.

Suddenly I saw my tram stopping outside Myers down the street, so we quickly said goodbye and I made a dash along to the next stop outside John Martins. The tram passed me, but I caught up, just managing to throw myself and my suitcase on to its platform before it set off again.

I felt like a visitor as we made our way out to the parklands and past the racecourse, which had turned into a campsite for soldiers – a very strange sensation after only a few weeks away! In fact I became quite nervous when the tram turned into Dulwich Avenue, in case anything else had changed. But nothing had. There was even the iceman grappling a big block of ice with his tongs and lugging it up a driveway. Then when I got off Mr Sweetman was doing his rounds at the end of our street in his smart blue van with *Greengrocer – Only the Best Will Do* on the side, and the scales hanging above the back step. He hauled on the reins with an exaggerated 'Whoa boy!' to pull up old Socks and stop for a chat, so I hopped on to the step, just like in the old days. I bought two shiny red-and-yellow Jonathan apples for the boys. Mr Sweetman gave them an extra polish on his apron and added a couple of lovely ripe strawberries for Betty. He wanted to sell me half a case of late nectarines for the bargain price of 2/-, to take in to Mrs Marryat, but I told him I only had another shilling to last the whole weekend. Anyway, Mother's second-biggest Globite case was packed with butter, cream and eggs (which I prayed were still intact) and getting heavier by the minute. And my sheets, as the Marryats don't have any spares. Mother told me to say they must keep them.

I'm sure Miss Browning's front curtain moved as I slowed down going past the front of my 'old' house on the way to the Marryats'! My heart gave a jolt. How odd to see another family's bicycle and tricycles lined up against the side wall, a scooter thrown down on the gravel driveway and a mournful, woofing black cocker spaniel at the front gate. A fuzzy-haired, wide-eyed baby was sitting up strapped into a shabby pram that was parked on the front verandah in the sun. That's where I last saw my friends … However, I got such a warm welcome from Mrs Marryat and all three children that I soon cheered up.

We got straight down to work to produce everything that makes a party special. The only small disaster was when Alec, who is full of mischief, blew into the saucer of glitter that Mrs Marryat was about to paste on the girls' party hats, sending the thousands of shiny specks scattering for yards in all directions, even into our hair. So the girls had to have crowns with no jewels.

Janet's big brother Michael brought her all the way up from Glenelg on two trams to see me for an hour that night. He sat looking bored at first, but toting little sisters around is what brothers have to do sometimes. Just my luck to have Heather instead of a big brother. (His friends could have been useful one day as partners for dances!)

When we finished dissecting the lives of our mutual friends, Janet assured me that I'm lucky to be away from the gloom in the city, since Adelaide feels it will be isolated from any help if there is an invasion here. Her parents seem to know there's so much going on that the public doesn't hear about – like American and Australian Navy ships moored off the coast, which make people quite fearful in case the enemy attacks them. At which Michael came to life and said that at one stage there were seven American warships that hadn't made it to Pearl Harbour in time, and had been sent on here until they were redeployed. (Another of my new words.)

Janet says people are hiding drums of fuel in the sand hills, and there's a big new air-raid shelter – a concrete bunker – under the grandstand at Glenelg Oval. Michael explained that if there is an attack the public have instructions to gather there, and they will be given food, blankets and so on, before being sent on buses to Strathalbyn, up our way in the Hills, where they will camp on the oval. All the support people, like the St John Ambulance crews, will stay in the bunker.

Thinking about what it would be like to be evacuated, I realised I am becoming calmer about the war now I'm away from the city. We haven't made nearly as many preparations for an invasion as the Marryats have. They've even replaced their glass light shades with shields made of tin, that wouldn't shatter in an explosion.

Actually, my family are already evacuees – just lucky ones.

Michael is really interested in ships and can't wait to join the

Navy, despite Terrence's death. So I told him how Father came home from his first overseas stint in Jordan and Lebanon on the *Queen Mary* last year. He said there were 10,000 men on board, crammed into steel bunks four high in each cabin. Hammocks were slung everywhere too. And everyone had just half an hour a day on deck, when they were forced to exercise.

Back in my everyday world I'm being called to put Johnny and Bob in the bath because Aunty Joyce has gone to Mrs Gurner's. The story of the party will have to wait. It went well – until nearly the end. How dare that pompous man barge in as if he owned the place, and leave poor Mrs Marryat in tears?

# 14

Rosemary was in charge of the games – the usual things like Pin the Tail on the Donkey, Blind Man's Buff and Musical Chairs. Mr Marryat, who was supposed to be on hand to stop the more boisterous big cousins from getting too wild, and keeping everyone out of the air-raid shelter, disappeared round the side of the house by Miss Browning's overgrown hedge with his pipe and matches during the last game, which was a chocolate frog hunt among the hydrangeas and agapanthus. Rosemary laughed to herself, imagining how Miss Browning might tell him off like a naughty schoolboy if she spotted him through the gap.

The bigger boys started organising a game of their own. The leader gathered his chosen group round him, with a stick for a gun, and announced they were going to play battles. 'We're the Aussies,' he told the three girls and the smallest boys. 'The Diggers. And you're the Germans. We've got the lawn and the orange trees, so you have to go down the back by the chook house and almond trees, and we'll invade you.'

A little girl of about four, one of the new neighbours, burst into tears. 'I don't want to be 'vaded!' she wailed.

Rosemary decided to leave the bigger children to sort it out. 'You come inside with me then,' she beckoned. Children of that age didn't need to learn how to lie down and pretend to be dead. She also scooped up Betty, who had spent the last hour waddling round after her like a faithful dog. They headed indoors to see when the party tea would be ready. After all, that's what children really come to parties for.

While Mrs Marryat and a couple of aunties placed candles on the cake and finished putting lollies in the pretty little baskets made out of tea packets cut in half and covered with crêpe-paper frills, Rosemary began filling cream horns with mashed-up strawberry jelly. She was doing quite a good job of topping each one with whipped cream when Betty fell over while trying to clamber on to a chair and help, bumping her arm. A big dob of cream plopped on to the mottled green lino, but it didn't matter because Elmer the curly-haired puppy (Billy's birthday present) soon licked it up.

Then, just as they were calling all the children into the dining room to eat, there was a ring at the front door. 'Can you get that, Rosemary dear?' called Mrs Marryat in a frazzled voice, balancing on one foot as she lifted a tray of sausage rolls out of the oven while shielding the puppy from the heat with the other.

Rosemary was confronted by the massive bulk of a uniformed man, a pen hovering over an official-looking notebook wedged against his great stomach.

'Corporal O'Flynn from the Volunteer Defence Force, Burnside Battalion. I need to speak to your mother,' he boomed.

She immediately renamed him Corporal Officious. 'It – she's not my mother,' she began to explain. 'I'm just – ' But he looked so forbidding that she stopped explaining and fled to the dining room to get Mrs Marryat. There the table was about to be attacked by the ravenous guests, poised like twenty lively young dogs straining at the end of invisible leashes while they waited to be told they could tuck in.

Mrs Marryat gave a despairing look around, as if wondering how to escape, then called one of her kitchen helpers to take over, and told the children they could start. 'But remember your manners, you boys!' she called over her shoulder. She asked Rosemary to stay by the door and not let anyone out to disturb her.

Corporal Officious had come to inspect the house with a view to deciding how many American servicemen the Marryats could billet. He explained the men would stay while they were working or training in Adelaide, until they were sent on active duty somewhere. Then they would come back whenever they got leave, just like a family member.

Mrs Marryat looked appalled. 'But I've got three young children,' she protested. 'And anyway, my husband's an air-raid warden, so we do our bit.'

'You know what the Prime Minister said: "All Australians at home must, individually, wage a war to the death",' the Corporal insisted. He went on to the bit in the speech about everyone making sacrifices. It was a wonder he didn't quote the Queen too, thought Rosemary; she had told women in London during the Blitz that their housewifely duties were just as important as the efforts of the armed forces. As if they'd believe that …

'No, I just can't do it. My two youngest are ill so often. They need a lot of extra care. And my husband's out just about every night, doing training or civil defence work.' Mrs Marryat's voice was uncharacteristically terse. She tried to add that she had joined the Toorak Gardens Red Cross and Community Club committee too, but the visitor didn't let her finish.

'What illness do the children have?' he asked suspiciously, consulting his list.

'Alec – he's the three-year-old – has dreadful asthma attacks, and since we came south he's been getting bronchitis,' she began. At that little Betty slipped past Rosemary, toddled over to her mother, and tripped on the edge of a mat just as she reached her. 'And this one – 'Mrs Marryat went on, with a catch in her voice, 'was born with her hips out of joint.' She hugged Betty to her.

For a split second Officious looked a bit sympathetic, turning his attention to Betty, a quite beautiful child with a mop of auburn ringlets. 'But I thought babies born like that could have an operation to fix the, er, condition,' he said. 'My nephew – '

'Blame this damned war!' Mrs Marryat interrupted him. 'We were living in Darwin when she was born, and with all those troops massing – you know, ready for a Japanese invasion – we couldn't find a doctor who could be spared to treat a civilian. Then, by the time we were evacuated down here, it was too late to cure her. She'll always walk like a duck.' Her face crumpled as she finished her outburst.

Officious drew himself up and his face became a mask. 'Not an acute condition, so no exemption,' he decided. 'There isn't any choice, I'm afraid. Now, let's see how many rooms you have.'

Mr Marryat, who had joined them by this stage, assured Officious there were no spare rooms. But of course when the volunteer soldier plodded off on a tour of inspection, he wasn't fooled for a second by Rosemary's makeshift bed on a couch in the sitting room.

'Visitor,' he noted. His face didn't even crack into a smile when Mr Marryat took him in to be half deafened by the happy horde of children in the dining room, most of their faces smeared with tomato sauce and cream. They were just in time to catch Billy and his cousin making rude gestures with frankfurts …

At the end of his inspection the Corporal announced the three children could all share a room, and that a separate dining room was not required. Which meant the Marryats would be assigned two American 'guests' to cook, wash and iron for. They would arrive within the week.

When Mrs Marryat headed to her bedroom in tears after his departure, the aunties and Rosemary had to take control and keep the party going smoothly.

*This damned war!* Rosemary repeated to herself angrily as she hurried yet another small child off to the lavatory. That was a term she would never dare use in front of an adult.

I won't go on about the party now; I'll write to Grandma later about that bossy corporal, which should be enough to get it all off my chest. Grandma will be sorry for Mrs Marryat, who has to billet Americans.

There are still a few other small things about last weekend that I want to report, though. I didn't mention that Miss Browning has let her poky sleep out to some desperate newly-weds. Apparently they could hardly fit their bed in there. She wasn't just being kind, I'm told. First she needs the money and, secondly, she's expected to make full use of her house to help the war effort. Imagine sharing the kitchen, bathroom and clothes line with her! I'll bet she bosses them.

Then, I haven't written about Billy and Alec's visit to the farm. Mrs Marryat didn't come, as she not only had a sick headache, but was also in a panic preparing her house for the Americans' arrival. She kept Betty with her. All four boys got on famously, and after gobbling down Aunty's lovely Sunday roast they ran about the farm until they nearly dropped. Johnny had been given strict instructions that he was not to let them disturb the cows or go anywhere near Bruce the bull, who lives in solitary splendour in the furthest paddock for most of the year, but that didn't seem to spoil the boys' fun. I did have to intervene when Billy decided everyone should go on a snake hunt, though!

The visitors were fascinated to find the train line that runs right along the far fence of the paddock where Lamb Chop is supposed to live, so I stayed with them to make sure they weren't tempted to get through the wire and on to the track. I showed them how to put their hands on the ground, so they could feel a train coming before they heard it.

Bob said, 'My daddy went away to the war on a train when I was small.'

'Shiny rails!' Johnny exclaimed, and everyone turned to look at him. 'I used to think he was always still there at the other end of those silver tracks.' I patted his shoulder.

Before I could give in to feeling depressed, though, Billy yelled, 'Here's one coming!' Sure enough, a long train crammed with hundreds of troops came through, so we all hung over the fence and waved. We got lots of smiles, waves and even blown kisses in return and the train driver gave an extra toot just for the boys. Guess what Billy wants to do when he grows up?

And for a minute the mystery boy turned up too! Suddenly, as the train approached, he emerged from behind the shed at the rickety siding on the other side of the track, in from the road. The siding apparently hasn't been used for many years except that occasionally parcels are thrown off for farmers. It doesn't have a name any more, but old-timers still call it Scott's siding, after our farm. I thought I saw the boy reaching up and waving, looking as if he was calling out something, though of course you couldn't hear for the deafening clatter of the train. Then the carriages hid him from us for a minute, and I fully expected he would have somehow jumped on board. But when the guard's van had passed, there he was, waving happily – much as we were. Someone had thrown a folded newspaper to him from a carriage window, and he glanced at his trophy before he headed slowly off into the scrub.

He didn't seem to look at us, but he must have been watching us from his hiding place.

Another mystery: the only worrying thing about the lovely afternoon was that we couldn't find Lamb Chop anywhere. The visitors would have loved him. Aunty said she'd tell Ian to look out for him. But now, three days on, he still hasn't turned up. Luckily Johnny and Bob stopped fretting for him this afternoon and started a game of chasey, but I'm puzzled, and keep listening for that familiar 'baaa – aa'.

Even Grandpa Jack seemed to enjoy having all those boys tearing around the farm. When Mr Marryat finally dragged Alec and Billy to his car and said goodbye, we all agreed they should come up again. At which Mr Marryat, who must still be quite shocked at what happened to Darwin, said if things got bad enough in Adelaide, he might be sending them up for the duration. He didn't need to spell out that he meant if the city is bombed.

# 15

'Did you read *this?*' Rosemary thrust the day's news headlines in front of her weary mother, who had just come in from milking with Joyce. They had battled that afternoon getting old Molly, one of the best milkers, back up on her feet after she slipped into a ditch. Joyce headed off to light the chip heater for the boys' bath, while Sylvia plonked herself on to a kitchen chair for a minute's respite.

*Here we go again, Les. She latches on to the smallest development. Knows too much. I reckon the Defence Forces could use her to plan their next moves.*

'You tell me,' she sighed. 'My head's spinning.'

'I hope you've got our tea waiting!' Joyce shouted from the bathroom.

Rosemary called back impatiently, 'I made a shepherd's pie with the rest of the cold lamb. It's ready in the oven.' She turned back to her mother. 'It says here that General MacArthur has taken control of all the combat units of the Australian armed forces. And the headline calls him "the Saviour of Australia". That's good, isn't it?'

'Yes, well opinions will be divided about whether he's a saviour. Lots of Australians are unhappy about an American in charge of our forces,' said Sylvia.

'But I think we've got to accept it if we don't want to be invaded, don't we?'

*She's forcing me to have a debate with her again. Oh, if only you were here, Les!*

Joyce was back. 'Goodness knows I don't worship the Americans, but I hope the papers are right about the saviour bit. Someone in town today said that the Government is planning to divide Australia into two zones, and abandon the north in a line above Brisbane if it is invaded.' She disappeared again, responding to a loud bang from the cranky heater.

Rosemary let the idea sink in.

*'Abandon the north*? But that's terrible!' she exclaimed. 'Think about it. We all know the enemy could get to the centre of the country, and come straight on down by train.'

'Now – ' her mother was trying to interject.

'Our cattle stations and farms and little towns would be the first stops – and then Adelaide!'

'Now, don't get all upset. It's just a rumour,' Sylvia told her. She was annoyed that Joyce hadn't kept that bit of news to herself. She thought of her husband.

> *You know, Les, I always say ignorance is bliss. Like we're not telling Rosemary about that awful Tokio Rose and her propaganda and vicious gossip, on the wireless at night.*

But Joyce never missed a chance to make everyone jittery. Tonight while they ate she reported on a letter that had come that day. It was from an old schoolfriend who had married a doctor and gone to live in Sydney.

'At the school that Beryl's daughter goes to – a private one of course – every girl has to carry a khaki canvas bag with emergency supplies in it, and their name and address sewn on the front in big letters in case they have to evacuate suddenly. We should make bags for you boys.'

Bob said he already had a schoolbag. Johnny had at least some idea of what sort of bag they meant, though. 'Can I fill mine with lollies? And my Meccano set?' he asked.

'You'll have clean underpants and socks, and dried food,' Sylvia hopped in quickly before Joyce could scare them to death with graphic details of fleeing from the enemy.

Rosemary chuckled to herself. *The first thing a mother would see to before you had to run away is that you had clean underwear!* But aloud she took her mother's cue. 'What else does the letter say?' she asked. The reply didn't help.

'She wants to know if we've received printed instructions about preparing for an air raid. You can put tape diagonally across the windows, you know, so they don't shatter with the pressure. Or you can tape on lace-curtain material or mosquito netting to stop the glass flying when it splinters. I think I'll write away for a copy.'

They must be even more frightened in the big cities like Sydney than in places down south; it might be the beginning of the end if the largest city was captured. When Rosemary thought about the conversation again as she drifted off to sleep later she reminded herself how tranquil their life was, and recited, *I will lift up mine eyes unto the hills, from whence cometh my help.* They couldn't possibly be in danger up here. Could they?

Suddenly her eyes were wide open again.

*FRIDAY 24 APRIL*

To think I was telling myself how peaceful it is to be here. I still can't believe what I am about to write.

<u>Lamb Chop has been turned into chops.</u>

We get a side of lamb from Uncle Norm's every week or two, in return for milk, cream and eggs. So, following the weekend roast leg I innocently produced grilled loin chops on Monday, braised neck and breast on Tuesday, a rolled stuffed shoulder on Wednesday, and so on. The penny only dropped tonight, while I was serving up rabbit with bacon and onions – one of my absolute favourites – after Aunty Ivy brought us two good-sized bunnies Ian had trapped. When I remarked how nice it was to have a change from lamb, I noticed a funny, sly look cross Aunty's face.

I waited, almost exploding with fury, until Mother took the boys out to pick quinces, then burst forth.

'You killed Lamb Chop!!' I accused Aunty. 'How *could* you?' She admitted she'd taken the opportunity to get Ian to remove him last Friday while I was down in town and the boys were at school; and she was quite unrepentant.

'But those little boys *loved* him!' I went on. Aunty's face closed up at the word 'love', so I stopped short of saying her children didn't get half enough of it. She replied that Lamb Chop was getting to be a darned nuisance, and if I knew anything about farms I'd understand that you simply can't have a full grown ram running round the place.

I stormed out, and have just finished having a good cry. Yes, I slammed another door. I hate Aunty Joyce and I hate Ian too. The only comforting thing is the boys haven't worked out what happened. And I'll make absolutely sure they don't.

Sylvia was also keeping something to herself – a letter from the Army's District Records Office. Her heart had leapt and then lurched when she saw 'Australian Military Forces' on the envelope, and her hand trembled as she opened it. But it told her nothing.

> 'I have been directed by the Minister for the Army to advise you that no definite information is at present available in regard to the whereabouts or circumstances of your Husband Number SX 12839 Lieutenant Lesley Hurtle LISTER, 2/15th Field Regiment, Eighth Division, A.I.F. and to convey to you the sincere sympathy of the minister and the Military Board in your natural anxiety in the absence of news concerning him.'

The next paragraph explained why 'some time must necessarily elapse' before there could be any news. In a blur Sylvia read about 'the nature of the recent operations in the theatre of war in which he was engaged' as well as 'the difficulties which have arisen in communicating with units which are located in territory now held by the enemy'. And so it went on. A full page of waffle.

> *Listen to those bureaucrats, Les. Why can't they save paper and just say, 'We don't know where he is or what has happened to him. We're sorry. Please be patient.'*

Finally there were the assurances that the 'utmost endeavour' would continue to be made, and any definite report would be conveyed to her by telegram. She sighed and put the letter into the wood stove.

> *Of course, Les; I got in such a flap that I forgot I'd get a telegram if there were any real news. Well, no point even telling Joyce or Rosemary about this one. I don't know which of them is worse – one or other of them is always getting her knickers in a knot over something.*

The weekend delivered a medley of pride, hostility, distress, tears – and happiness. First, Grandpa Jack put on his uniform and his medals on Saturday morning long before sunrise, squared his shoulders, tilted his slouch hat and strode into the town for the Anzac dawn service.

Rosemary, who had heard the scrape of the gate, asked her mother at breakfast who'd been coming or going so early on a Saturday. She was giving Joyce the cold shoulder.

But it was Joyce who replied. 'April twenty-fifth. Anzac Day. That was Jack off to glorify war with all the other old codgers,' she snorted.

'I thought he wanted no more to do with war,' Rosemary ventured.

'He's not glorifying war, Joyce. You're wrong,' said Sylvia. 'He's honouring his lost mates; the spirit of the Anzacs will never die, you know.'

*You're carrying it on right now, aren't you, Les?*

When someone dropped the old Digger off at his gate later in the day, Joyce couldn't help another snide remark. 'There's more than Anzac spirit in him,' she said, watching her father-in-law make his way a little unsteadily up his back path.

But Rosemary stuck up for Grandpa Jack this time, recalling the marches and services that she and Heather had been to with her father, and the overwhelming sadness of reciting *'We will remember them'*. 'I reckon that anyone who stands there listening to the "Ode to Remembrance" for the loved ones they lost deserves a pretty stiff drink afterwards.'

Joyce gave her a blank stare that she mistook for an unspoken question, so she began to recite. 'You know – "They shall grow not old as we that are left grow old." It – ' Trailing off and turning pale when she saw the embittered look on her Aunt's face, she tried to apologise for upsetting her; but Joyce was already marching to her bedroom.

And then on Sunday a shy but proud Heather brought Jim up to the farm.

'He's not all that good looking, is he?' Rosemary observed to her mother as the two young lovers ambled across the heifers' paddock, hand in hand.

'He's a lovely, wholesome-looking young man,' Sylvia remonstrated. 'And the two of them are obviously head over heels in love.'

*You'd approve of him, Les. Looks like a nice, clean-living*
*fellow. Quiet, but that's not a bad thing. My word, that*
*Rosemary's a picky young miss. Wait till it's her turn to get*
*a boyfriend.*

'It's just that he's got a big nose that makes his eyes look little, and he's rather short. I suppose he's all right,' she conceded, 'but he's no Prince Charming, is he?'

When Jim went off to kick an old floppy football with the boys after they'd all had a cup of tea and scones spread with the new quince jelly, a starry-eyed Heather asked Rosemary what she thought of him.

'Can't imagine what you see in him,' Rosemary replied flippantly. 'You always dreamed of getting someone really tall. He's a bit boring too.' She was only teasing, but Heather took her seriously, bursting into tears. Of course although Rosemary tried to tell her then that she had just been joking, the damage was done. Heather was quiet for the rest of the afternoon.

Then, when it was time for them to leave, Jim told everyone that he was enlisting, and would be going into training camp the following week. He'd finally decided on the Army. He would be at Woodside, which he thought was only about ten miles away as the crow flies.

You could have cut the silence with a knife.

'I'm sorry I teased you, Sis. Really!' Rosemary was the first to say something.

You could see Joyce's expression freeze again as the memories hit her. 'I hope it will all go well for you then,' she said with a stiff smile.

'My daddy went to the war,' Bob told Jim.

'And he was very brave,' added Johnny.

Only Sylvia had no words. Even though she hardly knew Jim, she got up and patted him on the shoulder, her eyes filled with tears. He and Heather looked so grown up and serious, standing there side by side. That night, alone in her bed, Sylvia talked to Les.

*The look in that steadfast young man's eye reminded me so much of you when you told us you were joining up, that I'm afraid I let my guard down. But don't worry; it's not often*

*that it all gets to me. I'm being strong for you, Les. Like you*
*told me to be.*

Johnny asked Joyce, as she tucked him up in bed, 'Mummy, how do we really know that Daddy was brave?'

'We just do,' she replied impatiently. 'All soldiers are brave. Now, go to sleep.'

# 16

*SATURDAY 9 MAY*

Oooh, I still love the extra bit of freedom I get on Saturdays! No bicycle riding, no schoolwork (even if it's a self-imposed task), no dressing for church. I've been lying here listening to all the different bird sounds, my favourite being the carolling of the magpies.

This week for the first time for ages we have heard good news of the war. There has been a huge battle in the Coral Sea (which I'd never heard of, but it's out in the Pacific, east of the northern tip of Australia), and the American naval forces with help from ours have driven the Japanese away from the south coast of Papua. Apparently lots of Japanese warships have been sunk. That's wonderful to hear – as long as I don't let myself think too much about all the people who have died – because New Guinea is the last stepping stone down to Australia if there's to be an invasion.

Mr Curtin is still doing a good job of stirring the nation. A report on his speech about this battle said that it brought tears to many a hardened journalist's eyes.

I never write much about the war in Europe, since you're not there, Father, but Mrs Gurner says the British Air Force is making massive raids on Germany, and the tide is beginning to turn over there. On the other hand, the Germans have opened a fresh offensive in Africa. It seems the news is never all good or all bad.

Jim went into training at Woodside, just across the Hills from here, on Monday. I wonder how often Heather will see him now? Perhaps it will be a case of 'absence makes the heart wander'; she might fall in love with someone else. He will have just a few months' training, then he's likely to be posted overseas, probably New Guinea.

We have had good rain at last, which means the new pasture should start to grow in a week or so. It's been such a bad drought that Uncle Norm's lambs have been feeding on windfall apples since the feed ran out, and we were getting worried the cows would go dry. Ian and Uncle Norm can start seeding now, just in time before the soil gets too cold. So everyone is pretty happy, especially Grandpa Jack. I even heard him humming yesterday morning in the muddy yard.

'Where there's muck there's money,' he said in a satisfied voice as he shovelled manure. Only he pronounced both muck and money to rhyme with chook!

Just then I stepped in a cowpat and slipped. I cried out, 'Ugh! Oh God!!' as I slid through a patch of black gluey mud, landing on my backside. At which he called me a useless bit of a girl, and told me gruffly that I should be thanking the Good Lord for His bounty, not using His name as a common swear word. I'm not making much progress with Grandpa Jack. Will he always despise me?

Not only were we late setting off to school by the time I cleaned myself up, but to make it worse Bob came in crying after he had a spat with the red rooster, and I had to settle him down. So I certainly wasn't singing in the rain. Can you imagine me riding the bicycle with its cart in this weather? Poor little Bob was crouching under a wheat bag. My borrowed black oilskin flapped against the wheels and kept getting tangled in the back one, while a waterfall dripped from the brim of my sou'wester, which came nearly down to my nose. I must have looked like a bedraggled crow.

And would you believe that as I pedalled home in the foulest mood, my head down watching the spray spreading out from the front wheel, who should appear at the siding but that strange boy!

◦▬◦

'Hey! You're getting drowned. Why don't you come in here till it eases off?'

A clear, strong voice broke into Rosemary's dogged, head-down onslaught into the driving rain. Looking round, she could see a figure huddling at the covered end of the derelict railway siding's shelter. That thatch of almost white hair left no doubt that she was about to meet her mystery boy at last.

She didn't hesitate. Abandoning the ungainly bike, she dashed to the shelter – practically into his arms. And soon he was helping her brush the little rivers and ponds of water from the stiff folds of her raincoat, as they introduced themselves.

'I'm Kyle. Kyle Selby,' he said. 'I've seen you around.'

'And I'm Rosemary Lister. You were in Miss Selby's classroom before Easter.' (She wouldn't list the other times she had spotted him; it might sound as if she had been looking out for him – which she had.)

'That's right, she's my big sister. I'd just arrived. I was at Ian's on Easter Monday too. I was thinking of coming over and forcing entry into that ladies' circle to meet you, but – '

'Did we scare you off?'

'No, I ran out of time because my sis was looking after me like a gaoler. She only let me out for an hour or two!'

Rosemary looked at him, puzzled, and saw he was smiling.

'I'm convalescing,' he added. 'Nearly died on the operating table having my appendix out a while back, so I've been put out to grass here, like a pensioned-off racehorse.'

'That's terrible! I mean nearly dying. Did it burst? Are you getting better?' She was aware that she was gabbling nervously.

'Just about right, thanks. I had to go back to hospital again in a hurry just after Easter because when they stuffed everything back inside me the first time, they left a few bits twisted. Only problem now is that my energy still runs out halfway through the day. I've hated sitting around like an invalid.'

'Grazing. Well, it's lucky they didn't send you to the knacker's!'

They were at ease with each other already, chatting away almost like old friends. He explained that he been enrolled to start mechanical engineering at university in March, but he only got to attend for a few days. When he eventually went back again briefly following the two operations, he realised there was no point going on. He would never catch up after missing so many weeks of lectures and practicals. So now he was doing light farm work instead of paying board. A bit later, when he was stronger, he might as well join up; probably in August, along with his older brother who was about to turn eighteen.

'How old are you, then?'

'I'm sixteen-and-a-half, but I wouldn't be the first to put my age up, would I?'

*Another one going!* Rosemary was surprised at the stab of disappointment. But she made sure she didn't show her feelings, just chatting about the recent changes in her life as well, without mentioning her father in case it made her lose her light-hearted tone. The two of them were in much the same situation, with their lives on hold, even if his career was more important since he was two years older.

To her surprise, he seemed to enjoy her story of Grandpa Jack and the 'mook'. So she told him how Bob had been bailed up by a fierce rooster when she sent him out to give the chooks some scraps. In a panic, Bob had thrown an egg at the rooster. It smashed on the bird's beak, at which the enemy backed off, croaking indignantly and dripping yolk. Her new friend laughed until he had to clutch his side and try to stop.

'You've had quite a morning then. I'm still learning about farms. You'll have to keep collecting stories for me, to save me dying of boredom,' he said when she finished.

'Oh – I thought you must have always lived on a farm here – because you know Ian.' Again she was puzzled.

But there was no mystery at all. 'No, my father is the bank manager at Ceduna, over on the West Coast you know, and I had to be closer to town for a while until I got the all clear from Dr Magarey. Since we haven't got relations in Adelaide, I'm staying on Packers' farm where my sister lives during the term. It's a wheat farm a mile or so up that little road there. They took me to Ian's on Easter Day.' He pointed to a dirt track that wound down the hill to the siding.

She was starting to ask him why he was here at this godforsaken siding, when the sound of an approaching train interrupted her. Kyle jumped to his feet. 'Here it comes! Over an hour late today.' He added, 'The Overland.'

'Must be too many troop trains on the line,' Rosemary shouted over the increasing din.

She remembered that years ago she and Heather used to watch the Melbourne Express, as people called it, with its first-class sleepers and dining cars. She always dreamed of travelling to far-flung places, but Heather never did. They had both liked trying to see inside, though, to find out what sort of floral arrangements they had on the dining tables, and check whether there was anyone posh on board. Some ladies used to have fur coats and hats with black nets and feathers. Once one was even holding up a little dog that matched her fur! Rosemary supposed there wouldn't be any fuss made these days.

The train bore down on them, a living beast with dragon's breath, eyes blazing, its cowcatcher a set of bared teeth. Soon there would be a glimpse of the fire in its belly, and steam would hiss from its nether regions, adding even more volume to the deafening clanking and groaning of its powerful body. When its whistle blasted as always before it came slowly out of the cutting, the boy ran close, just like that other time. Now Rosemary could hear him calling 'Paper! Newspaper!! Melbourne paper?' Sure enough, a gloved hand appeared from a window, and someone threw out a folded newspaper. Another followed. He scooped them up from the wet platform then jumped back under cover, with an ear-to-ear grin. She noticed he was moving more freely now.

'Two different ones!' he exclaimed happily, showing her the Melbourne *Herald* and a country rag called the *Border Watch* from goodness knows where.

She looked over his shoulder eagerly as he scanned the front page of the *Herald*. There were more details of the great naval battle, and they read bits to each other eagerly.

'Nine Japanese warships already sunk!' he exclaimed.

'Do you do this every day?' she asked him. 'Get papers, I mean?'

'Most days. We don't get good wireless reception back there behind the hill, and I hate losing touch with the world. Especially the way things are at the moment.'

'Doesn't the family you're boarding with get the *Advertiser*?'

He gave a wry smile. 'Frankly, I wonder if they could read it. Nice people, but they wouldn't know what's going on in the next town, let alone the other side of the world. Half the population has no concept of the war, except they know there is one. The Packers think people like us are crazy. I even read crumpled sheets of old newspaper that come in the boxes of groceries.'

'My Aunty Joyce and Grandpa Jack think I'm weird too,' she told him. 'Even my mother says you can know too much about the war. She tries to keep stories of atrocities from me.' Mention of those names reminded her that they would be way behind with the chores. She'd be in trouble if she were too late.

'I've got to go! It's our pickup day for the cream cans.' She jammed on the rain hat again and stepped out of the shelter, realising how reluctant she was to be leaving. *What if he doesn't want to see me again?*

But he was asking, 'Will you be coming past every day? We could meet here.'

'Weekdays, yes.' She saw his face light up, then immediately he blushed. She added, 'But Aunty Joyce did say she might drive the boys sometimes on the worst days. Otherwise they'll have to stay home.' Silently she wished for a resumption of the drought.

'I'll be away for the week of the school holidays, but then I'm here for a month or so. After that I'm going back to Ceduna for a while before I enlist.'

She pulled the bike in more or less under cover; it would be quicker to take the short cut across the paddock on foot, with her faithful iron steed waiting for her here in the afternoon. They said goodbye awkwardly as she poised herself to leap across the tracks; but she had one last niggling question. When she turned he was still watching her.

'How did you know I'm a newspaper reader? You said "people like us".'

He grinned. 'Detective work. Someone who goes to all that bother to arrange to get library books must be my kind of person. And then,' his smile faded, 'I asked Ian about you, and he told me your father is missing overseas. So you'll be following the news.' He turned abruptly and headed for the road.

TUESDAY 12 MAY
Quick note about a piece in the *News*, which the 'mystery boy' gave me. It says eighty sirens blasted out in Adelaide at 10.45 yesterday, to

signal the city was about to be bombed. I would have been terrified if I'd just popped into town to buy some new school gloves! Turns out it was an 'air-raid precautions test', but apparently hundreds of people didn't take it seriously enough to seek shelter. Our Premier, Mr Playford, says people have to be trained to keep off the streets. In a real raid they might have been killed by either the blast of a bomb or flying shrapnel and glass.

P.S. His name is Kyle.

# 17

After the simple statement, 'His name is Kyle', Rosemary was careful not to mention her new friend by name. In fact she wrote very little in the weeks during which she and Kyle shared news, stories and laughter. Her scrapbook began to fill with cuttings from half-a-dozen different papers.

She was keeping her mystery boy to herself. Partly it was shyness, of course, since she knew that when the news got out she would be teased in the same way she had often teased Heather. Her developing friendship with Kyle was the only part of her life that wasn't spread out like a map for all to study. And anyway, she told herself, he wasn't a real boyfriend who kissed and cuddled, he was just a friend. She mustn't get close to him in that way yet. When it all boiled down, though, she was afraid to get too attached in case she lost him. That's what the war did; it tipped relationships one way or the other.

As it happened, initially no one was even aware she was taking a little longer on the school run. Sylvia, Joyce and the rest of the extended family were too entrenched in their repetitive routines to check on her movements, and very little traffic used the old dirt road alongside the little siding these days. So, for a few weeks she and Kyle shared news, stories and even books regularly, debating the issues of the day in a way that always left Rosemary feeling alert and alive. *Perhaps my brain won't dry up like a prune after all,* she thought to herself one morning as she pedalled happily back to the farm. She realised too that the anger that had so often twisted her up was ebbing.

⊪⊪⊪

'Is he your boyfriend?' Johnny asked Rosemary.

'Of course not.' Rosemary tried unsuccessfully to look disinterested.

Johnny had observed her and Kyle greeting each other on arriving together at the door of Miss Selby's room at the end of term. Kyle had his luggage with him; he was going back to town with his sister for a week. Rosemary was returning library books and collecting a new bundle to last her through the school holidays. Johnny arrived as Kyle was giving her back a hefty tome about Egypt in the time of the Pharaohs, borrowed from her latest collection. The little boy looked eagerly from one to the other, trying to pick up clues as to how well they knew each other.

Kyle hopped in quickly with, 'We've met when I've been out walking. I have to walk for at least an hour a day until I'm strong again. I had an operation, you see.'

That diverted Johnny's attention. 'Have you got a big scar?'

'Yep; an angry-looking red slash. If there were no ladies here I'd show you.'

Johnny checked out the room. 'There's only one lady. Rosemary's not a lady.'

'Then neither is my sister! Here, have a look.'

Their secret was still safe, though Miss Selby was trying to hide a smile as she handed over the new set of books to Rosemary.

It was just as well Kyle was away during the holidays, because she would never have got free of the boys, who made constant demands, seldom letting her out of their sight. Marjorie, no doubt missing Valerie, who was now based permanently in Townsville, had practically moved in too, saying there was never anything to do at home.

Rosemary soon concluded that Johnny and Bob's cousin was selfish and spoilt. In fact none of the three would willingly do anything she asked when she needed a hand, yet they still expected her to have time to entertain them. She thought miserably, as the week wore on, of how she was missing her daily chat at the siding. But eventually her friend was back, and they traded stories again.

A few days into the term they were discovered by no other than Grandpa Jack, who turned up on foot just as they were waving goodbye to each other with the liveliness that only good friends show. *Nosy old busybody*, Rosemary said under her breath. Now the word would really get around.

But to her surprise Grandpa Jack winked at her.

'It's all right, lass, your secret's safe with me. You seen *The Wizard of Oz* yet? Came out last year.'

'Yes?'

'Well, we wouldn't want the Wicked Witch of the West puttin' a spell on you, would we? That Joyce 'as poisoned more than one nice friendship.' She gaped at him, but his face was impassive. Did Grandpa Jack actually have a sense of humour? He was right; Aunty Joyce would look just the part in a witch's hat and cloak!

'You could be useful to me if you'll stick around for a bit,' he went on. 'Train from town should be droppin' off a couple of parts for the separator an' a new 'ose, so you could maybe put them in your little trailer t' save me luggin' it all back.'

They filled in the few minutes' wait with small talk – tentative at first – about the miserable dank weather (you couldn't even see the opening to the cutting), and the number of troop trains using the line. Then Grandpa Jack found his tongue. When he came back from the Great War, he said, on a foggy night, he had jumped train at the cutting without anyone spotting him. He wanted to see his family right then, not waste another day or two going on to the city to be officially discharged.

'Lucky to have the line passing so close to your farm!'

'I was the envy of all me mates that night. Worth gettin' into trouble for it later.'

'Trains aren't as adaptable as cars though, are they?' Rosemary reflected. 'Too bad if you live miles from the route.'

But Grandpa Jack was sticking up for the railways. 'Lifeblood of the country,' he said. 'It's the trains that opened it all up, you know, even before I was born.' He expanded his image, sticking out a hand. 'Like these veins, they are. Whole network of tracks comin' and goin' round your body, an' you couldn't stay alive if they wasn't workin' properly, could you?'

'I like that! I can't help thinking of trains as living creatures, you know.'

'Well, 'ere's a regular monster. Let's see if it's the one I'm waitin' for.'

A freight train from the city was looming up out of the fog, slowing down with sighs and groans as it approached them with squealing brakes. Sure enough, after they had waited minutes for the last of the many wagons to pass by, half choking in the smoke-laden dampness, the guard was waiting at the door of the caboose with a paper parcel and a coil of heavy rubber hose that he launched in their direction.

'Damned lucky to get this 'ose,' said Grandpa Jack. 'Japs 'ave closed off our rubber supplies, you know.' They headed home in silence.

The following day Rosemary told Kyle about her conversation with Grandpa Jack.

'Lots of men used to hop on and off trains and hide among the freight during the Depression,' he told her. 'The guards turned a blind eye, I think. Should try it myself some time!'

It's weeks since I've written anything. Life has been busier than ever, with the boys home on holidays for ten days. Marjorie too. Then Heather came up with Jim again. She's obviously besotted. She's still a bit cool towards me, and I didn't help by suggesting jokingly that if Jim wasn't going to propose to her, she should do the asking, even though it's not a leap year. I won't write down what she said; it contained a word that ladies shouldn't use.

Feeling a bit guilty at upsetting her again, I helped Mother make a big fruit cake for her to take back; but I don't think she had any idea how much work I put into preparing the fruit. I even soaked it in the last of our sherry.

In the aftermath of the Coral Sea battle, we listened to Mr Curtin saying this victory is a good start, but Australia is by no means secure yet. I've cut out the stories of the battle too. Passengers frequently throw interstate papers off trains at stations – mainly the Melbourne *Herald*, an evening paper, but sometimes the *Argus* or even the *Sydney Daily Telegraph*, and I get given one sometimes. Everyone was so elated about the Americans sending the Japanese packing from up there, and sinking so many of their ships. This has been the first big setback for the enemy, and the first time a sea battle has been fought mainly with aeroplanes operating from aircraft carriers.

I've never written about Mrs Marryat's American billets. They are airmen called Larry and Glen. Apparently they were involved in this battle – although civilians are not supposed to know details like that. Mrs Marryat says they have swanky, superior airs and wear lots of smelly lotions. They are so over-polite that she never knows if they are genuine; she doesn't like them much. They disrupt her life by coming and going at a moment's notice (not that they can help that), then when they are back here they really live it up. Larry in particular rolls in drunk at all hours. Worst of all, they keep talking about 'canned beans' and milkshakes when she serves up a grill and three veg, or a cup of tea!

Mrs Marryat says that, unlike her, most families are highly enthusiastic about helping out by billeting soldiers. Some get upset if they only get one when the neighbour got three, and others have even divided off part of their back verandahs to make sleep outs to house them! When she rang yesterday she told me a story to pass on to Mother, because it concerns our friend Mr Bolton and local families taking in Australian troops recently.

This is what happened. When our district was chosen to give emergency accommodation to several thousand men from the 6th and 7th Divisions of the AIF while they were en route from the Middle East to New Guinea last month, the whole operation was arranged by Mr Bolton and his Emergency Communications team in about three days. A team of air-raid wardens – including Mr Marryat – worked all through one night till dawn, identifying households with spare beds. Then just five phone calls from Mr Bolton activated the emergency summons machinery – the network of 'runners' I wrote about once before.

When the runners got the call at lunchtime to deliver a thousand billeting notices, three hundred boys and girls arrived at the Town Hall on their bicycles within an hour of being contacted! In only forty-five minutes they had delivered every last notice – right into someone's hand, not just into letterboxes. If someone was out or away they consulted the neighbours before they made decisions. By nightfall, beds were found for all the soldiers.

How exciting! I would have been doing that if I still lived in Cleland Avenue.

Rosemary's meetings with Kyle continued, with only Grandpa Jack aware of them – so far. To her surprise, he seemed to be enjoying sharing her secret, such as it was. He had even started venturing some opinions about the progress of the war.

Then Marjorie, home for a few days after coming down with a mild dose of the 'flu, and at a loose end, came pottering by on her pony one morning while Rosemary sat with Kyle on the siding's one remaining rickety bench. They were taking in the day's frightening six-inch headline: JAPS IN SYDNEY HARBOUR. It was a mistake to startle and look guilty when the girl suddenly appeared in front of her. Rosemary knew from the gleam in Marjorie's eyes that soon the whole district would be talking about the teacher's brother and Joyce's niece.

'So that's where you get to!' Marjorie exclaimed. 'No wonder you've never got time to do things with me.'

Rosemary introduced her to Kyle, almost succeeding in not looking flustered. She tried to divert Marjorie into talking about the day's news.

'Someone threw out yesterday's Melbourne *Argus*. See here – two Japanese submarines have been sunk right in Sydney Harbour.'

But Marjorie wasn't interested. 'Sydney's on the other side of the country. Submarines are not going to sail up the Nairne creek, are they?' She peered at the page more closely then.

'Now, you can tell me about the crowning of Miss Red Cross if you like. *That's* news! But papers never put good photographs in these days, do they?'

'Newsprint rationing. They're not allowed to waste paper on social notes or print any photos that don't directly concern the war,' Kyle told her.

'Of course that's war news. Isn't it, Rosemary?'

'Well – ' Rosemary didn't know what to say. 'Um, why did you come to our place?'

'I thought you might have some spare time, so I came over to ask if you wanted to learn to ride Millie after lunch.' As she spoke she tugged on Millie's reins, and the pony gave a little skip. 'But your mother – '

She knew it was silly to be nervous about horses, but Rosemary's stomach rolled over at the thought of getting on one. She quickly thought up an excuse: 'Oh, I'm sorry, but I've got to help get the butter made today because we want to send some to town when Aunty Joyce goes tomorrow. We're getting an amazing price for it at a shop at North Adelaide. All we can supply.'

'All right, I believe you; that's what your mother said. Anyway, I can see you'll always be *much* too busy to do interesting things with me.'

'You can come back and help if you like. Actually, I quite like patting down the butter into the moulds and wrapping it. It reminds me of making mud pies.'

'Dairymaids never get a day off,' Kyle joined in. 'Pity I can't volunteer for a riding lesson, but I might open up my wound again if I fell off.'

'That's right – you're the one who had the operation. I saw you at our place on Easter Day.'

The three of them went their separate ways, Rosemary acutely aware of Marjorie's triumphant look as she cantered off with her gossip.

TUESDAY 2 JUNE

Beryl, Aunty's friend in Sydney, actually got through to us on a trunk call late yesterday. Since I was the only one in the house she talked to me, in a very agitated voice. I thought she must have tragic news to tell us, because long-distance phone calls cost so much that you don't ring up simply to chatter, especially these days. But she was just all worked up about the three midget submarines in Sydney Harbour. I'd already read about them: one was sunk by a depth charge, one got entangled in a submarine net, and one escaped. It was fascinating to hear a firsthand account, because there's never much detail in the papers of course.

Beryl lives close enough to have seen the vivid explosion when a small boat called the *Kuttabul* was torpedoed and sunk. Not only was it a bright moonlit night, but she said there were vivid shafts of light from searchlights as well, and soon the air was filled with the shrieking of sirens and the roaring of planes. She and her daughter huddled under the kitchen table all night, with a mattress piled on top of it. She says some of her friends have fled to the Blue Mountains. Apparently the roads heading away from the coast are jammed with anything that has wheels – the up and down lanes both being used by vehicles heading out.

I don't blame her being upset! All I could do was keep making sympathetic noises as she poured out her story. Of course, everyone in Sydney is shocked. They were only tiny submarines, but the chilling thought is that they must have come from a mother ship waiting out there somewhere. Like a shark sending out its young to start feeding.

The papers and wireless reports have been stating the *Kuttabul* was just a 'superannuated Sydney ferry-boat' and of no military importance. But Beryl says the facts are circulating that it was being used as a naval depot, and nineteen young ratings were killed on it. Another cover up.

Aunty thanked me for passing on Beryl's news. She has thawed a bit lately – perhaps because she liked my latest thought about war: if women were in charge there wouldn't be one. Her solution would be to put the leaders of the countries at war into a paddock and leave them to fight it out. She even seems to have forgiven me for being so insensitive on Anzac Day. (Every time I hear or read 'Lest we forget' I cringe. As if poor Aunty would forget ...)

# 18

The opening winter rains were followed by days of pale sunshine and crisp, still nights. One Saturday in late June when Chuck had come into town and Jim was starting a rare weekend's leave from Woodside, Heather and Violet took them for an excursion into the foothills, all of them well rugged up and laden with picnic rugs and a basket.

Jim knew Waterfall Gully well, but it had taken some effort for Violet to persuade Chuck to leave the comforts of suburbia. 'You'll like it up there. The water will be positively gushing. No, there won't be thousands of people there – it isn't Niagara!'

At the tram terminus some of the passengers who had been disgorged disappeared into the last of the houses or down side streets, leaving others to hike doggedly up nearly three miles of steep and winding road to the waterfall. But, guided by Heather's memories of exhausting childhood walks with her father, the foursome soon took a gentler and less used track that had once ended at Mügge's dairy. Passing old market gardens and orange orchards alongside Waterfall Creek, and scrounging a few windfall oranges through the fence, they found a secluded spot in a little gully. A pair of blue wrens flapped out of the undergrowth as the men put down the rugs in a sunny patch on the tender new grass that sloped down to the water. The girls spread out the food, the vacuum flask and cups, and Chuck's obligatory bottle of Coca-Cola.

Unexpectedly, Chuck was the most appreciative; holding his

peeled orange in one hand and a big wedge of cake in the other, he tackled them alternately. 'Just look at the size of this orange! You know, I've never seen them actually growing on a tree before. Truly! And your landlady sure bakes a fine fruitcake,' he enthused, taking another large bite even as he wiped juice from his chin.

Heather looked at him in disgust. *Didn't your mother teach you not to talk with your mouth full?*

Violet laughed gaily, patting his little round paunch as she explained that Mrs Jones had only allowed them to make the Vegemite sandwiches – from a stale loaf of bread, and with the merest scrape of butter. It was Heather's mother who had given them the fruitcake on her last visit to the farm.

'Wasn't going to let that old dragon find it. I hid the tin in the wardrobe and pinched a knife to cut it,' said Heather. 'Oh, and my sister helped make it too. She's touchy at the best of times, and she'd be really cantankerous if she knew I didn't give her some of the credit.'

'Ah, sisters! I miss young Lavine and Dolores so much. Aren't families just wonderful?' Chuck exclaimed.

Violet asked, 'Don't their names rhyme? I thought they were Lavine and Doreen.'

A look of annoyance flickered across Chuck's face for a split second. 'You're right. It is Doreen. Dolores is just a pet name,' he explained.

Heather thought he had once called her Delphine. She couldn't help feeling, not for the first time, that Chuck was being less than genuine. But it was none of her business.

'Well,' said Jim, changing tack, 'we'd better get back to your family's farm soon, Heather – the next time the powers that be at the barracks decide not to just give Saturday leave to the League footballers and ignore the rest of us. We could stock up on real country food again. Though I don't just love you for your fruitcake of course!'

Heather blushed; he had never actually used the word 'love' before. Not that she had any doubt about his affection …

Jim must have noticed and looked a bit uncomfortable. His next change of subject was even clumsier. 'Aren't we lucky to be here picnicking as if we didn't have a care in the world, even though there's a war on out there?'

'Y'all are such *pessimists*!' said Chuck. 'You know, now us Yanks are here there's no need to get in a lather about an invasion. Look at our awesome conquest over there in the Midway Islands a couple of weeks ago! We sank even more ships than in the Coral Sea. Boy, did our planes send them Nips packing!'

'That's all very well,' Jim retorted. 'But Newcastle was bombed by a Japanese submarine just after that, you know. And not just a midget one.'

'Oh yes!' Heather jumped in. 'The same one shelled some of the Sydney suburbs too, and hundreds of houses were evacuated. My Aunty Joyce's friend keeps sending her news, and this time she was absolutely seething with rage because one of the blasts cracked both her front windows.'

'I'd be more than seething. I'd want to kill them with my bare hands,' agreed Violet.

'We-ell,' drawled Chuck. 'Enough of all that. I reckon my little flower and I oughta take a stroll upstream.' He hauled Violet to her feet, winking at Jim in an undisguised fashion.

Jim took the hint. 'I'd say that paddock over there might have mushrooms. I'm a champion mushroom spotter from my childhood. Shall we go and look?' he suggested to Heather. So the two of them headed in the opposite direction from the other pair, holding hands and smiling at Chuck's lack of subtlety.

Sure enough, they found a dozen or so big field mushrooms. Heather wrapped them in her scarf, though goodness knows if Mrs Jones would cook them for the boarders.

'*Mmm*! Grilled steak with mushroom sauce!' drooled Jim.

'No, I want mushrooms, eggs, fried tomatoes – and sizzling bacon,' countered Heather. 'I wonder when we'll ever see bacon again, now that we're all getting ration books.'

'Rationed rashers? Well, I thought the coupons were just for clothing – so far. Not like in England. But bacon's only a dim memory, rationing or not. Even before I left butchering, we hadn't had any for months. They reckon the Yanks are eating up all our meat.'

'Chuck certainly looks as if he doesn't go without much!' giggled Heather.

They settled on the spreading roots of an ancient, gnarled redgum beside the creek – still carefully out of sight of Violet and Chuck. But not quite far enough; Heather was embarrassed to hear squeals, giggles and gasps that left little doubt as to what her friend and Chuck were up to. Then Jim's arm was round her and he was kissing her. She felt herself going rigid.

'It's okay,' he was whispering. 'I won't do anything you don't want to. But I do love you, you know. And I want to get to know you a lot better before I go away.'

She relaxed and kissed him back then. So little time to enjoy each other … Suddenly, led on by thoughts of what the next months and even years might mean, she remembered Rosemary's jibe about proposing – which now actually seemed like good advice. (Not that she'd admit that to her sister!) She found herself telling him firmly, 'I'm not like Violet, you know. If you want much more than this you'd better marry me.'

Their next embrace left the mushrooms badly squashed.

Rosemary and Heather were weaving similar threads into their life stories on that Saturday afternoon – and, by coincidence, in each case the setting was the bank of a lively creek. But while one relationship had deepened, the other tenuous alliance was put on hold.

Kyle came down over the hill after lunch, and asked to take Rosemary for a walk. It had in fact been a relief once their friendship was out in the open, with Rosemary actually finding she enjoyed the gentle teasing of her family. In the last three weeks Kyle had come to tea twice, tried his hand at separating cream and making butter, insisted on helping her learn lots of Latin vocabulary, and served with her on a Red Cross produce stall in the main street one Saturday morning. Ian had even invited them to join him and his new girlfriend as a foursome at a farewell dance for some boys who had enlisted, in a nearby family's woolshed; which made them feel accepted in the community. And of course they snatched a few hours here and there to simply talk and be together. That might not amount to a red-hot romance, but it had become a firm friendship.

Today was different though, for this was Kyle's last day. 'I'm going to miss you,' he told her with a wry smile and a squeeze of her hand. 'But it's not for too long. I'll try to get back up here before I go into the Army, and after that – well, who knows?'

They sat by the creek for an hour, Kyle's arm encircling her, and went over all the possibilities of the next segment of their lives: first his final visit home to his doting parents, next his training; and then the big unknown. Where would he be sent? When would Rosemary get back to town and school? Was the tide really turning in the war? For a while they just stared into the rippling water, deep in thought. Then, when the sun left the gully and a cold breeze forced them to stir, Kyle jumped to his feet.

'I hate public partings, so I'm going to say goodbye now.' He kissed her, and they clung to each other for a minute before he guided her back under the fence and up to the house.

'Anyway,' he said with false cheerfulness, 'this is only *au revoir*, not goodbye.'

Rosemary put on a smile too, and acted out a casual farewell for the benefit of the hovering boys and her mother, whose shadow could be seen behind the kitchen curtain net. 'See you later!' she called after him with a cheery wave.

'Ha ha! I saw you kissing Kyle down by the creek,' a jubilant Johnny told her in front of the whole family at the tea table.

*Your little girl's growing up,* Sylvia told Les with a sigh as she snuggled into her warm bed and cuddled her hot-water bottle.

*You should have seen her go red when Johnny teased her about young Kyle Selby. He's a nice lad and a good pal to her – she needed a friend up here. She hasn't known him for long. In fact I didn't know about him until Marjorie told Ivy she'd seen the two of them together. Anyway, she's too young to be in love, thank goodness.*

It seemed such a shame that both girls had made friends with boys who would be off to war. Now, a young farmer would be exempt. She could see why Jim was going; but Kyle was such a bright boy, and so young. Perhaps she should have suggested Trades School for him. Someone at church had a son doing that, learning things like machining, welding and toolmaking. There was such a grim urgency to get people trained to run munitions factories that there would soon be three teaching shifts a day.

*Imagine doing the midnight to morning shift. My word, these are unhappy times. By the way, it's absolutely freezing up here when we go out to milk. At least you're in a tropical climate, aren't you?*

Reminding herself that Les was going through his own hard times, she made her thoughts take a happier path, a strategy that usually sent her into a relaxed sleep. She painted for him the lush greenness of the paddocks now, and the cows heavy and angular with their unborn calves. They'd had some fine, dry days, but Grandpa Jack said there was a big westerly change on the way. Her mind was beginning to drift …

*I didn't tell you most of us have rotten colds. Hope you're well, Les. Oh yes – we'll all be sending birthday wishes to you across the sea tomorrow. Joyce asked Grandpa Jack to kill a young rooster as a special treat for tomorrow's Sunday roast. No, of course we'd never forget.*

A blow of her stuffed-up nose, and she let sleep claim her.

*SUNDAY 28 JUNE*

Time for a catch-up; it's been ages since I even opened this diary. We've had a week or more of cracking frosts and calm, pale sunny days; but now winter has really set in. It's been a dreadfully wet, windy day, and I'm feeling a bit down in the dumps after saying goodbye to Kyle yesterday. Yes, I know he hasn't featured in my diary since I actually got to meet him, but you can't be too careful, can you? I'll admit now that my mystery boy has become a very good friend, and I'm going to miss him a lot.

What's more, today is Father's birthday, so we're all struggling to keep our spirits up. But writing always makes me happier, as if I'm in touch with the people I write about. So, Happy Birthday, Father. I made you a quite passable sponge cake, even though Aunty sniffed disapprovingly when she saw it. We're all thinking of you today.

What more can I write after upsetting myself by putting that on paper? Going on about the British in North Africa being driven back to the border of Egypt won't help and, anyway, I've pasted cuttings about it into my scrapbook. Grandpa Jack and Aunty looked quite crushed when they heard that Tobruk had been re-captured by the Germans. After all the effort soldiers like Uncle Brian put into defending it last year …

I think I'll just ramble on because I can't sleep. We listened to Mr Curtin's speech about the 'season of austerity' that he has called for. He said, 'Forget about that new hat to match the material you have bought. A blue shirt will cover you – don't think about having a grey one to match a grey suit.' And he called a darning needle a weapon of war, because it would save us from buying new things. Well, he'd approve of my hand-me-down pink gloves.

The way rationing works is that everyone will get a hundred or so coupons a month, and various items use different numbers of coupons – if they're actually in stock. There are lots of rules too. There are to be no evening frocks or cloaks manufactured (except wedding gowns), no children's party dresses, no double-breasted suits – and, in fact, not even cuffs on trousers, or buttons on coat sleeves. As if denying Australians a few thousand buttons will win the war for us! Not that it would matter to us; Grandma's got a shoebox full of buttons. She must have saved every one ever used by our family for fifty years! Waste not, want not …

We refuse to use the *Austerity Cookbook* that Beryl sent from Sydney. Its author actually thinks that we should get used to Asian style dishes because they have lots of rice and vegetables and not much meat. I don't mind a sweet curry occasionally, with sultanas in it, but we're not desperate enough to try most of these concoctions. Like Aunty said, let's stick to plain old meat and veg.

I know, we're lucky to have any meat at all.

I'm going to tuck up under my eiderdown and look at some of my schoolbooks now, since it's obvious nothing will happen today – as usual. I'm trying to follow the course in as many of my subjects as I can, in case I can get back to school later. Trouble is, I finished reading the history and geography books in the first few weeks, and I can't possibly do the maths on my own. Never was much good at long division, let alone compound interest. Algebra – what a joke! But Latin is easy, because it's a dead language, and my pronunciation doesn't matter. I think I'm doing enough reading and writing to pass English, and sometimes I even do some grammar exercises, like parsing sentences. Proper noun, verb, adjectival phrase …

I've just sneezed, which smudged the ink. We're all getting colds, one by one. Bob's has turned into bronchitis and he has a deep cough, so we have been putting mustard plasters on his chest before he goes to bed. I remember how comforting the warmth of them used to be, so now I can make them myself from brown paper warmed by the fire and smeared with sloppy mustard.

*MONDAY 29 JUNE*

That entry came to a sudden end because something *did* happen! Heather and Jim turned up unexpectedly in the middle of a hailstorm, drenched, bedraggled, shivering. While Aunty tossed on a batch of scones they dropped a bombshell: they are engaged!!! They will be getting married on August 15 when Jim finishes his training, during his very short pre-embarkation leave before he is sent goodness knows where. They haven't even had a chance to buy a ring yet.

That's less than seven weeks. I'm so excited!

Heather is young at eighteen, but I've always reckoned she should grab the first person who proposed to her, in case she got left on the shelf. After all, she's a rather ordinary person.

'Can I be your bridesmaid?' I pleaded when she had changed into a set of my clothes and we had lit the big sitting-room fire. 'Have you forgiven me for being so mean when I met Jim?'

Heather was so wound up and happy that she said of course I could be her bridesmaid, along with Violet, and that she knew I really liked Jim. She'd just got a bit overwrought that day because she was feeling nervous about introducing him. So we're friends – until we irritate each other next time.

Of course, Mother is all of a dither, thinking about the wedding.

Shops have run out of imported satins and laces, even if you had enough coupons to buy such items, so it is going to be hard to turn Heather into a lovely bride. She says she doesn't care if she has a proper wedding or not. But I think she does. One thing is for sure; Mother won't let her get married in an ordinary short dress like lots of girls do, especially those who get married in a hurry, or who are away from their families.

Then there's the church. There wasn't any dissent when Holy Trinity in the city was suggested, because that's where our great-grandmother was married way back in the early days. And Grandma too.

Aunty, who really is becoming more positive in her outlook, told Mother not to worry, because everyone would try to help in some way. She's right; people are doing amazing things for each other to get us all through this war that goes on and on.

Even Grandpa Jack did his bit last night. He took Heather to the bus in Nairne, and then drove Jim all the way back to camp. (By rights Jim should have been on the special train that takes the men back from Adelaide every Sunday night, so he got dropped at the station to mingle with the others when they arrived.) Of course Grandpa Jack was grumbling that he'd have to walk everywhere for the next week till he got more petrol coupons, but you got the feeling he was happy for us all.

Father will be so pleased to hear this news when we get back into contact. Wouldn't it be lovely if he was home for the wedding?

Well, dreams don't cost anything.

# 19

'So, the church is booked for five o'clock, and Keith is paying the deposit on the Masonic Hall. Just as well – this wedding is going to leave you penniless, Sylvia. Now, let's run through your list again. How far have we got?' Joyce, happier than she had been for a year, was at her organisational best.

Rosemary kept hovering nearby, trying to remind them about the bridesmaids' frocks, but no one answered her. Sylvia stifled a sigh, instead telling Les, *She'll soon learn that Heather is the centre of attention for once, not her.*

However, Sylvia had misjudged Rosemary (not a rare event), for her daughter was prepared to be patient. Involvement in a wedding was the most romantic thing that had ever happened in her life, even if it was only her sister's. She was also ready to give advice if anyone ever asked her, but so far they hadn't.

This development had jolted them out of the rather comfortable routine they had all settled into. Five days after the big announcement they were already making good progress, with a number of items put away in the front room, and the boys threatened with a fate worse than death if they played in there, or put a single finger on anything.

'The main thing is that Mr Forbes is putting aside the satin. He says it doesn't look like curtain lining, so people don't have to know.'

*Les, don't be upset that we resort to making do with second grade materials and used goods these days, will you?*

'Yes, weren't we lucky he had just enough?'

'The luck is that all our coupons pooled together added up to the right number,' Rosemary butted in. 'But there's still Violet's and my bri – '

'And when the mail order pattern arrives,' Sylvia went on, 'then we'll be busy.'

'If I run out of white cotton, Mrs Gurner has plenty.' It was Joyce interrupting this time.

Sylvia went back to her notes. 'Shoes and gloves. Grandpa Jack to re-sole my best summer shoes for Heather. Rub chalk into your kid gloves.'

'Yes, they should come up nice and white for her.'

'Right. Now, Rosemary's going to write to Grandma and ask if she still has that long petticoat from your wedding, Joyce.'

'It's half written,' said Rosemary. 'I'm asking about tiny pearl buttons too. Now, what about – '

'We've got more than enough old and borrowed items, and the something blue will be the sapphire pendant that Les gave me when Heather was born.'

*You were always such a romantic, weren't you, Les?*

The disjointed conversation went on like this for a few more minutes. They must make the cake soon, to let it mature. Guest list. Invitations … Leave them for now. Flowers could be decided on much later; someone would be sure to help out with them. And as for the reception food, they'd shelve that problem for a while too. Might start saving tea, though; the word was getting about that it would be rationed before the week was out, and probably sugar would follow.

'So, what else have we overlooked?'

'I *keep* trying to remind you,' said Rosemary. 'The *bridesmaids'* dresses.'

'The two of you might just have to wear different outfits,' said Joyce. 'Anyway, there's time yet. We can save up next month's coupons, and I'm sure Grandma will send hers too. Old people don't need many new clothes – not like me with the boys.'

Suddenly Rosemary realised they had forgotten something of major importance. 'Has anyone thought about the veil?' she asked.

'Oh goodness,' Sylvia started to fluster, 'now that's going to be a problem. Lace has such high coupon value, even if you can get it.'

'Have you thought of mosquito netting? You don't need coupons for that, you know,' Joyce suggested.

'Well, if anyone had enough lace for us to edge it with, it could be all right. Let's ask everyone we're talking to. You know, Rosemary, I think we might send you to town on Monday. You could – '

'Yippee! Can I stay overnight, and see my friends too? *Please?*'

'Seeing friends will be the last thing on your agenda. You can collect the material from Mr Forbes, and we'll give you a list of little bits and pieces like hooks and eyes to get. You can look at his dress materials, but no promises. And you can ask about lace.'

By night-time, Rosemary had organised her visit. The shopping list had grown by a dozen items, the Marryats had agreed happily to put her up for the night on Monday, and she had even arranged with Janet to call in on her old class just before the end of the school day. All in all this diversion would help take her mind off Kyle's indefinite absence. She sang as she lined up the cream cans for the morning and reassembled the separator.

Hearing her, Sylvia smiled, and spoke to Les.

*It's all going well now. You always said you wanted your daughters to have nice weddings, and this one will be just beautiful.*

Wouldn't he be so proud of his two girls when he saw the photos one day?

'Photos!' she exclaimed aloud. 'We haven't teed up anyone to take a wedding portrait. Perhaps George Bolton can help with that.'

*TUESDAY 7 JULY*

I've had such a good time! I'm dog-tired, so I'll start a summary, but I may fall asleep before I can elaborate. I went down alone yesterday on the midday bus, and called in at my old school and the Children's Library, then headed to Dulwich. Collected and paid for the wedding dress material (welcomed like an old friend by Mr Forbes) and got a sample of some lilac taffeta that might do for my frock and Violet's. Not the most popular colour, but I think it will suit us both. An appropriate match for Violet's name too. I couldn't buy the right sort of lace to edge the veil though.

Next I had a good talk to Miss Browning, since old people don't like you 'flitting in and out like a moth' (as Aunty Florence apparently once said about Mother). Details to come! I spent a lovely evening with the Marryats too. Best of all, Mrs Marryat left Alec and Betty with a friend after Billy went to school the next morning and took me to see *Fantasia* at the York before I headed back home. It was wonderful, reminding me again how I've been missing films and music and – well, all sorts of things.

What else? School. That was the one disappointment, because I didn't realise how much I've changed in these last few months. My old classmates seemed so rowdy and giggly: was I once like that? They had just run a toffee day to raise money for the Schools' Patriotic Fund, and they bullied me into buying up the leftovers, whether I wanted them or not. I ended up with ten lumps of sticky goo (the sort Father calls jawbreakers) in paper patty pans for 1/3 d, which was supposed to be a bargain. Apart from Janet walking out to the gate with me to have a proper chat, no one had anything sensible to say. Well, there was one thing; poor Mrs Pearson had a heart attack. I'm very sorry to hear that. I feel annoyed that some of the girls thought it was funny.

On my way to the tram, when I detoured to say thank you to Miss Whyte at the Library, we had a nice chat about books. She said Miss Morley is scouring the country to get enough books for people like me. She has even made trips to Melbourne and Sydney to scrounge more stocks. The service is growing like Topsy. We agreed, though, that I'm getting a bit old for most of the children's books – I've read so many of them anyway – so she said she would send me some of the classics, like *David Copperfield* and *Jane Eyre*. I told her I like poetry too. She said I could write to her about poems whenever I sent books back, because she loves poetry.

Miss Browning came bustling out of her front door as I neared the Marryats' house, to waylay me. 'Rosemary, dear, how are you and your family?' she asked – and invited me inside! After ushering me into her neat but shabby sitting room (all very brown) she asked politely whether there was any news of Father. Everyone does that even though they know there isn't. She told me how the street wasn't the same without us girls running down it to the tram, or Mother and Grandma in and out all the time. She must be practically a hermit if those were the highlights of her life. How boring to be an old maid; I suppose she wasn't attractive enough to get a husband.

Of course Miss Browning was eying off my big parcel of drapery items and wanted to know what had brought me back to Cleland Avenue. So I told her about the coming wedding, in great detail, just to entertain her a bit. I'm so glad I did, because when I mentioned the veil, she hesitated for a moment before she said, 'I think I can help your mother there.' She bustled out of the room, returning a minute later with a card of the finest, most ornate lace to edge the veil. I immediately envisaged a tiny old lady with gnarled fingers making it: sitting in a rocking chair by a fireside, concentrating intently on its intricate pattern of delicate flowers and tendrils, and checking it for even the most miniscule flaw.

When I exclaimed that it was just glorious, she said it was Maltese lace, quite old. She clammed up when I asked how she had come by it. 'Mind you, it's only on loan,' she said brusquely, as she led me back up the passage to the door. 'Tell your mother she'll have to just tack it on. I'll trust her not to cut it and to get it back to me without a single torn thread.'

She was still watching me as I went into the Marryats' gate, and from the look on her face – a mix of sad and stern – when I turned to give a little wave, I got the feeling the old lady must have already been regretting her kind deed.

When I brought the lace home today, Mother thought it was a bit strange of Miss Browning just to lend it, but was thrilled with it of course. Heather is going to look so beautiful! (Especially since the veil will disguise her face until after she is pronounced married, when it will be drawn back. Yes, that's really catty, and I won't say as much to her.)

Another good thing about my quick visit was hearing what is going on locally. The only bad news was that nice old Mr Harrison died of pneumonia a couple of weeks ago. The butcher has taken his dog, Rover, who will have a luxury diet of meat scraps for life, of course. A bone a day too …

Mrs Marryat still isn't keen on her two Americans. The thing that really annoys her is that they never raise a finger to help, or play with the children; one evening they just sat and watched her struggling on when Alec had an asthma attack and she got in a flap about serving their meal on time. They have finished their leave and flown off for now, goodness knows where. Larry apparently tried to butter up Mrs Marryat when she got annoyed at him for putting muddy footmarks on her newly mopped kitchen lino, by giving her a delicate pink silk scarf. But she refused it because she's sure, from something that Glen let slip, that it was stolen from a street-side stall in the Philippines. I reckoned she's being a bit too goody-goody. I told her she should accept all gifts, and hand them on to me if her conscience won't let her keep them!

The big contingent of Australian soldiers who were billeted in our district have gone too, en masse, leaving many sad households who came to think of them as family after three months. I asked if men like Corporal Officious who came on the day of Billy's party were going to war too, but apparently their regiment consists mainly of older or medically unfit men, or those in reserved occupations. Mr Marryat calls them 'the old and the bold'.

Mrs Marryat laughed when I brought out toffees for Billy, Alec and Betty, and four more to give the children next door (all but the baby). She said people are tumbling over each other to hold fundraisers – from bazaars, teas and competitions to raffles, concerts and picture evenings. This weekend the family is going to a Patriotic Carnival at Norwood. I told her it was probably even worse in the country, with the same few people being asked to help all the time.

Apart from the fundraising, there are lots of events to entertain the troops too. The latest one, yesterday, was to be an American gridiron match at Adelaide Oval. Father would have been there with his ears back.

I kept a toffee each for Johnny and Bob, and had the last one myself on the way home in the bus. But I was a bit worried when a stab of pain shot up one of my back teeth as I sucked. Looks as if I may have to get to a dentist soon. That's the sort of thing you neglect when you just exist from day to day like we do on the farm.

One more thing. (I haven't got sleepy after all, and I can't believe how much I've written. Maybe I have spare energy now that Kyle isn't in my life, though he's often in my thoughts.) Last Saturday, July 4, was the American National Day, and our 'guests' celebrated all over town. The American Officers' Independence Ball was held in the Town Hall, and Heather says Violet went with Chuck. Her mother had made her a wonderful gold-embossed silk gown from material he apparently bought on the black market. The description reminded me of the gifts Father promised us ... The ball was the social highlight of the year, with eight hundred guests! Heather says she wasn't envious, but I wonder about that.

Violet stretched lazily before curling up again to dream for a little longer in that no man's land between sleeping and waking. Dawn was the best time of the day. She could block out work and worries, and relive special moments of her life. This morning she called up delicious memories of the recent Independence Ball – the happy crowd, bright music, and the gilded ceiling, as high as a three-storey building, hung with massive, glittering chandeliers. Oh, and the marble pillars that made you feel as if you were in a palace. She was dancing with Chuck, her midnight-blue skirt swirling elegantly, its gold threads matching his buttons and insignia. There was no doubt, as several admiring girls pointed out to her, that the Americans in their dove-pink trousers and olive-green jackets that fitted like skins were so much more stylish than their Australian counterparts.

Having brought her to the ball in a taxi – an unheard of luxury – and presented her with an orchid to pin on her shoulder, Chuck had introduced her with impeccable manners to the official party, and then to other officers. He made her feel like royalty. She in turn had held her head high, confident she was a worthy partner for him. How proud she had felt to be standing beside him as the American National Anthem was played. When he had jumped to attention with his right hand over his heart she hadn't smiled or fidgeted like some of the other partners.

After recreating the whole scene, right down to the sumptuous supper, Violet indulged in her favourite fantasy. Now she was the newlywed Mrs Charles Payard, throwing streamers and waving farewell to her devoted family and envious friends from the top deck of a luxurious passenger liner. The war having been won, of course, she was joining a thousand other happy war brides to start a new life in America. She would miss her family and friends, but soon they could all come and visit.

This half-wakeful state diffused a blessed amnesia about a few aspects of her present situation she wanted to ignore. If only Chuck would propose marriage, as Jim had to Heather ... But the closest he had got was to apologise that he couldn't make a commitment about the future because soon he must go away, if only for a short time. In fact there was the vague suspicion that sometimes he was not being quite straight with her. In the latest instance, she had caught up with him unexpectedly near the GPO last weekend when he was about to post a letter. Why did he jump a bit and quickly shove it in the box – just as if he didn't want her to see it? Well, there would be a simple explanation; she mustn't appear to be prying into his life.

The one thing she could not ignore for another minute, though, was the wave of nausea building inside her. She hauled herself out of bed, cursing silently, to creep out to the lavatory. It was so far down the back path that she and Heather used to joke that on a clear day you could almost see it from the back door. At least no one would hear her out there. Perhaps all that gunpowder was getting to her at last. Or maybe it was just that Mrs Jones's food was not only unappetising but positively bad for her digestion; why, even her monthlies were all out of kilter. She'd heard someone on the assembly line at work say that malnutrition sometimes did that to you ...

# 20

*TUESDAY 14 JULY*

One month to go! You wouldn't think we were running a dairy farm, if you saw the activity going on and the amount of wedding paraphernalia piling up in the sitting room. It's lucky that some of the cows are dry and calving hasn't started yet, as this gives us a bit more free time. There's not as much gardening to do in winter either, and most of the hens are moulting and off the lay. (Aunty culls the occasional 'old boiler' and threatens the half-feathered ones that if they don't lay soon they'll be chicken soup.)

Mother and Aunty have talked incessantly about THE WEDDING for two-and-a-half weeks now, to the point that Grandpa Jack raises his bushy black eyebrows and the boys groan whenever anyone mentions the gown, cake, flowers, food, etc. And it's always, 'Rosemary, you're the same height as Heather now. Come and put this on while I measure the hem.' Or, 'Rosemary dear, can you just heat up some of the pea soup for tea? We won't stop to cook. Well, if the boys don't like that they can have bread and dripping – with some Vegemite.' And so on.

I've had about enough of the whole topic of matrimony too, after helping write out the invitations on dainty little cards this week. 'Mr and Mrs Leslie Lister request the pleasure of the company of Mr and Mrs Maurice Swift' – etc. I won't go on and on about it. Today I'll just describe the wedding gown, now completed. It's fun being the model for that, because I can twirl around in it and dream of my own wedding one day.

Luckily the new clothing regulations don't apply to wedding gowns. Designs are limited by what materials you can get hold of, of course, but we have begged, borrowed or bought everything we need. The neckline is square with a little V cut out of the front (very fashionable) and there are tiny covered buttons heading down from the point of the V to the waistline. When the material is really plain – as curtain lining certainly is! – it's important to have some fussy little features like this. In addition, the sleeve edges and the bodice just above the waistline are finely ruched, the pleats held in place with piping. Mother was clever there; she used furniture cord. The skirt is fitting at the hips, falling then with a nice swirl, and there's a long train too, which Violet and I must learn to hold elegantly. The veil is also long; Miss Browning's lace makes it look divine.

I'll finish with clothing of a very different quality – Army socks again. A report in the paper the other day said that the Fighting Forces' Comfort Fund has received 2593 garments, of which 1396 were pairs of socks. Our local group got a letter from men in the 7th Division, now in New Guinea, thanking us for our efforts. My name was on the list, and I winced again to think how bad my socks were. (I've never begun another pair.) Imagine how popular I'd be if a soldier on a route march got a blister on his heel because my left sock went straight into holes. So I laughed when Johnny came home from school with this verse:

> *Dear Lady,*
> *Thanks for the socks, they are some fit,*
> *I use one for a helmet and one for a mitt.*
> *I hope to meet you when I've done my bit,*
> *But where in Hell did you learn to knit?*
> *Yours etc.,*
> *Tommy.*

Sylvia's hand shook as she tore open another letter from the District Records Office. *Now, don't panic. Bad news comes by telegram, not letters,* she reminded herself again. This time Rosemary had brought it in, and was standing expectantly by her side.

It simply stated that with reference to the letter Sylvia had received recently, Les 'must now be posted as missing'. It conveyed the Minister for the Army's sincere sympathy once again, followed by the standard sentence about appreciating Sylvia's 'natural anxiety'.

'What's this previous letter they talk about? I didn't see that,' said Rosemary sharply.

*She doesn't miss a trick, Les.*

'Oh, it was just a circular saying that if they ever got any news they would inform us,' she replied. 'And don't get on your high horse, because you know that if I got any news, you are the first person I'd tell.'

Rosemary burst into tears. 'I was just hoping for something a bit – a bit more – *you* know what I was hoping.'

*FRIDAY 17 JULY*

There are two news items. The first is a letter saying that Father is now officially listed as missing. This should be so important to us, but in fact it only confirms what we already thought. Well, it's certainly better than having him presumed dead, but we're agreed that it doesn't change anyone's circumstances. The letter was such an anti-climax after these long months of waiting; it made Mother grumpy and me despondent.

I've promised her I'll try to keep cheerful, so here's my attempt at some happy writing.

News item number 2. When I collected a new batch of books from Miss Selby this afternoon, she had a message from Kyle for me. He asked her to explain that the reason he hasn't written is that he has unexpectedly got the chance to help out for a month or so as a rouseabout on the cattle station north of Ceduna where his brother works. That's until they both leave to join up. It's a relief that he still wants to keep in touch. I've sent him an invitation to the wedding, even if he can't come.

The promised Bronte novel was among my library books, and I was pleased to find a little book of Australian poems there for a change too. Flipping through it before tea I came across two Great War poems by Mary Gilmore. (I think she's quite old.) I looked to see if she was as negative back then, and sure enough, one poem paints very grim pictures of the horrors of war, while the other seems to be highly critical of politicians.

She is certainly a good poet though. The first poem is called 'The Satin of the Bee', and each verse, after describing a ghastly scene of devastation that I'm trying to forget, ends with the couplet

> But the satin of the bee
> Flashes in the sun.

That contrast between the beauty of the world, which I see so often up here, and what men at war do to parts of it – and to each other – makes me so sad.

The other very short poem has the strange name, 'These?' I might have passed it over, but for the word 'mice' catching my eye. I remembered that this diary began with me comparing us to mice hiding in holes. And Mrs Gilmore has a similar idea – only it's expressed much better than I could have, and aimed at our politicians, not us:

> Are these our people's leaders? These
> Whose babbling voices
> Sound in familiar keys
> Like farmyard noises.

*The world churns like a maggot pit*
*Turmoiled in strife,*
*While the mice-minded sit,*
*Nibbling at life.*

Strong words! Surely she wouldn't damn the work of Mr Curtin and his party in this way? The politicians all seem so dedicated in working to save our country. (Grandpa Jack says I'm not critical enough, but I'll learn.) I love the term 'mice-minded'. I've decided to send a note back to Miss Whyte to see if she can get me some of Mrs Gilmore's more recent war poems.

There is one more little development in our wider family's life that I keep forgetting to put on paper. Months ago I mentioned a nice girl called Wendy, from my old school, who was back on her farm and missing city life like I am. Well, I only saw her once or twice after that, in Nairne, just to say hello. She did get that job at the brickworks. Then, to my amazement, when Ian picked me up (with Kyle) to go to a woolshed dance about a month ago, Wendy was his partner! I caught them gazing into each other's eyes when they thought no one was looking. I hope it lasts.

I'd better go and load the bike cart with a couple of tyres, the old hose that split beyond repair with the first winter frost, and a few other oddments. Why? Since there's an urgent need for rubber in manufacturing, there will be a rubber drive at the school tomorrow, run by the Schools' Patriotic Fund. Johnny is fanatical about collecting paper, bones and any manner of items that can be re-used, because you get SPF medals and different-coloured badges according to how much you contribute. So Bob will have to walk in the morning; I told him that's his bit for the war effort.

There! This is an almost cheerful report; my only slip-up was Mary Gilmore's fault.

Perhaps it was the distraction caused by the coming wedding, or the fact that Les had not been listed as 'presumed dead', but July seemed to bring a lessening of tension about the war. Most of the news in the papers was about the situation in Europe, and Sylvia, Joyce and Rosemary agreed they really couldn't get too upset to learn the Nazis had extended their Russian offensive towards the Don. The reports of 'light land skirmishes' with Japanese Units in Papua were a little more disturbing, but it was best to ignore the fact that the press typically downplayed the severity of incidents. Anyway, you never knew what to believe these days. Who was it who said, 'The first casualty of war is the truth'?

*Or are we just getting hardened to it all, Les, and forgetting how bad things still are?*

Sylvia pondered this a little guiltily.

One Australian would certainly have agreed with that verdict: the Prime Minister. He had just accused Australians of complacency, arguing that despite the recent naval victories, 'we still face invasion and the horrors that accompany it'. He demanded that Australians devote every waking hour, and if necessary their lives, to the war effort.

Sylvia shrugged after hearing that broadcast, resolved to put it out of her mind. Naturally they would be very frightened in Canberra, where the seat of government was a likely target, wouldn't they? Of more immediate importance was the marshalling of a battalion of willing helpers to make pies, pasties, sausage rolls, sandwiches and little cakes for the wedding reception. Working out how to get them all delivered to town on the day required about the same level of strategy as organising a battalion of soldiers.

Sometimes her distracted state of mind worked in the family's favour. All right, she agreed – while accepting the offer by a nice woman she had met at the last Mothers' Union meeting to deliver a carload of food to the hall – Rosemary could take Johnny and

Bob plus the Gurner girls to see *Little Nellie Kelly* at the Saturday matinee. Yes, even if she'd seen it last Christmas in town. At least it wasn't one of the dozens of war films beginning to flood the market. What with these and the newsreels that showed graphic details of battles, there was little escape from the world's troubles. Anyway, it would keep all the children out of their hair while Mrs Gurner helped with the yards and yards of hand sewing on all their wedding gear. Since the film had Judy Garland in it too, all in all the outing should cheer Rosemary up.

*SATURDAY 25 JULY*
Good news!!! Wendy's brother survived the sinking of the HMAS *Perth* in March, and is listed in today's paper as a prisoner of war. Lucky Wendy. It's strange that I mentioned her just last week.

This is an 'unconfirmed list from an enemy source'. At last the Japanese are starting to give out lists of names from Asia, as the Geneva Convention expects them to do.

There is also a trickle of information from Java, with lists being compiled from names provided by some escapees. Sifting through them set us quivering, but in fact there is little new information. The lists are not fresh casualties, they mainly post people officially as missing, like Father is. The first list was of 160 South Australian names, followed the next day by a RAAF list of 171 dead and missing.

So now some families are publishing statements in the paper, with photographs. For example, 'Mr and Mrs J. Beare of Swaine Avenue Rose Park have been informed that their only son Edward is missing ... believed to be in Java.' The Beares go to my old church, and I always remember Teddy because of his name. I hope he's all right.

Heather and Violet are just arriving. It will be fun having dress fittings – one tonight, then a final try-on tomorrow after the alterations are done. I want my dress to match Violet's perfectly, despite Aunty Joyce saying that what we wear doesn't matter.

Violet will have to sleep on the couch in the sitting room, among all the wedding stuff, as the sleep out that Heather uses is small, and cluttered with fifty years of junk.

'Stop wriggling, girl! Of course I'll stick a pin into you if you don't stand still.' Pre-wedding nerves were getting to Sylvia, and although Violet's frock was the worst fitting of the three, she was taking it out on Rosemary.

Rosemary sighed loudly, exaggerating a statuesque stance as the lilac taffeta was swathed around her. She was privately thrilled that the basic, slim style of dress demanded by the new guidelines made her look older than she was, and she rejected Joyce's suggestion that her skirt could have a net overlay to give it a softer look. She was determined not to act childishly, but her mother was making it hard for her, treating her like a ten-year-old.

She was puzzled too. She glanced quickly at Violet again, but Heather's normally vivacious friend was sitting quietly on the couch with her frock on her lap, her face pale and pinched, and her thoughts obviously many miles away. She must be really lovesick! Or jealous maybe?

When Violet had put her frock on it hung on her like a bag, except around her firm bustline, until Sylvia had expertly pinned and tucked it into its sleek sheath style. 'Why, you must have lost some weight, Violet!' she exclaimed. 'I was sure I had your measurements right. I'd think Mrs Jones was starving you, but Heather isn't fading away.' And Violet had mumbled something about having a bilious attack over the last week or two. So Sylvia said she'd leave a fraction of room at the waistline, just in case Violet filled out a bit when she felt better.

Rosemary decided that Violet must have been telling the truth about the gastric upset, because she heard her vomiting in the lavatory in the early hours of Sunday morning, when the boys were still asleep and her mother and Joyce were out milking. But their guest seemed to have recovered later, because she and Heather had been laughing merrily together as they melted some ends of lipstick in a tobacco tin on the stove. They had scrounged them from family and friends, and kept adding further lumps gouged out of discarded tubes, until they achieved more or less the desired colour. Then it was a matter of pouring the mixture back into some of the tubes to set.

'There! We may not have Evening in Paris perfume, but Lister's Lustrous Lipstick is going to be a real winner!' Violet laughed.

'Why can't we buy things like lipstick and perfume these days?' Rosemary asked.

Heather knew. 'Because the chemicals in them are needed for medical purposes.'

'You can use our makeup on the wedding day,' Violet assured Rosemary with a friendly smile. 'I'll do your face for you.' They both sat down to discuss their part in the wedding service, and Rosemary decided that nothing was wrong after all. Moreover, she was forced to admit to herself that Heather's best friend was a thoroughly nice person.

That night, after the girls had left, she overheard Sylvia say to Joyce, 'You mark my words, I know the signs. That girl has a little bun in the oven.'

'Well,' said Joyce. 'Perhaps we should have been planning a double wedding then.'

# 21

*TUESDAY 28 JULY*

I'm thinking a lot about what I heard Mother telling Aunty Joyce. Chuck will have to marry Violet in a hurry if it's true, to avoid the shame of her being a very pregnant bride. Wouldn't be the first one though; I remember Mother saying once that many a girl has clutched a larger than usual bunch of flowers in front of her, to hide a telltale bulge.

In keeping with my attempts to be as adult as possible regarding the wedding, I've made up my mind not to question anyone about this. I'll just to watch and see.

Our first calf was born in the night. It's a little heifer and so sweet. I was pleased to see that Grandpa Jack took Johnny and Bob with him when he went to check on Dorrie, the new mother. He is doing so much more with the boys lately, like teaching Johnny to milk, and just letting them follow him around and chat to him. That's especially good for Johnny; he seems to have withdrawn into himself a little recently. And it helps us, now that we are so much busier.

Several Japanese flying boats raided Townsville a couple of days ago. Valerie sent a message to say that she was on a train when the first planes went over. It had to stop in case the enemy pilots saw it moving and bombed it. Apparently the planes did no real damage, but as in other cities on the coast, lots of people have packed up in a panic and headed inland. It shows that the enemy is still around, doesn't it? Mr Curtin is right; we can't relax yet. I wonder if Aunty Ivy will tell Marjorie about this. If she does, perhaps Marjorie won't be so blasé about the war having no effect on us, with her sister in danger.

We are so lucky here – hardly deprived at all. Valerie's last letter, which was passed round the whole family, said that Townsville is bulging at the seams with troops (some say there are 200,000 of them!) and that food is very scarce. Civilians have to queue for hours for just about everything, and then accept whatever is available. Valerie says she's coming home soon for a good feed.

On a brighter note, Bob is feeling very proud of his donation of old tyres to the rubber drive at school. For his writing lesson today he had to copy a note of thanks, which said 22,000 tyres were donated round the state in a ten-day period. He wrote it very well, except that he got his 2s and an S back to front. Now Johnny says waste paper is desperately needed; well, I can help him with a pile of newspapers ...

My train of thought leads me to Kyle, of course, and the way he used to beg for papers at the siding. I can almost see him there when I ride past. I'm missing the extra news I used to get, but I'm not game to stand there myself and call out. I think I'd just get wolf whistles!

Violet felt better already, having made the decision to tell Chuck her news – *their* news. (Though, truth to tell, she was burying a smidgin of trepidation.) She had made up her mind on the weekend after seeing how happy Heather's family were about Jim. It was a pity her own parents hadn't seemed all that enthusiastic about Chuck on the only occasion she had taken him home, but they would get to see what a good catch he was when they knew him better. She thought that perhaps they had tried to discourage her for fear that they would lose her to America's Deep South.

She had been rehearsing her speech, to be delivered at the most intimate moment of the evening. *I've got something to tell you, Chuck. Something wonderful*... But Monday night passed without her hearing from him, so on Tuesday she rang his officers' mess to remind him that she was waiting to see him. The result was the briefest conversation, with Chuck saying breathlessly that he couldn't talk right then, but would be back in touch soon. 'Love you, honey,' were his last words as he hung up.

Now it was Wednesday, and she'd been waiting ever since she got home to hear from him. Mrs Jones's telephone was strategically placed in the hallway, so she could check that her boarders were putting a penny in the tin on the little table whenever they made a call. And in order to listen in, no doubt.

Violet paced the small space between the two beds and the door, trying to decide what to do. Three steps across, three steps back ... *Love you, honey.*

He might be at the Covent Garden. That's where they had nearly always gone when he was free on a weeknight. Perhaps she would surprise him. But what if he – ? She tried hard not to imagine him in another girl's arms ... After all, he often told her she was the only one, so she should be ashamed of herself for having doubts. But he had such a charming smile for all the ladies, so if he had met someone else, she'd rather know now. What's more, she wasn't going to just lie down and accept defeat. There was too much at stake.

Heather put an end to her dilemma by bouncing in to say she was meeting two or three of her old school friends at the Arcadia Café for a cup of coffee – a sort of impromptu hens' night, arranged that day when she bumped into one of them on her walk home from work. Did Violet want to come too, or was she seeing Chuck?

Relieved to have a second string to her bow, her friend said she would meet Chuck first, and come on down to the hens' party if he had to leave early. And so the two of them repeated the familiar ritual of prettying themselves up prior to the inevitable rush to the station, and the usual chorus of 'Yes, Mrs Jones, we'll be home by ten!'.

'Funny,' Heather observed as they parted at the front door of the Covent Garden, 'there don't seem to be so many Americans around tonight.' She was right; when Violet climbed the stairs and tentatively put her head into the restaurant, the place was half empty. Puzzled, she headed to the french doors and peeped out to the tiny balcony – not much more than a doorstep surrounded by window boxes really, and with hanging baskets dangling overhead – where they had sometimes shared a private moment away from the throng. It was in fact a relief that Chuck wasn't there. If I found him here with another girl, I think I'd jump right off, she thought. A shiver suffused her body.

'Hi there, beautiful!' She sprung round – but it was only one of Chuck's friends coming into the dining room, followed by a small knot of fellow officers and some girlfriends. They invited her to join them as a waitress in a crisply starched uniform guided them to seats at their usual table.

'Hi there!' she returned, forcing a smile as she closed the balcony doors. (She hadn't taken long to learn the sort of greeting these Yanks liked.) 'Have you seen Chuck?'

The man's look of embarrassment made her blanch. After an open-mouthed silence he drawled, 'Why, didn't he tell you then? He's gone with the unit he helped train, Miss Violet, up to Queensland. It left first thing this morning.'

Violet plonked down on the nearest chair, just staring at him. After a minute she managed to ask, 'How long are they gone?'

'We-ell, that lot won't be back this way at all, like. Heading for the frontline pretty soon, I reckon. Up in the islands. We're all moving on.'

As the first wave of shock passed and her body and brain came to life again, Violet sprang to her feet and dashed for the stairs. But the American was quicker, grabbing her arm before she could descend.

'I gotta tell you this, Miss. Not fair to keep you in the dark – give you false hopes. He's married, you know. Got a wife and two little kids back there in Louisiana.'

He just managed to hold on to her as her world spun and she fainted dead away.

*SATURDAY 1 AUGUST*

There's news, but I'll tell it in order for once.

Now that it's only two weeks to THE day, there's a touch of panic setting in. Not surprisingly, Mother and Aunty Joyce have been starting to wonder how on earth the farm can be kept running while we are all in town for the wedding. Sure, we can ask the neighbours to call in and handle the milking alongside Grandpa Jack for a day and a half, but calving will be in full swing too, and there really needs to be someone around all the time who can call for help. Apart from doing the basic chores.

Can you imagine Grandpa Jack? At least once a week he declares, 'We need another pair of hands round this place.' He's not game any more to say that it should be a man! And to give him his due, he is the only one who recognises how much I have been doing over the last month. Mother and Aunty have never stopped to think about it while they fussed with the wedding clothes, planned the reception and saw to a thousand other details. So when Aunty got short-tempered with me today (she's got a chesty cough and she's irritable) because the drain outside the back door was blocked with slimy leaves, he stuck up for me!

'That girl is doing the jobs of a farmhand, cook and washerwoman already. You're workin' her fingers to the bone, you two. We need another pair of hands ...'

Well, he is about to get his wish – but when he hears about it, he's not going to be pleased! You see, Aunty got a phone call today from that Miss Marshall who was trying to get the Government to start a Women's Land Army. She says the Land Army officially came into being a few days ago, although she's supposed to wait for a conference in a week or so to set her plans in motion. Meanwhile she is quietly placing girls on the land, and she's sending us someone – tomorrow night!

All we know about our girl is that her name is Audrey Sprod, she is twenty years old, and she's coming from New South Wales. She will be on a train that should pass through Nairne about 8 pm; it's been ordered to stop, even though it's an express train from Murray Bridge to Adelaide.

I wonder how much she knows about dairy farming?

We've been cleaning out the sleep out for her.

The only other thing worth mentioning is that Miss Whyte has sent me a new poem by Mary Gilmore, who was apparently made Dame Mary several years ago because of her work for women's rights as well as her poetry. It's very moving. I like it so much because at last she seems more tolerant and accepting – but still so protective of those she loves. It's called 'Nationality':

> *I have grown past hate and bitterness*
> *I see the world as one;*
> *Yet, though I can no longer hate,*
> *My son is still my son.*
> *All we at God's round table sit*
> *And all men must be fed;*
> *But this loaf in my hand,*
> *This loaf is my son's bread.*

Miss Whyte says Dame Mary is one of the strongest voices for Australian women in this war. I hadn't ever thought about us having a voice. Those last two lines remind me so much of Aunty Joyce when she stated that all she lives for is to put bread on the table for her sons, and keep their heritage for them. I might show it to her, now that I'm getting on a bit better with her.

◼

A southerly blizzard streaming straight up from the Antarctic howled as Rosemary huddled inside the cabin of the old buckboard next to Grandpa Jack. They'd heard there had even been a rare dusting of snow on top of Mount Lofty that morning; what a night for their new hand to be arriving!

'Put your coat away, woman, you can't go out on a night like this with that cough of yours. *I'll* go and get the blasted girl,' Grandpa Jack had told Joyce in an exasperated voice at 7.45.

Joyce looked doubtful. 'Well, you'd better take Rosemary with you. I wouldn't blame the girl for refusing to get into a vehicle with the likes of you.'

Jack grinned, showing an unsightly gap where he had two side teeth missing. 'You reckon I'll be rude to the lass, an' she might get on the next train an' go back where she come from. Well, I'll – '

'You'd better be civil to her then, Jack. I'll blame you if she doesn't last the distance.'

'If you'd listen an' not interrupt, I was goin' to say that I'll put up with 'er if she pulls 'er weight. An' I 'ope she's a big strapping lass with some weight to pull. She'll be doin' a man's job.' As he spoke he was casting an unfavourable glance at Rosemary's still slender frame.

I'd like a shilling for every time they talk about pulling weight, thought Rosemary.

Next they had an argument about whether to take the car or Ian's buckboard, and Grandpa Jack won again. 'I'm just not takin' your car out with them worn tyres on an icy road at night. You better stick to goin' to the shops or one of your fancy afternoon teas in it till I can get you some new tyres. And anyway, why should Princess Audrey get special treatment?'

So there Rosemary was, a few minutes away from the station with Grandpa Jack – when a train thundered past them in the dark. 'Gosh, that's terrifying!' she exclaimed. 'Aren't they allowed to have any lights at all?'

Her question was ignored. 'Damned thing's early. Can't never rely on timetables, can you?'

The station was in total darkness too. The noise of the train was fading and the waiting room and the stationmaster's room were locked up. At first they couldn't see anyone when they stopped near the platform. 'You stay 'ere while I'll go an' 'ave a look,' ordered Jack.

As he thrust himself out into the gale, Rosemary glimpsed a head poking round the far corner of the building by a little shed, where poor Audrey was sheltering as well as she could, probably feeling as if she'd been abandoned at the end of the world, not just the end of a platform.

'Hmm,' was all that Grandpa Jack said when he half pushed his new passenger up into the cabin next to Rosemary a couple of minutes later, and threw her suitcase into the back. Rosemary introduced herself, getting a quick look at a pale, very scared face framed by wispy, mousy brown hair. She could feel that the shivering body squashed next to hers was rather bony and not very tall – not entirely to Grandpa Jack's specifications.

# 22

SUNDAY 2 AUGUST

I don't know about having a stranger join your family like this. Audrey looked absolutely petrified when Grandpa Jack and I picked her up at the station, and she has hardly strung half a dozen words together since. She's from a suburb right on the Harbour in Sydney, called Balmain, so she certainly doesn't know anything about country life! We tried to make her feel welcome, of course, with Mother getting hot cocoa for us all while Aunty Joyce showed her to her room and spread an extra rug on her bed. Bob was asleep, but Johnny poked his head round the door to stare and then give a half friendly 'Hello' too. When I had chased him back to bed I asked Audrey why she wanted to join the Land Army. Remembering how much I loathed the idea of farm life just a few months ago, I genuinely wanted to know the answer.

I'm not much the wiser yet, because she just shrugged and mumbled, 'You know – life on the land,' then stared into her mug. I don't know whether she might have added something about it being an adventure, or making an effort for her country, because Grandpa Jack hopped straight in. (Up till then he hadn't given her much more than his usual grunt.)

'We'll give you life on the land all right. Five o'clock we start roundin' up the milkers – that's in winter. Sylvia can give you a shake when she gets up.'

'I'll do no such thing, her first morning,' Mother flung back at him. She's getting as bold as Aunty. 'The girl's had a long trip. She can have a proper sleep the first night, and look around a bit with Rosemary later in the morning. Plenty of time to start learning about the dairy in the afternoon.'

Then Aunty had to add, 'Rosemary can show you the ropes today, but mind you, I'm not paying you £2 a week just to do housework or mind the boys or anything like that. You have to be a farmhand – that's one of the rules.' Golly, she and Grandpa Jack are a tough pair.

I tried to lighten things up by joking, 'What a shame! I thought someone might take over half of my jobs.' And that hit the wrong note too, because Grandpa Jack glowered at me and told me that since he'd be teaching one girl to handle the cows he might as well teach two. So tomorrow I'm to tag along too.

So much for thinking that Grandpa Jack was warming towards me. As he headed home to bed I heard him muttering, 'Both scrawny as emus. Useless females.'

'This is a cow. This is the business end of the cow. Right? You start by washin' 'er udder with the warm water. Not just for cleanliness, though that's important too. You 'ave to stimulate the cow to want to let down the milk, an' so the first thing you need is warm 'ands.'

Rosemary and Audrey were getting what Grandpa Jack called 'all the good oil' on milking. Of course, not much of it was new to Rosemary, but she made sure Grandpa Jack saw her listening attentively. Producing milk was all a matter of hormones, apparently – people's as well as the cow's. Hormones were produced in the cow's pituitary gland, and they released the milk into the individual milk-secreting sacs. If a cow got upset in the morning, then came in with a distended udder in the evening, you had a 'snowball's chance in hell' of milking her. So Audrey got the full lecture on keeping the herd calm at all times, and was shown as a top priority how to turn on the temperamental wireless. 'An' don't change the station. None of that jazzy stuff, mind you!'

'Mozart?' suggested Audrey.

'Cows like the crooners. Bing Crosby an' Frank Sinatra.'

Lesson two, predictably, was about not passing on your own anxiety or anger. 'An' what goes on in *your* mind an' body matters too. If you feel like kickin' the cat, or you're 'avin' a bit of a weep, she'll pick up your mood an' you won't get nowhere with 'er. So keep it locked away.'

'That's a tall order,' whispered Rosemary, thinking of how Aunty Joyce must have felt after Uncle Brian died. Audrey, who still looked a bit tense, agreed.

It helped if you talked to the cows, in a monotonous sort of voice. Bluebell, one of the most placid cows, had been chosen for the demonstration: 'Okay now, Bluebell, your turn first, same as always. In you go now. Good girl – you always show the others how nice it is to get rid of that 'eavy bag of milk, don't you, old love?'

Then the girls had to have a go at milking. Rosemary was pleased to see that Bluebell's tail was safely hitched up where she couldn't get up to any mischief with it.

'Remember, serenity and tranquillity. Don't make 'er toey,' Grandpa Jack intoned from time to time as they took turns pulling at those rubbery teats while stifling giggles. He added, 'You can even sing to 'er if yer like.' But when Rosemary started humming 'You are my sunshine', old Bluebell looked round at her with her big brown eyes bulging as if in surprise, and they all decided singing wasn't a good idea.

Audrey, who was beginning to relax, showed some potential. Grandpa Jack grudgingly agreed that quite small people could be good milkers, as long as they had strong arms. 'I started when I was six or seven,' he told them proudly. 'An' young Johnny's goin' to be good too.'

'Blast!' Rosemary, who had jumped sideways when Bluebell shifted a back foot, had accidentally jolted the bucket so that milk sloshed over her shoes. Which brought her brief career as a milkmaid to an abrupt end.

'In a right tizzy again. Didn't I say no bad language or temper? You better stick to the apple pies,' Grandpa Jack growled. 'Knew the minute I saw you that you was too 'ighly strung for this job.'

Rosemary began to bridle; but before she could think up a suitable retort, Grandpa Jack was already redeeming himself. With a definite twinkle in his eye he went on, 'Mind you, a woman who can make a good apple pie – or an apple cake like yours – is worth two farmhands.'

*TUESDAY 4 AUGUST*

So far, so good. I wouldn't say that Grandpa Jack – or Aunty Joyce for that matter – have actually taken to Audrey yet, but she's holding her own. Grandpa Jack has stopped referring to her as the Princess now she has turned out in overalls. She looks as if she's going to be okay at milking, unlike me. Grandpa Jack confirmed what Aunty Joyce decided months ago; I have the wrong temperament for the job, and got sacked after I swore. Grandpa Jack was just waiting to have a go at me because he hates to hear a female swear. Though I think he almost winked at me when he finished telling me off. Anyway, we're all agreed, including Bluebell the cow, that I'm not calm enough to be good at milking. Apparently the adrenalin that flows round your body when you are uptight in any way produces a smell that upsets the cow, and then she won't let down her milk. It's the same as a horse or dog knowing whether you like it or not: if you're scared they can smell the fear.

I'll jot down a few items I've been saving up to record, as I have a feeling that with the wedding getting close there soon won't be a minute for writing. The main one is that the replies to the invitations are flooding in, and I'm getting excited about all the people I will see again. Especially Grandma! Uncle Keith, who will give Heather away, is bringing her down from Whyalla. It won't be a very big wedding; times are tough and so many men are away. (I wonder if Father might after all be getting our letters about it.) So there will be just our closest relations, including Aunties Florence and Agnes – we're all bedding down at one or other of their houses, a few old family friends, Jim's relations and the bridal couple's best friends.

There has been more 'light' damage from raids on Darwin. I reckon damage can never be light if you factor in the terror of having a bomb hit your house or shop. There are reports of bitter fighting at Kokoda in New Guinea too. Mother was talking to Mrs Bolton, who said their neighbours are devastated because a soldier whom they billeted earlier in the year has been killed up there. Isn't that sad? And finally, there's a very good photo in today's paper of ships that were involved in the Midway battle. They look so dark and bulky and grim.

That's all the news. It's funny, but a part of the front page is missing from today's paper. Used to wrap up rubbish, I guess.

I know I hardly ever write about Father these days. The truth is, with this new, busy life of ours, I think about him less too, and I feel bad about that. I wonder if other people are like this. I do long to have you back, Father.

Audrey says the bathroom's free. She seems a lot happier tonight. No wonder she looked half dead when we picked her up; she had been sitting on trains for days, from Sydney to Melbourne, and then on here, and hardly sleeping. Fortunately the passengers got tea and cakes, or cold, congealed eggs and sausages from time to time off trestle tables laid out on platforms by various women's groups. Each girl had a slip of paper with the farmer's name and location on it, and nothing else. The last of the others had been let off near Murray Bridge, and Audrey had no idea when she would be dumped out, because of course she had never heard of Nairne. Who has? She can smile about it all now, though, and says, 'Well, our new motto is "Anywhere, any time", and this is as good as anywhere.' I like her.

�»═«

The headline 'Details of Atrocities in Hong Kong' had jumped out at Sylvia when she took a quick glance at the morning paper. Shuddering, she quickly tore that bit off the front page and threw it in the stove before anyone else could read it.

Despite her frequent assurances to Les that she was being strong for him, she was in fact becoming jumpy and more frequently flustered as the wedding day approached. A plane flying overhead last night, the sound of its engine fluctuating as it moved in and out of clouds, had been enough to make her insides do a backward somersault. Surely it couldn't be an enemy plane? What if something terrible happened to spoil their happiness so close to the big day? What if ...? She tried to bury the half-formed dread that Les's death would be announced, and they would all be in mourning.

But today, when action swept away the doldrums, she felt in control again.

'Rosemary!' she called. 'I want you to get lunch for Jack and Audrey. Just give them cold meat and the leftover potato salad and plenty of bread. Joyce and I are going over to Ivy's to finish icing the wedding cake.'

*THURSDAY 13 AUGUST*
I've had the loveliest surprise. Kyle wrote to say he's reaching town tomorrow – AND he will be coming to the wedding!! It will

be wonderful to see him again. He hasn't said where he is going next, or when. I'm pretending he's not going to enlist, but he almost certainly is.

I had no idea how much planning goes into running a wedding, but we're on the home run now. There was nearly a last-minute hitch when it occurred to Aunty Joyce that she can't leave Audrey alone in the house here. Luckily Valerie is home on leave for a few days for the first time since she went to Queensland, so she will be 'borrowed' for a couple of nights. I wonder how those two will get on?

We're off to stay with Aunt Agnes tomorrow afternoon. Grandma and Uncle Keith and his family get to stay with Aunty Florence. I'm not sure which will be worse – the sweet potty one or the dreary sharp-tongued one! But Johnny and Bob are happy, because Aunt Agnes's house at Croydon backs on to the railway line that goes to Outer Harbour, and they'll be able to hang over the fence and watch trains. As if they don't get enough of their rattle and tooting and smoke up here.

It will be a miracle if I can even fit in the car, what with the ton or so of food that we will have. Luckily the frocks and cake went last week, and the flowers will be delivered by someone from the CWA.

Speaking of the CWA – Audrey certainly is a city girl. Yesterday she asked what CWA stands for, and when we chorused that it was the Country Women's Association, Grandpa Jack snorted and said, 'You really did land 'ere flat-footed, didn't you?' Then I had to ask what that meant!

Heaps of wedding presents have been arriving, as we are going to store them all here. Knowing what was in short supply in Heather's glory box, I've bought her a collection of kitchen gadgets like strainers and a potato peeler, plus a *Green and Gold Cookery Book* – 'Containing Many Good and Proved Recipes' – that also has lots of household hints and remedies in the back. Mother says housewives have sworn by it for nearly twenty years. Violet's gift is unconventional, but a generous and thoughtful one. Apart from providing new silk stockings that she once got from you know who, she has made some lovely underwear and a nightie for Heather's trousseau out of some remnants of parachute silk that a relation got hold of.

Of course most of the gifts are much more ordinary (I wonder how many toast racks and teaspoons there will be) and probably more expensive. Maybe several vases. Lucky Mrs Jim Smith! No wonder girls long to get married.

But I don't think I've ever mentioned that there is no point in Heather and Jim setting up a home anywhere yet, since Jim has to report to the Wayville Showground as soon as the honeymoon ends and then will be going away. We all think that's a rotten way to start married life, but it can't be helped. Heather will carry on with her job and stay at Mrs Jones's with Violet as usual, because of course it's so hard to get a house. It's just as well married women are allowed to keep working in some jobs these days. I keep wondering if Heather knows that Violet is having a baby – that's if she really is.

I also wonder where the lovebirds will be honeymooning. They're doing a good job of keeping that a secret. We're guessing Victor Harbor; its guesthouses are very popular. I stayed there once with a friend's family. We went on the horse tram that takes you on the causeway out to Granite Island, where you can watch for penguins. Then if you're at a loose end and it's not beach weather you can walk round to the old whaling station. When I said that to Mother she laughed and said, 'Yes, well they'll be wondering how to fill in a whole three days.' That made me blush.

Briefly, the good and the bad on the war front. First, the US marines have made a very successful offensive against the Japanese in the Solomon Islands, at a place with an odd name – oh yes, Guadalcanal. The paper says the American Navy is brilliantly prepared. But then there is a warning from the Japanese Government to Australia and

India that is described as 'sabre-rattling'. I think that sounds scary, but Aunty reckons things are improving a bit, and that it's the Japs who are getting rattled, not the sabres.

Anyway, there will be only one thing on my mind from now on for a few days: the wedding at last!

# 23

'Aren't we lucky it's such a beautiful day?' Aunt Agnes exclaimed to Rosemary for the fifth time, hovering in her doorway when a friend with yet more wedding presents was trying to get past. Rosemary agreed once again, and drew her great-aunt back, managing to be patient only because it was her specific job to keep Agnes occupied while Sylvia and a cousin's wife did the hair of the rest of the bridal party. Hers was already stiffly swept up on top and curled around the ends, so that now she held her head self-consciously while she tackled a small mountain of sandwich bread and fillings. Someone seemed to be coming or going all the time, and everyone must be offered a snack. *And all men must be fed,* she recited to herself. The amazing Aunty Joyce had left everything laid out before taking the boys and all their good clothes with her to the hall in town, where she was going to put the final touches to the decorations and check on every last detail before they headed to the church.

'Come and I'll do your makeup, you two,' called Violet. She had arrived bright and early, ready to set out all her accumulated cosmetics. Suddenly Rosemary was swept by a wave of excitement. She had never had her face made up before!

Sitting back while her powder, rouge and lipstick were applied, she observed Violet quietly, but could see no sign that anything was amiss. Either her mother had been mistaken, or Violet was a very good actress. There was no more time to think about that topic, though, because just then Aunt Agnes caused a diversion by absent-mindedly letting in her yappy fox terrier, Larry, which headed like a cannonball for the frocks laid out on the armchairs, causing instant chaos.

'Rosemary! *What* did I ask you?' sighed Sylvia in a peeved tone after she had restored order and firmly placed Aunt Agnes down in her shabby brown-velvet chair.

Soon Heather was swanning around with her veil in place and makeup complete – looking comical, since she still had on her Harris Tweed skirt and orange cardigan. Then in no time, it seemed, the laughter-filled morning had gone, the sandwich platter was left with only wilted lettuce, and the bridesmaids were helping Heather step into her gown. They gasped as the last buttons and hooks were fastened, and she turned to face them. She was calm, radiant, beautiful – the perfect bride!

*She looks smug,* thought Rosemary, and felt a twinge of guilt: what an unkind word smug was. She only meant that her sister looked contented, and deservedly so.

Fortunately Aunt Agnes was dozing off, leaving Rosemary free to dress. She slipped into the sleep out abutting the second bedroom, where Sylvia was giving Violet's frock a final once-over. She didn't mean to eavesdrop, but only a damask curtain on the bedroom window separated the two rooms.

'Just as well I left it a bit loose, isn't it?' Sylvia was saying. 'In fact, if you slip it off for a minute, I think I'll just unpick those little front darts and give it another press.'

There was a rustle of taffeta before the silence was broken by Violet's tearful voice. 'You've guessed, haven't you?'

'I had a bit of an idea,' admitted Sylvia. 'Does Heather know?'

'*No.* I didn't want anyone to know until after this.' Violet sounded panicked now.

'What about your young man?'

It was the wrong thing to say, of course, because Violet began sobbing quietly.

'That's right, Heather said he's away at the moment. Now don't get yourself upset, dear, or you'll spoil your makeup and get puffy eyes. Everything will work out.'

'It can't work out! Someone – one of his friends – told me he's married, and he's got two children.'

Heather was calling for help to get her necklace done up, so Rosemary crept out. By the time she came back within earshot, Sylvia was saying, 'There! No one will have any idea. You look just lovely. Now, give me a brave smile.'

Ten minutes later, as they all crowded into the cars, Heather's friend had hidden almost every sign of her broken heart; though her smile looked somewhat brittle. She waved along with the rest of the group when they had to stop for a train crawling through the level crossing at the end of the street. A whole carriage-full of nurses, on their way to a troop ship no doubt, hung out of the windows singing 'Wish Me Luck as you Wave Me Goodbye'.

*MONDAY 17 AUGUST*

Oh, what a beautiful wedding! I made a wish and slept with my piece of cake under my pillow last night, and today I've been wandering round in a state of bliss, either humming the wedding march or staring into space. Mother has just laughingly told me I'm in love with love. I don't mind admitting that Heather's wedding was just the happiest, saddest, most romantic event I've ever been to. (I'd better not let Valerie hear that; she says there's a lot of nonsense goes on about getting married. I reckon she needs a boyfriend.)

I'm not sure I like the idea of everything that goes with married life – but I hope I'll get married one day.

Kyle was waiting outside the church among a group of outsiders who were just having a stickybeak. I couldn't miss that hair of his, sticking up in the wrong places despite his efforts to neaten it. He came up to me as we went into the porch, quickly squeezing my hand. I was relieved to see he is just like I remembered him – gorgeous! He leant over and whispered I looked wonderful, before slipping into a back pew. But Johnny spotted him, so soon Aunty Joyce was beckoning him to come and sit with them. And there was Grandma too, in an aisle seat and holding a satin horseshoe she had made for the bride. She looked as happy as I've ever seen her.

The service was lovely, so full of meaning. They say just about everyone cries at weddings, but I think we all shed a few more tears than is normal, because of what this war is doing to us. You know – the 'For better and for worse' bit, and especially 'Till death do us part'. So many of the guests were thinking of the people who were not with us, which made the service extra poignant. (That's my word of the week, which came to me when we saw all those nurses heading off to war.) Even some of the men had to blow their noses or rub at their eyes suddenly when the minister talked about love being a bright beacon in these dark days. Uncle Keith said afterwards that the hay fever season must be starting early. I've never thought about it before, but I suppose older people were remembering their weddings too; Grandma was sitting still as a statue, with a faraway look on her face.

Fortunately the rest of the day was just a happy party. Even Aunty Florence smiled and cracked a joke or two! I made sure I didn't stay close to her for long enough to get a lecture.

The fun started as we all walked up North Terrace from the church to the reception, falling into a loose formation behind the bride and groom. Suddenly a group of airmen, led by a pipe band, marched out of King William Street. Kyle says they were from a Spitfire squadron. Anyway, they turned the corner just ahead of us, making for their headquarters. They are camped at the

Exhibition Building up the road, and apparently are constantly seen (and certainly heard) parading. When their leader saw us he smiled broadly, yelled at his men to halt, and asked where we were heading. Jim said, 'The Masonic Hall.' There followed a lengthy drum roll, then bagpipes, a trumpet and drums started up and they set off again, leading us up the street in grand style! We all called 'Goodbye!' or 'Thank you!' when we reached our destination. As Aunty Joyce said, money wouldn't buy such pomp and ceremony.

It was wonderful to see Kyle again, and to hear a few (too few) of his stories from his amazing month in the outback. Like when a dingo carried off one of his boots in the night while he was camping! (Must have smelled interesting.) It's a shame we haven't been able to share adventures together.

It made me so happy to introduce him to Grandma. My two favourite people together. Apart from Father; no, I didn't forget him on the day. Grandma loves that infectious smile of his, and they found lots to talk about – just like Kyle and I do. It was certainly a night for talking! Whenever I wasn't busy doing bridesmaid-type things like handing round the cake, listening to the speeches and so on, I spent the whole evening just catching up with family and friends.

Oh – I should have mentioned that before the proper bridal toast one was proposed to the 'three flowers'. That is, Heather, Violet, Rosemary. It was fun.

Of course, I only knew about half the guests. It was strange to see all of Jim's family and friends, and especially to hear Jim's father welcome Heather into his family. There was the usual sentimental talk about how Mother wasn't losing a daughter, but gaining a son. Finally Uncle Keith, taking on Father's role, said to Jim, 'Mind you look after her, young man, she's very precious.' I'd never thought of Heather as precious ...

By the end of the reception some of the men were sounding quite merry, almost as if they'd spent a few hours at the pub. Which seemed strange, since I knew liquor is not allowed to be served in public halls, and there were only soft drinks in jugs on the tables. So I sat back and observed, as I'm learning to do. Sure enough I solved the mystery. One or two at a time, the men would saunter along to the lift down the passage, press the button, and disappear into it when the doors opened. I could only think that the lavatories must be on another floor. Why did men need to go so often? Then I saw that the indicator wasn't moving away from the first floor. Sidling closer, I caught a glimpse of Uncle Keith pouring a shot of whisky for Jim's father! He had set up a little bar in the lift ...

The time went so quickly, what with the cutting of the cake, and the dancing. Yes, Kyle danced with me, which was blissful despite my embarrassment about having two left feet when it comes to dancing. Soon Violet and I were helping Heather to change into her going-away outfit. It wasn't a new suit, but Mother had put a fur collar on it, making it look very smart. Then came the last tradition – throwing the posy.

The unmarried girls gathered, most of us calling to the bride to throw her flowers to us. And guess who caught the corsage? Violet. I could see that Heather had aimed it right at her, and looked really pleased when her best friend caught it; she could hardly have missed. Of course everyone cried out, 'That means you'll be the next bride!'

Poor Violet. I have to admire her so much, because she kept that bright smile on her face right to the end, obviously determined not to spoil her friend's perfect day. But I could see the pain in her eyes when we had waved Heather and Jim goodbye, and she set off home with her parents, her own posy and the bride's drooping from her hands.

◦┃▬┃◦

Naturally Sylvia had kept Les fully posted on almost every aspect of the big day. But now, as she sat carefully unpicking Miss Browning's Maltese lace, she was conducting a review, to fill in the many details she had been too occupied to relate as they happened.

*We all put on happy faces, Les. The only time I let my guard slip was when they sang 'O perfect love'. I thought we had checked everything in the service so the likes of Joyce wouldn't get all melancholy; but I forgot about the lines*

*'Grant them the joy which brightens earthly sorrow,*
*Grant them the peace which calms all earthly strife.'*

*That was just too much for me. But I cried silently.*

*It was easier for the young ones to be jolly of course. Young Rosemary looked so pretty and happy. Her friend Kyle is a nice lad, but she'd better not get too fond of him, because he's off into the Army like just about everyone else. I saw how enthusiastically he kissed her goodbye. I don't know what will happen to little Violet though – the poor silly girl. I expect her parents will send her to one of the homes for unmarried mothers, probably the Kate Cocks one, and she'll have the baby adopted. Even so, she's ruined her life, hasn't she? She'll never marry well now.*

Of course, Les should have led his daughter on to the floor for the wedding waltz, before handing her over to Jim. Sylvia recalled the awkward moment before at least six men had descended on Heather to claim the privilege.

*Then when Jim got a look in, and everyone started dancing, you should have seen the two of them. They could have been alone in that hall, the way they drifted round, their eyes locked together. Clinging to each other passionately, because soon they will be torn apart. (Now who's getting melancholy?)*

What else was there?

*Oh yes, I've told you about some of the speeches, haven't I? They were all very good, but Jim's father couldn't help saying, 'So live life to the full while you have the chance.' The poor kids – they've got three days of married life until Jim has to report back to camp. Still that's two days more than some newly-weds are getting at the moment.*

Sylvia, who had stopped praying months ago, had suddenly started again. *Dear God, bring him home to us safely, and put an end to this agonising wait.*

# 24

*TUESDAY 18 AUGUST*

The wedding is nothing but a memory already. But how vividly I will recall Kyle's farewell to me ... Now, though, it's back to the same old routine.

On pulling up my blind, I have just seen a sight to make me laugh out loud. Valerie has materialised out of the dawn mist on Marjorie's pony, Millie, which is far too small for her – and Audrey is perched like a doll on top of Caesar, Uncle Norm's biggest Clydesdale! A couple of very pregnant cows are ambling along in front of them. I needed something to lift my spirits, after tossing and turning half the night.

Those two are already behaving like firm friends. I was a bit surprised until I thought about it; but although Valerie seems to look down on girls who stay on the land just to marry and be farmers' wives, she also admires people who use their initiative, and who are 'doing their bit'. There's no doubt Audrey falls into that category. Of course, she may end up marrying a farmer. She'll have all the credentials.

Aunty Joyce is being quite nice to her now. She even said a few days ago that she'd take her down to town one day, since she's never seen the city.

I'll have to hound Johnny and Bob to get dressed for school in a minute; I can hear them having a scuffle that sounds like a pillow-fight. If I don't stop them soon, guess who will be cleaning up a snowfall of feathers and mending a pillow or two?

Jim and Heather will have to part tomorrow. Isn't that sad? Kyle is going to be just a memory too, because he rang yesterday, not long after I finished writing my story of the wedding, to say he had to leave last night, after only a few hours' notice. He is going to Puckapunyal in Victoria, where he will do artillery training. I have memorised his Army number – SX 49929. He is amused that his card lists his regular employment as 'jackaroo', after only a month's experience doing odd jobs on a station. And the other funny thing is that, since he has put his age up to eighteen, he has realised that his birthdate is recorded as only two months behind his brother's! Now, that would have been a miracle birth!

I won't get to see him again; and can you imagine me trying to say goodbye on the phone with Johnny at my side, grinning?

Kyle told me he'd be passing by on a train in the middle of the night, but he had no idea when. So as the long night wore on I listened to half a dozen of the juggernauts, trying to distinguish the rattle-rattle-clank-clunk of passenger trains from the heavier buffet-crash-thud-BANG of a goods train. (I'll admit I looked up buffet in my dictionary, because I've become very slack about my 'new word a day' resolution.) The heroine of a novel would probably be brave or foolhardy enough to spend the night on that sodden, windswept platform, waiting for her beloved to go by. If I had been there, I'm sure Kyle would have stuck most of his body out and yelled at me. The last thing he said was that one day he'd jump right off one of those trains, and into my arms. We both know where he got that idea, of course.

Valerie left midweek, but not before trying to give Audrey advice about asserting her rights. 'Make sure you get a proper uniform allowance. Women who enlist get extra coupons. You should get money for equipment too – and penny postage.'

Audrey didn't seem too fussed about any of that. 'I think we get a badge and uniform after three months' trial, if we're going to be permanent. But we haven't enlisted, we're only enrolled; we're privately employed so they don't count us as part of the Army.'

'Well,' Valerie warned, 'no one is going to give you thanks for all your work or pay you any respect if you don't stick up for yourself. You mark my words.'

Audrey was in fact sticking up for herself very nicely. She was already becoming indispensable on the farm, thanks to her willingness to knuckle down and learn anything from riding a horse to digging trenches. 'Gee, I ache!' she exclaimed once; but she never gave up, and was getting stronger by the day. She had met lots of local people too, and helped form a hockey team whose other members were also new arrivals – either Land Army recruits or girls from the telephone exchange. I suggested they should call themselves the Landlines.

She quietly made it clear by her attitude that she wasn't going to be bullied by Grandpa Jack. Not that he made it easy for her. For instance, one day when Joyce was showing her how to treat a cow that had what he called 'a crook quarter', he blamed Audrey for poor Lily's predicament.

She wasn't in the least flustered. 'What do you think, Mrs Scott?' she asked.

Joyce quickly jumped to her defence. 'You know as well as I do, Jack, that cows often get mastitis, especially Jerseys. I'm sure Audrey isn't neglecting their hygiene.' She turned her back on him and went on explaining to Audrey that if the infection spread to all four teats, septicaemia would set in; and then there was no hope for the cow, which would have to be sent to the abattoirs for slaughter – if they could get it there before it died. That would be bad news, not just for Lily, because an old jersey didn't have much salvage value. Not like a bigger breed, a shorthorn for example. Audrey took all this on board, and more.

An unexpected consequence of Audrey's presence among them, once she had settled in, was that they all began to talk to each other more. It was as if the newcomer, with her forthright yet friendly manner, knew how to cut through the constraints that both bound the family together and made them keep their silence.

She had made the connection straight away that she and Rosemary had both been transplanted by the war, and got right to the heart of the matter. 'I gather you'd rather not be here,' she said to Rosemary over the butter churn one afternoon.

'Right first try. I suppose I should feel guilty. You know – that I'm not throwing myself wholeheartedly into coming to my aunt's and my country's aid.' That was something she hadn't even been admitting to herself.

'I wasn't thinking that. I don't blame you being upset about having to leave school; your aunty says you were going to be a top student. Not like me. I couldn't wait to leave my job.'

'Which was?'

Audrey grinned. 'I worked in ladies' underwear in Grace Brothers – and you can imagine how often someone told me the joke about the lift attendant who said, "Ladies' underwear – going down."'

'That's the sort of humour Johnny likes!'

'I was just thinking,' Audrey went on, 'that I'm the opposite of you. Your mother has dragged you here, whereas mine is upset I came.'

'Didn't she want you to leave home?'

'She liked having a daughter who wore a smart black skirt and crisp white blouse. She's embarrassed to tell everyone that I'm a common farm labourer! She said, "Can't you do something more uplifting?"'

They giggled together about the uplifting qualities of brassières.

⊪

The next morning Audrey turned her attentions to Grandpa Jack. 'So where did you serve in the Great War, Mr Scott?' she boldly asked while they were mounding up the day's accumulation of manure. Rosemary was nearby, coaxing a tottering bull calf to drink from a bucket. And although you could sense that Grandpa Jack's brain went straight into defence mode, ready to repel unwanted questions about what happened at the front, he only grunted once before he told her about his posting to France, the areas in which he had fought, and how he was sent to London after nearly dying of the 'flu early in 1918. 'It was just a bit ahead of the epidemic that set in worldwide – an' the end of the war. Me lungs collapsed, so I never got back to the front.'

'You were one of the lucky ones then. Like my father; he got evacuated with a leg wound.'

'Lucky?' Rosemary queried.

Yes, Grandpa Jack informed her gruffly. Lucky. It meant they got back to their families alive and without much permanent damage. But his face twitched and contorted as he spoke, and the girls fell silent.

A minute later he took up the topic again. 'Just about everyone that wasn't killed was wounded,' he said. Then went on vehemently, 'I begged Brian not to join the infantry this time round – I couldn't explain 'ow bad it was though. Anything but the infantry, I said. But 'e was pig-headed an' wasn't goin' to take my advice. An' now Joyce blames me for his death. Says I pushed 'im into it.'

A night or two later Audrey had the women talking. When something had come up about boyfriends, she told them with a wry smile that hers had suddenly dumped her and gone off with her best friend from their schooldays. Joyce and Sylvia exchanged glances and, to Rosemary's surprise, Sylvia was looking uncomfortable.

'They've got a habit of doing that. Fickle lot,' said Joyce. She was still fixing her eyes on her sister, challenging her to respond.

'Well, at least you're blaming him too, not just me,' Sylvia came back.

Rosemary looked from one to the other. 'Are you going to keep us in suspense?'

They poured out the story, not always in agreement, but both seeming willing to clear the air at last. It seemed that Joyce had been the childhood sweetheart of a young man called Ted from a farm up the road, and it was more or less assumed by all that they would eventually marry. Ted was a real charmer. Then one day he started taking notice – lots of notice – of Sylvia, who had begun to grow into an attractive young woman under their very noses; more appealing than her rather angular sister. The two fell deeply in love.

'But – you married my father,' said Rosemary.

'The war came,' Sylvia explained. 'The Great War. I was young. Too young to marry before Ted went away, but I sort of promised to be there when he came back. Only when he did come back – '

'Let me guess,' said Audrey. 'When he came back he didn't love either of you.'

Sylvia shook her head and looked to Joyce to finish the tale.

'He was never right in the head again,' Joyce explained in her usual curt way. 'Flew off the handle at the slightest provocation. Some weeks he was so down he wouldn't talk to anyone. Then he took to drink. But he still loved Sylvia, and said she was promised to him.'

'So what happened?' Rosemary and Audrey asked in unison.

Rosemary thought this plot was shaping up nearly as well as *Jane Eyre*, which she had just finished.

'He was so fierce sometimes he scared me. I was going to leave home to get away from it all,' Sylvia took over. 'But I didn't have to.' She took a breath and finished: 'He took his father's car one night, and went out drinking. Then on the way home he drove the car through the railing of a bridge – and was drowned in the river.'

Joyce eventually broke the silence that followed. 'I think it's time we all went to bed,' she said.

'I do love your father, Rosemary,' Sylvia assured her as they went to their bedrooms.

### FRIDAY 28 AUGUST

I'm still reeling a bit from Mother's story about her first love. You never know what's around the next corner in this life, do you? Imagine, if Mother had married Ted, I would never have been born. And then there's Aunty. She must have stayed single almost forever after the war until she met Uncle Brian. Lucky she did. I've been told before that Uncle didn't ever look for a wife until his parents died and the farm was going to be divided up.

There's really no news, but I may as well fill in an hour till bedtime by writing, as I'm currently out of books. Heather went straight back to work as if the wedding never happened. (Yes, they did have their honeymoon at Victor Harbor, but naturally she wouldn't tell me a thing about it.) Jim has already left. He had to report to the Showgrounds at Wayville, where the men all slept on straw palliasses – some of them in the pigpens! He said he's now a number, not a name, because once you belong to the Army, you don't have any rights. They were not told when they were leaving till the last minute. So Heather just got a phone call, and no real goodbye. Jim's gone to a jungle training place called Canungra in Queensland first, and soon he will head to New Guinea. What more can I say? We all knew this would happen, but it's sad all the same.

It's no different with Kyle. The Army now owns him too, and will tell him exactly what to do. I haven't heard from him since he left. But I'll keep dreaming of him, however long it takes.

What a letdown all this is, after the excitement of the wedding. My life is so *ordinary*!

The only activity now is on the home front, where our days – and nights sometimes – are dominated by cows. We have had twelve calves so far, seven heifers and four bulls that are healthy, plus a stillborn bull. Aunty is very happy with this ratio and hopes it will continue, as she needs to build up the herd to keep the farm viable. We've been taking turns to name the heifers; I've chosen Freda and Phoebe so far, for adorable twins. Aunty thinks those names are a bit fancy. She called her calf Betsy.

Unfortunately I've found out what happens to the baby bulls. They don't get names.

The dead one was immediately skinned, to be fed to Uncle Norm's dogs. I didn't get upset, as I know there's no room for sentiment. But I made more discoveries. The new calves are only left with their mothers for the first few days, while they are drinking a very rich milk called colostrum, which is essential to their growth. Anyway, it mustn't get into the ordinary milk, as it would discolour it. Then, because it is cheaper to feed the calves an artificial formula called Denkavit and begin to use their mothers' milk for cream straight away, the little darlings are taught to suck from the teats on the Moo Bar that I wrote about before. Sometimes you have to stick their heads in a bucket of milk and get them sucking on your finger at first, until they get a taste for the formula. If a calf won't suck at all you can put something sweet like jam or treacle on your finger. It feels so strange!

The bulls don't even get much of the colostrum, however, and are just force-fed as much Denkavit as possible after the first day.

That's the good bit. When I saw Audrey rounding up the little bull calves on Monday, I asked her where they were going.

'It's the calf pickup on Monday mornings,' she told me.

'Pickup? Where do they go?'

'We keep the heifers of course; it's only the bulls that go. Here – hang on to this little fellow, will you? Someone buys them and then they are sold on to be fattened up until they are big enough to be butchered as veal. Or some are just slaughtered for their skins.'

She looked at my horrified face as she shoved the last bellowing calf into a pen by the gate, and said, 'You didn't really think they can all grow up to be bulls like Bruce, did you?' I had to admit I'd never thought it through. Just like I didn't understand about Lamb Chop, and got so furious with Aunty.

*SATURDAY 29 AUGUST*

Still bored. It's a disgusting wet day. I'm going to a birthday party later though – a friend of Ian's. Till then, another scribble.

We haven't followed the war news much lately; someone would soon pass on good news if there were any. But I did glance at another lecture from Mr Curtin, who is still going on about the 'She'll be right' attitude of a lot of Australians. He said he was disappointed the enthusiasm for the war effort of so many people seemed to be waning; because we are still in danger. I believe him. A week or so ago I spotted a little report marked 'Somewhere in Australia', about a ship shelled by an enemy submarine in Southern Australian waters. Of course, the reporters are not allowed to say where, but Grandpa Jack thinks it was a passenger ship somewhere in Bass Strait, between Victoria and Tasmania. That's much too close for comfort.

I asked Grandpa Jack how he knew things like that, when he didn't seem to read the paper very much, and he said the grapevine's the best news network of all. Then he told me something I'd certainly never heard, something that at first I found hard to believe. I'll try to make this sound like him:

'F'r example, 'ave you 'eard that the country's first casualties due to enemy action wasn't in Darwin? They was 'ere in South Australia, down the coast at Beachport.'

'What do you mean?' (That's me.)

'Well, back in '40 it was, two or three ships was mysteriously lost between Adelaide an' Melbourne. Then in the winter last year, German landmines started to wash ashore down the South East, or fishermen towed them on to the beaches.'

'Who told you about them?' I asked, and he said impatiently that his mate Ralph's got relations down that way. His look warned me not to interrupt again.

'An' one day they brought one in at Beachport. All the locals crowded round to 'ave a look at it – enormous brute they said it was. But when the naval experts got there they shooed 'em all away. Said it was 'ighly dangerous. They towed it away from the town an' attached detonators to it. Only the detonators didn't go off, so the big boss dispatched two Able Seamen to check. They crept up the beach –'

I couldn't help it. I exclaimed, 'Oh no! Did it go off?'

Grandpa Jack nodded solemnly. 'It suddenly exploded, an' blew 'em to smithereens. So they was the first victims of the war to die on Australian soil.'

I don't suppose many people know that story. Phew! I haven't been able to get it out of my mind. I wonder how many more mines are floating round out there?

I was talking about the telling-off from the Prime Minister, wasn't I? I don't agree that our efforts to help have lessened. Johnny and Bob are even taking rags and the silver foil from Grandpa Jack's cigarette packets to school for the waste collections, as well as paper and bones. I must say the playground is looking like a junkyard. Johnny has a yellow lieutenant's collector badge with several bars, just like the service medals servicemen get, and a silver aeroplane one. He is now aiming for gold. But so much paper has accumulated round the state that a temporary halt has been called, because depots are jammed. The last time I talked to Mr Marryat, he said the Education Department got rid of 500 tons of old reports, dockets and correspondence!

I have overlooked one bit of exhilarating action coming up. Now we have Audrey here to help out, Mother and I are going down to town for a couple of days next week to fix up accounts from the wedding, see to a few other business matters, get me some new shoes and return Miss Browning's lace. Of course we'll meet Heather too, and will call in on the Marryats for a few minutes. We're going to stay with Aunt Agnes again, so Mother can see if her neighbour will keep a good eye on her for a small weekly payment. She knows Father would want us to make sure his aunt is not neglected. Before we leave town we can treat ourselves to an afternoon at the pictures, so I'm already checking out what's on. I'd like to see Joan Fontaine in *Suspicion*, which has had a good review, but Mother likes Bob Hope's slick humour and wants to go to *Nothing but the Truth* at Wests. She'll win, of course. I can't wait to be independent …

# 25

'What beautiful daffodils! Do come in and have a cup of tea.' After a moment's confusion during which her hand had flown from straying strands of her long unkempt salt-and-pepper hair down to her apron, Miss Browning had regained her composure. To entertain was probably a rare event for her, but her curiosity to hear all about Heather's wedding must have helped her to overcome her qualms.

'I've had a nice thankyou letter from Heather,' she told Sylvia. 'But of course young people never have the time or patience to tell you what you really want to know, do they?'

Time and patience … There was a long wait during which their hostess tried out several vases before settling on a pretty variegated pink and purple carnival glass one for the flowers they had brought from the farm. Then, since they reminded her of her cups and saucers with daffodils on them, she searched for her special tea set in a deep, dark sideboard in the adjoining room. But eventually Rosemary and Sylvia were sipping tea and politely munching stale shortbread biscuits.

They took turns describing the wedding, prompted by the old lady – 'And the flowers? Ah, spring bulbs and wattle. Edged with tulle, how lovely. Now tell me about the young man' – until she was satisfied.

As she fingered the exquisite lace they had returned, she started telling them about *her* young man. His name was Alfred Lee, and they had become engaged before he went away to the war – the Boer War, not the Great War. They were going to be married before he went; a date was chosen and preparations were well under way, when she began the new century by going down with diphtheria.

'So he sailed away before I was well enough to go through with the ceremony. He told me to have everything ready for when he returned. But he never came back.' Miss Browning stood up and gathered three sepia photographs from the mantelpiece, all a bit faded. The first was of Alfred, a serious-looking young man; next, a dainty woman with a sweet, soft look who must be Miss Browning herself; and finally a group of mounted soldiers with the caption, 'Second South Australian Contingent, left Australia 27 January 1900'.

'And so the lace?' Rosemary finally broke the silence.

'His parents had brought me back the lace from a trip they made abroad; the family were quite wealthy merchants. They always treated me like a daughter, you know. I wasn't as young as most brides, because I had nursed my mother for years until she died. She had consumption. A cruel disease … Now where was I?'

'Alfred's parents,' Sylvia prompted, sounding a bit choked up.

'Oh yes; I was fortunate to have two loving families to look after me in the years that followed.' She had a far-off look in her eyes for a minute, until she added, 'Then one went, and another, until I was on my own.'

*That's the woman I thought was a witch* … Rosemary felt tears prickling at the back of her eyes and blinked rapidly. They finished their tea and said goodbye in a sombre mood, promising to keep in touch until they could return to be neighbours again.

'So we've had wars to mess up our lives for three generations,' mused Rosemary as they headed for their old house to have a word with the tenants about some repairs.

'The Great War was the worst. But after any war finishes there simply aren't enough men to go around,' Sylvia told her. 'Older women or war widows have almost no hope.'

*… and I used to scorn Miss Browning for being an old maid.*

'One in ten men of marriageable age in Australia died in the Great War you know,' Sylvia went on. 'And nearly three times as many were wounded or gassed.'

'Like Grandpa Jack. Now it's happening all over again. The human race hasn't learnt much, has it?'

Sylvia wasn't listening, her mind still on marriage matters, not the state of humanity. 'Now, an unmarried mother like Violet may as well not even try for a good man.'

Rosemary raised an eyebrow. By now they all knew Violet's story, but she and her mother had never discussed it.

'Damaged goods, you know,' Sylvia explained.

*MONDAY 21 SEPTEMBER*
*Note to myself:* write update about changes to my life! When I get time …

Violet had been taken off the assembly line and promoted to a section where they made explosives. It was a pity she would have to leave months before the baby was due in January – as soon as her condition became obvious – because shortly after she had joined the union it had even been suggested she would make a good shop steward. Her departure would be unpopular, coming at a time when more munitions workers were desperately needed.

So far she had avoided having to tell anyone at work of her predicament, the fawn button-through frock that was their uniform being loose fitting. But her horrified parents had learnt the truth on the weekend of Heather's wedding when she had stayed with them. And once they had got past the recriminations ('How could you be so *stupid*? I'll wring that man's neck if I get hold of him ...'), they were now being moderately supportive. At least, they had reluctantly agreed they couldn't force Violet to give up her baby, and would let her stay with them until the time came, rather than being concealed in one of those homes where she would be treated like dirt. She could even give birth at the private hospital at Parkside where most local mothers went, as long as she was willing to put on a wedding ring, dream up a husband in the forces and call herself Mrs Somebody. Though, goodness knows what the neighbours would conclude ...

Violet was still thinking out the implications of all that.

Heather was the one friend she had confided in, finally breaking her silence on the night after Jim went away. They were snuggled up in their beds although it was still early, their overcoats spread atop their thin blankets as always; that was the only place where they could be both warm and hopefully out of earshot of the objectionable Mrs Jones. Understandably Heather was miserable, and Violet tried to listen sympathetically, comforting the forlorn bride of five days. But it all became too much when Heather complained, 'I won't even be able to go out with other men now I'm married. You're going to have all the fun, as usual.'

'*Fun!*' Violet exploded. But indignation quickly turned to tears as she poured out her sad tale. The more they talked, the more the reality of her situation hit home. An hour later, when there was no new angle to explore, and they wearily put their light out, Heather offered one last crumb of comfort.

'You'll meet someone wonderful one day, you know. You deserve to.'

But Violet sobbed, 'I'll never trust another man as long as I live.' She was crying so loudly that Heather tried to stop her in case Mrs Jones overheard and started snooping.

Neither of them heard the squeak of a loose floorboard out in the passage.

*SUNDAY 27 SEPTEMBER*

Today is one of those sparkly sunny days that make you glad you live in the Hills. I never thought I'd say that, but the new leaves on the gum trees are glowing reddish-gold, the grass is what Grandpa Jack rather wistfully calls Irish green and the willows against the sky down by the creek have turned to glistening silver lacework in the sun's rays. And the birds!

It's a month since I last wrote in here properly, because I'm much busier now.

I'll explain, since I don't think you're getting any letters at all, Father. Now that Audrey is proving so useful, Mother has agreed to an idea that has been quietly brewing in the back of my mind for ages, and which Mr Marryat brought to the fore on our post-wedding visit to town. At his suggestion I've enrolled to do correspondence lessons in three subjects for the last term – Maths, English and Latin. The languages are my favourites of course, but I need to make major progress in Maths if I'm to aim at my Intermediate Certificate next year.

With my life taking a turn for the better, I'm going to be occupied with more than chooks and chores from now on. (Well, you can be sure I'll still have plenty of chores.)

The English tutor wanted me to send samples of my writing, so after doing a composition entitled Country Life (that's the sort of thing I thought she'd expect) I wrote about Dame Mary Gilmore's patriotic poems, and included some quotations, just like I've been doing in this diary. She was very impressed! The best poem of all was sent to me recently by Miss Whyte. It's called 'No Foe Shall Gather Our Harvest', which ties in so well with our present circumstances here on the farm. Apparently it is very popular among the troops, and has even been set to music, though I haven't heard it. I really like the declaration in the last lines:

> *And we swear by the dead who bore us,*
> *By the heroes who blazed the trail,*
> *No foe shall gather our harvest*
> *Or sit on our stockyard rail.*

Mrs Gilmore – I mean Dame Mary – explained in a footnote that only strangers were entertained in the parlour, and real friends talked to you down at the stockyard. That's so true!

If Aunty reads that one she'll get angry and then gloomy like she does whenever there's bad news. The other day when we were laughing about something silly she told us we need to remember we're not out of the woods yet. She has a point.

My usual update on life at the farm and in the wider world is well overdue.

1. No, I can't include anything about Father in the news. But there was an article a couple of weeks ago suggesting that the initial number of deaths in Singapore was not very high, so that gives us new hope. Based on reports leaking out, such as one from an escapee who was fed and hidden in huts by the natives, and got to a nearby country in a canoe – Vietnam I think – the experts think a lot of men are working in the countryside on projects like roads and a railway; I can't help thinking that life outdoors might be better than being stuck in a prison. For goodness sake, if they know that much, when are we going to give us more details? It has been over seven months now.

2. I don't think older people feel things as much as my generation. Mother is looking pretty contented, and despite the lapses I've just mentioned, Aunty doesn't seem to be brooding as much as she used to. I suppose time is starting to heal her wounds, and things are

getting a bit easier for her. Not only has the Government at last introduced widows' pensions, but the farm is actually making some money; in fact, when Mother and I went to town we took out a few Savings Bonds for her. Mother's bought some too, with rent money she has stashed away, as it all helps our state reach its quota. We're meant to invest the money we save by not being able to get all the extravagant things we used to buy. I thought of this because Bob caused a laugh and some embarrassment last week when he 'borrowed' Aunty's certificate from her dressing-table drawer and took it to school for his morning talk! His teacher made sure I brought the precious document home in an envelope, suggesting we find a better hiding place for it.

3. Johnny seems a bit unhappy at times. I've discovered he is fretting about the fact he doesn't know anything about what his father did in Africa, or how he died. Actually he told Audrey this (everyone seems at ease confiding in her) and she said he should ask his mother. But of course, he already has, and she won't talk about it. I wish we could help him. I've been letting him use my Derwent pencils – my set of twenty-four is one of my prized possessions – but that's not likely to help much, is it?

4. Audrey, who has been quite cheerful, despite her heavy workload, is almost part of the family too. But something changed last Monday. She was very quiet that morning at breakfast. She even looked as if she was going to cry once, when Aunty Joyce teased her about being home late after going out with Ian, Wendy and some others. (They have a good time, that lot. The few single men who are left are in their element, with all the girls at the telephone exchange and now some Land Army recruits to choose from.) Then at mid afternoon she came bustling in from the paddocks to ask whether there were any letters for her. There weren't – Aunty

said nothing gets through on a Monday. At which she really did burst into tears.

We all asked whatever the matter was. Well, it turns out it was her twenty-first birthday! She didn't expect us to know, of course, but the awful thing was that no one in her family had even sent her a card. Poor Audrey. Mother and I quickly whipped up a three-minute sponge, dusted it with icing sugar and scratched around in the sideboard for some old birthday candles, luckily finding just enough. Johnny and Bob made her a card from the bottom of a stocking box edged with pinking shears, and we dredged up some little gifts, which we wrapped as nicely as we could. I gave her some nice lavender soap, but it was Aunty who had the best present hidden away (obviously not in her drawer!) – a box of Winning Post chocolates. As Grandpa Jack said when we held the surprise party at teatime, 'Those things are scarce as hens' teeth!'

'Hens don't have teeth!' Bob exclaimed; which got most of us laughing.

By the time we had sung 'Happy Birthday', Audrey was smiling too. Fortunately, several cards and a present – a nice hand-knitted lambs' wool jumper – arrived the next day.

5. Kyle has written to me once, but no address was given, and he didn't say much, except to describe the train trip a bit. (He really has a bit of a love affair with trains.) Apparently each station is known for the food it provides: it goes something like: sausages at Murray Bridge, chunky corned beef sandwiches at Bordertown, rissoles and mash at Dimboola, eggs and bacon somewhere else. The older men say that after a few trips you don't need to check the signs because the menu tells you where you are. Can Kyle really be 'enjoying the experience of Army life'? I don't think men are very good at expressing what they feel. But Aunty said Uncle Brian

was never allowed to write anything interesting. If a serviceman said where he was – even if he was just at a camp in Australia – or gave details of what he was doing, that bit was chopped off or blacked out.

I won't get any more news through Miss Selby either. She asked to be transferred to her home town of Ceduna, so her parents will at least be in touch with one of their children.

6. Just after Aunty told me about the censorship, Heather got a letter from Jim with words and phrases neatly cut out of the page! We haven't seen her for a while. She was going to come up this weekend, but she rang to say she is feeling a bit off colour. I think she's pining for her darling Jim who should be about to sail to New Guinea. The fighting is very fierce there; she must be worried about him.

Ever since our visit to Miss Browning, and hearing her tragic story, I've had a real sense of foreboding that something awful is going to happen in our family. Of course, I'm not going to say that to anyone. I hope I'm wrong.

That's it from me until something important or exciting happens.

# 26

Nobody, not even Jim, knew of Heather's pregnancy; she hadn't decided yet whether he would be more excited or worried by the news. Since they had been together for less than four days after the wedding, there was absolutely no doubt about the due date of mid May! On the weekend, when she went up to the farm, she would decide whether she might surprise her mother. In these early weeks, the young bride was weary but self-satisfied. Even if her man didn't come back, she would always have a part of him.

Of course it only took Sylvia a couple of hours to work it out. A feeling of deep contentment crept over her as she observed her older daughter eating her lunch.

'So, you clever old thing,' she said after the others had sprinted out to retrieve the washing off the line as it started raining, 'when will I become a grandmother? Let's see – somewhere in May?'

Heather gaped at her. 'How could you know?'

'It's the beetroot. You screwed up your nose and pushed it aside. When I was first expecting you, the only thing I couldn't stomach was beetroot. It's so acidic. Then that same dislike suddenly swept over me in the same way four years later – and I knew I was pregnant again.'

'I was going to tell you soon. I was just waiting – '

'I know. Waiting till you were sure. So you haven't had any morning sickness yet?'

'Not really. I'm just terribly tired for no reason.'

'Well, you look after yourself, my dear. You'd better get to a doctor for a checkup if you're so tired. Of course it's courting fate to tell too many people before you pass the stage where you might miscarry.'

'That's another five or six weeks. No, I won't tell anyone yet.'

But Rosemary was already coming back in behind them with a heap of shirts and tea towels for ironing. 'Tell anyone what? You always did keep secrets from me – and that's so mean!' Then when Heather and Sylvia exchanged half-questioning, half-amused looks, the penny dropped. 'Oh!!!' she screeched. 'You're having a baby!'

'So much for secrets,' Sylvia sighed. 'Trust you, Rosemary. Anyway, now that the whole world is about to find out – let's celebrate!'

*SUNDAY 4 OCTOBER*

Well it only took a week for me to have some good news: I'm going to be an aunty!!

True to form, Heather wasn't going to tell me she's expecting, but Mother guessed anyway. I'm glad because it's so nice to have something happy to think about.

The baby is due in May, and of course Heather is hoping like mad that Jim will be home by then. But I don't think the Japanese or the Germans consider fathers, mothers and babies when they plan their next move to take over the world. Heather may have even left it too late to write to Jim with the news; he must be embarking for New Guinea already. Apparently there's no contact once troops go overseas. And even if he does find out before he goes, he may have quite a big baby – even a toddler – to get to know on his return. It depends how long it takes to win this war. (I think most of us, even Mr Curtin, for all his goadings about working harder, now think we will win.)

We discussed all of this over afternoon tea, and Grandpa Jack's contribution, delivered with his crooked grin was, 'As long as there's not a string of children when he gets back.' Heather thought that was quite unnecessary; as usual, she has no sense of humour. She doesn't understand Grandpa Jack yet either.

She hasn't decided how long she can work for, or where she and the baby will live. She could try to get a little place of her own (almost impossible) or a flat on the back of someone's house. And if nothing's available, she could come up here. Mother is obviously keen on that idea, but goodness, we'd be crammed in like sar – no, I must avoid the same, tired old words – let's say, like the soldiers on those troop trains!

Since I'm writing, I'd better see if there's anything else worth noting. I cut out a report marked 'Somewhere in New Guinea' that says the Australians on the Kokoda Track are now close to the Owen Stanley Gap. But I know so little about that country that this news didn't mean much to me.

So I asked Grandpa Jack what he knows about the fighting up there. He says it must be dreadfully hard, hacking your way through dense jungle and ploughing along through the mud – all with a sixty-pound pack on. Coping with dysentery too. Someone who came home wounded says he was rescued by two of the natives, who carried him down the mountain for miles on a door made into a stretcher and then hid him until it was safe to get treatment for him. The soldiers call them 'Fuzzy Wuzzy Angels'. Isn't that nice?

Grandpa Jack says people don't appreciate how brave our soldiers in New Guinea are. He reckons that unless you've fought in Europe, they think you're just a second-class soldier. But, in fact, he says, you'd have to be a better fighter to survive up there than he was in France, where you spent half your time stuck in muddy trenches or collecting dead bodies. Well, I wouldn't know.

What else? It's only slightly amusing to see the paper has decided to publish 'Recipes to Stretch Potatoes', since that staple will be scarce until November. L-o-n-g potatoes! And there's a shortage of Modess pads. Well, we'll all survive that too – especially Heather.

My tooth is starting to play up again, and I'm praying like mad it will settle down. If not, I'll have to get myself to a dentist. Mother was annoyed when I told her, and said I should have arranged to go to Mr Petie, our family dentist, when we were back in town the week after the wedding. I replied that it wasn't so bad then; and anyway, I had too much on my mind at that stage.

Ian is someone else who has become absent-minded, and is not concentrating on his job. He must definitely be in love! He forgot to get the boys from school as arranged when he was in town last Thursday. And then he left a gate open the other day, so that his whole mob of sheep got into a wheat paddock. The normally mild Uncle Norm was apparently furious. But Grandpa Jack cackled and said, 'When I was a lad, an' courtin', I let our bull in among the neighbour's best young heifers. An' the calves they got for free from that mistake won all the prizes in the Show for years down the track.'

That started a string of 'When I was young' stories. At times like these I stop feeling anxious.

Which reminds me that early in this diary (before I heard how he jumped from the train) I said that surely Grandpa Jack could never have been young. Well, I discovered, while unwillingly doing some dusting, the postcard on the sitting room mantelpiece, which has 'Kisses from France' on it, is one he sent home to his wife in 1917. It has a fan surrounded by roses and purple pansies, all embroidered in silk, and a very sweet message on the back.

I think that's all.

Oh yes – I got 19 out of 20 for a Maths test!

Mrs Jones had been biding her time ever since she had heard Violet crying that night, and Heather saying, '*Shoosh*! You don't want Mrs Jones to get suspicious.' But the landlady was finding plenty to be suspicious about: the liveliest and most wayward of her boarders, who had disregarded most of her rules, hardly went anywhere any more. A couple of months ago Violet had been off her food, but these days when she came home from work she ate every scrap on her plate and scrounged more if she could. Then she shut herself in her room, a far cry from the brash way she used to dash off night after night to meet some American with a dreadful name. Chas? Chad? She had always been as cool as a cucumber if she missed the last train home on a Saturday and was caught trying to get someone to open the door or a window hours later.

Her swanky friend must have got much more than goodnight kisses in exchange for perfume, stockings and flowers. Now he had deserted her. While Mrs Jones had a pretty good idea there was more ailing Violet than a broken heart, getting proof was another matter. She could do without her sort; she had standards to keep up. But the irritating girl was always buttoned up in that overcoat of hers because she said she couldn't get warm. (The other boarders seemed to understand there was a shortage of firewood due to petrol rationing; but, oh no, not Madam Violet. Always standing up for her rights, that one. Well, she'd soon tell her what was right.) So, how was a body going to find out for certain?

That Heather had turned even quieter, and looked quite washed out after a day at work. She might be expecting too. Come to think of it, there hadn't been half as many sanitary towels soaking in the enamel bucket in the laundry lately. But then, Heather was married, so that was all right.

And so one Sunday morning, when Heather had left for the farm and the two sisters were out, Mrs Jones pretended not to know that

Violet was in the bathroom, and barged right in. Violet squealed and tried to curl up in the bath. *'Get out!'* she screamed at Mrs Jones. 'How *dare* you come in!'

At least Mrs Jones had the grace to withdraw, but not until she had taken a long, deliberate look at that distended abdomen. 'Come and see me when you're dressed, young lady,' she ordered. 'I'll be waiting.'

*FRIDAY 17 OCTOBER*

Another change in our lives. Heather is giving up work and coming to the farm to live for a while. Mother and Aunty are going down for her on Sunday. She was going to keep on for quite a bit longer, but last week she went to the doctor for a check-up, because she is always so tired. And it turns out she is anaemic. That's not good for her or the baby, so of course Mother has taken her under her wing, and says she needs to be up here so she can rest and be fed lots of red meat and vegetables and (of course) dairy foods. She'll enjoy being pampered; she always did.

Heather says she would have left the boarding house anyway, because Mrs Jones has been absolutely beastly to Violet. When she found out that Violet is expecting (which should be none of her business) she shouted at her that she is a dirty little slut, and that she wouldn't have her there a day longer, corrupting the nice girls who obeyed the rules and didn't get themselves into trouble. So poor Violet was given an hour to be out. Her father came and bundled her with all her belongings into his car, and Heather hasn't been able to see her since.

One bit of good news is that Heather got a letter from Jim, written the night before his ship sailed, and he did receive her news about the baby. She will only say he is over the moon at the thought of being a father; nothing I could do or offer would get her to read out his letter …

I heard on the wireless that there have been 'sharp words' from Mr Curtin about the attitude of Australians to the war. He says the situation is still very serious. Sometimes when I hear such things, that dark feeling sweeps over me again. But on the whole we are all getting on with winning the war in whatever way we have chosen, and are pretty cheerful on the surface at least. Amazingly, the other day I even heard Aunty Joyce of all people tell Mrs Gurner, 'Mustn't grumble. Getting round with long faces doesn't actually help anyone, does it?'

That leaves poor Johnny as the only glum one round here. I worked out the other day that he is being teased by a little kid called Greg at school because he hasn't got a father. Then a big bully was giving his arm a Chinese burn on Wednesday when I arrived to get the children, and he was trying not to cry. He's a very sensitive child. I told him he should boast that his father is a war hero, but I can see he doesn't believe me. And when I told Aunty and Grandpa Jack about it, they agreed with each other for once: he'll have to learn to fight back. I don't think retaliating is the best strategy with bullies; you'd just end up with your face pulped. But Mother says I mustn't stick my nose in.

# 27

'Good morning, Mrs Lister. Hello, Heather. You look very comfortable there!' called Audrey, who was coming back from next door for the last of her belongings. Sylvia and Heather, as warm and sleepy as a couple of lizards sunning themselves by the old stone wall, returned her wave.

A few days ago, while Audrey was on loan to help rebuild the sagging haystack at Ivy and Norm's, she had been invited in for lunch. Then, when she looked round, she said half jokingly that she should move over there to sleep, since they had two spare bedrooms – and the idea had been hailed by all as a stroke of genius. Her new hosts were enjoying her company, but she still spent most of her time in Joyce's and Grandpa Jack's employ, and had already stayed for tea one night. The family were not falling over each other quite as much as they had been, since Heather could now have a room to herself.

Sylvia was basking, not only in the late spring sunshine, but in contentment that she was playing a little part in nurturing a new life. She and Heather had washed their hair (thank goodness Velvet soap hadn't gone off the market) and given each other a rinse with saucepans of warm rainwater. Now they were drying their fair tresses in the mid-morning warmth. Sylvia had begun to embroider little nightgowns; Heather was knitting her first matinee jacket. Sylvia's thoughts turned to Les.

*It's such a lovely day. Spring's been a bit late arriving up here in the Hills, but the frosts finished weeks ago and everything's in full swing now we're into November; in fact, it almost feels like summer today. So pretty here too. There's pink heath and wildflowers along the creek, young fruit on the trees in the orchard, and Norm's wheat crop is looking good. Everyone's hoping for a record harvest now the drought is over. New life all around of course – gangly calves, sweet lambs, chickens. Oh, and the magpies are swooping. But then, they're only protecting their young. I'm thinking a lot about when our girls were small.*

'Les is going to be a wonderful grandpa,' she told Heather. 'He'll want to play football with the little fellow and make him a wooden train or truck; he's that sort.'

'But it might be a girl,' Heather reminded her.

'Well, as long as it's healthy. Which it will be, now that we've got you looking so well. A girl could have one of those little pull-along lambs. And all tiny tots love a hobby horse.'

Rosemary had arrived with a tray of morning tea for them. 'I reckon I've worked out what your last slave died of,' she addressed her sister. But Heather was unflappable these days, and only retorted that when Rosemary had a minute to spare she might like to start knitting some bootees. The reply was entirely predictable.

## SUNDAY 15 NOVEMBER

Heather is looking a lot better, now she is getting good food. Mother quipped that Mrs Jones must have been mixing too much Mex into the mince! The doctor says everything is going well. Apparently he can tell the baby is growing normally. Our star boarder has been with us for four weeks now, and is eating like a horse, sleeping about twelve hours a day, and hardly lifting a finger, except to wipe a few dishes or cut up the vegetables. What a life! You should have seen her and Mother sitting in the sun drying their hair yesterday, while I waited on them.

To be fair, they did offer me a cup of tea too, but I refused it. No, I wasn't in a sulk, though they thought I was; the truth is my tooth aches so much now that I can't drink anything hot or very cold any more. Mother gave me a Bex powder that has done no good at all, and has made me an appointment in town to get it filled next Wednesday. That can't come soon enough.

No word from any of our men. A few families are getting postcards from husbands or sons who are prisoners of war in Singapore. And others are hearing their loved ones named on a radio programme that is beamed out of Saigon. (They always play the record of Vera Lynn singing 'We'll meet again', which makes everyone weepy.) But nothing from Father. It makes me emerald green with envy when someone gets news, I must admit.

As usual, no one in the family wants to talk about the war with me. The adults give a sharp 'Shh!' and clam up if I come in and they're talking about burnt cities and bodies. The news is a mixed bag. Three big American cruisers have been lost in the battle for the Solomon Islands, but on the other hand the Allied forces have finally had a victory there. Heather even ignores the good news, like the Japanese troops being forced from their positions in New Guinea; they have apparently run out of food and turned back 'within sight of the lights of Port Moresby'. (That's from my latest cutting.) She should be hanging on to every word, since New Guinea is where her husband is!

I'm glad the general mood is happier, of course. The American Minister in Canberra has recently told President Roosevelt that thanks largely to Mr Curtin's inspiring leadership, the 'black blanket of despair' has now lifted in Australia. Thank goodness!

There's good news from Africa too, with the Allies avenging the defeat at Tobruk, and routing General Rommel and his Afrika Korps at a place called El Alamein.

It turned hot and windy this afternoon – a reminder summer is on the way. Grandpa Jack calls it 'a real stinker'. He thinks there will be a thunderstorm later. I came in to write this to get my mind off my pain, but that hasn't worked. Thump, thump, thump ... I'm going to get some cloves to suck now (Aunty Joyce's remedy for toothache) and then I'm off to bed. I don't even want tea.

�«▬»

When Rosemary, pale and wobbly, appeared in the kitchen and began rummaging among the spice tins and packets, Johnny said, 'You look funny, Rosemary.'

Bob looked up from his jar of tadpoles and laughed. 'You've got a fat cheek! Mummy, look at Rosie's bumpy face.'

Joyce in turn took one glance and went to find Sylvia. A minute later the two of them had decided that poor Rosemary probably had an abscess that might burst and poison her whole system. She must get down to the dentist the next day. They couldn't use the car though, because the new tyres on order for ages had still not arrived, due to Government red tape about registering the family as 'essential users'. A front tyre had blown out that week, while the spare had died months ago, leaving Grandpa Jack almost ready to pay four times the set price on the black market. It wouldn't be fair to ask Ian for the buckboard except in an emergency, so Sylvia would phone the dental surgery first thing and say they were coming on the midday bus. Mr Petie would be sure to fit them in later that afternoon.

Rosemary was still awake and in agony long after the rest of the family had gone to bed. Distant thunder rumbling to the north and occasional flickers of sheet lightning along the ridge were a further distraction, even when she pulled the curtains closer and hid her head under the blankets. Then just as she began to doze at last, a jagged shaft that lit the whole room was followed instantly by a terrifying crash of thunder.

She lay counting the seconds between lightning and thunder as more flashes and bangs followed, and waited for the rain. But it never came; it was a dry storm – the most dangerous sort. She knew why she could hear footsteps and low voices in the house: if you lived in the country you never went to sleep in a thunderstorm.

When another sort of light began flickering through the gaps at the edge of the curtains she sat up to investigate. The sky just over the rise towards Uncle Norm's was glowing. Then she smelt acrid smoke. At the same moment as she shouted out to her aunt that there must be a fire, there was an urgent pounding on the back door. Audrey's frantic, breathless voice called, 'Norm's haystack's alight. Come as quick as you can!'

'No, not you girls! You're not fit to fight a fire – you look after the boys,' Joyce ordered Rosemary and Heather, who had appeared together. Overalls and a jumper hastily thrown on over her pyjamas, she was struggling into her boots, with Sylvia in nightie and overcoat only seconds behind her. A minute later, after Joyce had made Sylvia pull on some trousers if she didn't want to be lit up like a Christmas tree, they had both picked up the buckets and wheat bags that were always at the ready near the dairy, and were running through the back gate.

Since the boys didn't wake, Heather sat on Rosemary's bed and the sisters watched the changing skyline anxiously, as flames and sparks now shot skywards. For a few minutes the flames died away. 'I think they've got it under control,' Rosemary sighed in relief.

But no sooner had she spoken than they heard shouting, with the wind gusting up and even bigger flames billowing. The shed, which was close to their boundary, was suddenly silhouetted in the weird orange light. The sisters rushed to the kitchen window for a better view.

Explosions followed. They could dimly see the outlines of the firefighters. Engines were roaring as neighbours arrived and the tractor and buckboard were shifted.

'It's like watching a film!' exclaimed Rosemary. 'You know, you feel so useless because you can't hop into the screen to help with the rescue.'

'You're just plain odd,' was Heather's reply. 'I've never actually had the urge to get into a film set.'

'That's because you lack imagination. What if someone was attacking your hero?'

Once again the fire was abating, and the shed seemed still to be intact. They could see a tall figure – probably Ian – up on its roof. Soon Heather yawned, saying she needed to get back to her beauty sleep. But Rosemary, whose prospects of sleep were no greater than before this crisis, waited up to hear what had happened, head slumping on the table. A last burst of flames lit up the kitchen walls before the shouting finally abated.

It was 4.30 before Sylvia and Joyce returned. The men were going to guard the embers until daylight, and then Audrey would do a shift. 'It could have been much worse,' said Joyce. 'Rosemary, how about a pot of tea before we get the cows in?'

Rosemary headed groggily over to the stove, poked the coals back to life and added some paper and kindling.

They took turns to tell her how they had poured water round the edges of the haystack, beating at the licking flames and glowing ashes with their wet bags, while the wind gusted round them, blowing embers over their heads. The heat was terrible! Of course the loss of the newly revamped haystack was disappointing. Not a tragedy though, since there was abundant feed again this spring and they would make lots of hay at the end of summer.

But just as the fire seemed to be out, the roof of the shed had started to go up. There was panic again: if it took hold and the wind increased the next stage was Uncle Norm's house. Thanks to hard work and a bit of luck, the tractor and shed had been saved. There was just one casualty, the buckboard. Although they had shifted it, a stray ember must have blown in its open window, so by the time they noticed, the vehicle was well alight. That meant that neither farm had a means of transport, unless you counted the tractor, an ancient bicycle or two – or shanks' pony, Grandpa Jack's term for walking.

Rosemary suddenly felt faint with pain and weariness. 'I was hoping someone could – I don't think I'll be – well enough – for that bus trip tomorrow.' She put her head down on her hands, tears oozing from the corners of her eyes.

Sylvia gave her a dose of brandy with some aspirin, and helped her to bed. 'You should have told us you were too sick to make the tea,' she said. As Rosemary drifted into a stupor she could hear her mother and Joyce discussing how they could best get her to a dentist. They would see if Jack had any ideas.

*MONDAY 16 NOVEMBER*

I've had an adventure. Too achy and exhausted this afternoon to describe what happened, but I'll start writing the story as soon as I feel a bit better. I'll just say that my tooth is out, and although there's a *boom, boom* pounding through my entire skull, that's nothing compared with the sharp stabbing of that abscess. More tomorrow perhaps.

'Well I wouldn't be *askin'* you if it wasn't an emergency, would I? The girl's in a bad way. If she was a cow I'd be putting 'er down!'

Even Rosemary had managed half a wan smile at that. It was still only 7 am but, with Joyce and Sylvia busy milking, Grandpa Jack was already on the way to solving her problem.

It was so frustrating, listening to one side of a conversation. 'Not a bad idea, that. I'll ring the station. Okay, she'll probably turn up on your doorstep in a few hours. Thanks again, mate.'

'Well?' Rosemary asked anxiously; but Grandpa Jack was a man with a mission, stopping only to say, 'Ralph and I fought side by side in the Somme in '16. An' you don't never forget the debts you owe each other. Knew I could rely on 'im.'

He had given the telephonist another number by now, and was soon telling someone at the other end that he had arranged for Rosemary to be seen by a dentist in Mount Barker, but had no transport to get her there. Yes, *of course* it was urgent. 'The girl's sittin' 'ere 'alf crazy with pain. It's a cruel thing, an abscess,' he insisted. 'That's it – Scott's siding, the old one where they drop off goods sometimes. Two mile the city side of Nairne; by the cutting – that's the one.'

'Right!' he eventually addressed Rosemary. 'City-bound troop train's comin' by at about 8.15, an' it's goin' to pull in at the siding for you. You'll 'ave to be ready to 'op straight on. Next stop's Mount Barker – only about six mile, but it's a bit slow windin' through the Hills. You'll be there by nine, an' I'll tell you 'ow to find the dentist. Okay?'

'I suppose so. But how do I get back?'

'Same way. When you turn up the stationmaster will get you on the next train. You'll be 'ome by lunchtime with a bit of luck.' Grandpa Jack tore a page from one of Johnny's workbooks. 'Now 'ere's a little map. You'll find Ralph's rooms 'alfway down the main street. You've got a tongue in your 'ead, anyway.'

'Do you think someone could come with me?' Rosemary was looking at him doubtfully. This was all a bit daunting.

'Well, the rest of us 'ave been up all night. After the boys 'ave gone to school – it's okay, Mrs Gurner's takin' them – we're all goin' to bed for a few hours.'

Heather hadn't stayed up. She would ask Heather ...

But Grandpa Jack was a mind reader. 'An' your sister's not supposed to be exertin' 'erself. Where's your spirit, girl? You'll be all right. It's not all that 'ard to catch a train, is it?'

(Heather's a lazy cow, thought Rosemary.) 'No, I suppose not. Well – thanks for all you've done, Grandpa Jack.'

As he left Jack muttered, 'Anyway, when I was a lad we'd walk into Mount Barker of a Saturday night. When we was courtin', that is.'

A minute later Rosemary was shaking Heather awake. 'Hey, they're going to stop a train at the siding to get me to a dentist in Mount Barker. And you've got to come with me.'

# 28

*WEDNESDAY 17 NOVEMBER*

Where should I start? Uncle Norm's haystack was struck by lightning on Sunday night, and it was a bit frightening to think how much worse the fire damage could have been. But I'm not going to write about that here, because by coincidence my composition topic for English this week is 'Fire!'. I'm going to use my imagination and pretend I was out there in the middle of the night fighting back the flames and helping save the shed with the buckboard in it. Even if it's not all true, a carbon copy of the story should remind me of what really happened.

(Another reminder to myself: if I want a really good mark, try to avoid clichés as well as weak similes.)

There are two other stories to be told, mine and the tale of bravery I'm saving up to tell Johnny when I have time alone with him. I'll write it down one day after I've caught up with my schoolwork. Tonight I'll start with me standing at the siding, waiting for that train, and Heather yawning at my side, when we should have been sitting down to breakfast.

Mother says I was selfish to drag Heather out of bed to go with me, considering her 'condition'. She would have stopped her going if it hadn't been milking time when we plodded down to the siding. I do feel a tiny bit guilty, and I must say Heather didn't come too willingly; but I reckon it didn't hurt her to give me a bit of support for once. Getting out of bed early to go on a little train trip isn't going to make that much difference to her, is it?

We only had to stand there for ten minutes – Heather munching on a chunk of bread she grabbed on the way out – before we heard the puffing and rattling of a train, followed by its usual warning toot as it emerged from the cutting, the early sunlight turning its smoke yellow. Sure enough a troop train was slowing down for us. The guard popped his head out the door of the nearest carriage and helped haul us both on board.

It was like stepping into another world – and not an inviting one. I had often glimpsed all those soldiers crammed in like sheep in saleyard pens, but a glimpse doesn't immerse you in close-up sounds, sights and smells. Especially smells; I've just checked my dictionary as my English tutor suggested last week, and have come up with the word foetid. It means foul, offensive, stinking. Not that those poor men in shoddy, filthy uniforms could help being the way they were. They still wore the uniforms they had fought in overseas; one apologised that they hadn't been able to wash properly since they left Brisbane over a week ago. The only water they could get between stops at stations for meals was the odd pannikin full taken from the boiler up the front if they ever got the chance.

Apart from them all looking so weary and unshaven, I could see at a glance that some of the men were wounded, and others sick. But they were all so nice! We were given a right royal welcome as they steadied us when the train set off with a jerk, a jolt and a screech, before settling into a swaying *clackety-clack*. Then they helped us into seats that had been hastily vacated.

'What the hell are youse two angels doin' 'ere?' asked the grinning redheaded beanpole of a young man next to me.

'You mind your language now there's ladies on board, Blue,' someone butted in. And a man stretched out full length in a luggage rack called down that we'd better watch out for Blue – he'd be wanting our names and phone numbers any minute. Not him though; he was on his way home to his wife and little boy for the first time for eighteen months.

'Yeah,' another voice broke in, 'and she'll keep you more than busy, won't she?'

'Never mind the wife. All I want is a hot bath and a good feed.'

After we'd managed to explain why the train had stopped for us, in between their banter, I got lots of expressions of sympathy. Now I knew the worst of my ordeal would be over in an hour or two, I felt as if what I was going through was nothing compared to the state of some of these men. One, who looked a bit like Kyle, and no older, had lost an arm … Some of them were feverish too. A few had a pink rash, while a couple had familiar-looking scabby spots. Sure enough we were asked, 'Have you both had chicken pox? That's what we reckon Morgs and Chippy have got.' Heather remembered we had both had it when we were little – luckily!

I chatted with them in as friendly a way as I could. (It was getting harder to talk, as my jaw had by now practically seized up.) After all, they could have been members of our family coming home. But Heather sat very stiffly. She complained after we got off that the atmosphere was so claustrophobic – her big word again – and made her feel quite sick. I don't believe her; she hasn't had any real morning sickness.

The guard came back and squatted by the end of my seat for a few words. 'So we've got some stowaways on board!' he said. 'Hope you're not up to mischief like the last one I caught.'

He told everyone how earlier in the year a girl of fourteen had hidden away on a troop train coming across the Nullarbor from Perth to Adelaide. She was running away from home, and the troops covered her with a greatcoat every time a provost came by. (They are the military police, and the word's pronounced 'provo'.)

'What happened to her?' I asked.

'She would've got away with it,' the guard replied. 'Those provosts are as thick as two bricks sometimes. But the silly girl caused her own downfall. After all they had done for her – smuggling food in to her and all – she stole a case, a watch and two shillings. So when the blokes found out that she was a thief, they dobbed her in. Last thing I heard, she was taken to court as a neglected child, and sent to a reformatory.' The guard stretched and went on his way.

The men obviously liked having a new audience for their stories, and listening kept my mind off my woes until we got to Mount Barker. Here's another yarn.

When a couple of the men were on a troop train in Queensland, going to Toowoomba, someone had smuggled an eight-gallon keg of beer on board. They hid it cunningly in a small space next to the lavatory at the back of a carriage, and replaced the wooden panel so it was invisible. Apparently the provosts, who knew it was somewhere on the train, spent the whole trip trying to find it, with no success. As the guard had said, they were a bit thick. By the time the train pulled in, the men were all very cheerful, and the provosts just the opposite!

Of course Heather had to exclaim, 'Ugh! Fancy putting it next to the lavatory!'

When I told that story tonight, Aunty Joyce gave a sniff of disapproval and called them larrikins. But Grandpa Jack cackled and said, 'It's 'umour that's always kept us Aussie troops goin', you know. Laughter and pranks was our secret weapon.' I think he would have gone on to tell a few of his exploits, but Aunty Joyce, who was in a spoilsport mood, put an end to our talk.

One more detail interested me. It seems some of those men were quite drunk, not just merry. Eight gallons is a lot of beer! When they all disembarked, there followed a fierce brawl on the platform between the Australian troops and some American ones, with the result that some of the recent travellers were arrested by the provosts and bundled into a cage at the rear of the train, while others were carted off to hospital. I was told that later the prisoners would be paraded before the public in order to shame them thoroughly.

I've heard before that resentment of the Americans is growing. If our soldiers see them in picture theatres and suchlike, they give them filthy looks. It's apparently worst in Queensland. There must be lots of reasons – apart from the usual explanation that those hordes seem to be taking over half our women. (Reminder: I must ask Heather how poor Violet is. She never tells me anything.)

When we disembarked, to the sound of hearty farewells, we found the dentist easily. I won't admit to Heather, but I could have done it on my own. Mount Barker is only a little town. Once again I was treated very well, considering the dentist couldn't help nearly killing me in yanking out my tooth. (Oooh, that awful grating, grinding sensation as it was prised out ...) I sent Heather off window-shopping for half an hour, so she couldn't call me a sook if I cried or yelled. On the whole I think I was quite brave, and only recall emitting one strangled groan.

Now I have to keep my mouth disinfected, but all the nasty stuff is draining away well since it was a top tooth, and the gum is healing already. Mother tried to feed me invalid mush for a day, until I rebelled. Egg flips don't make me flip, but I really can't cope with fricasseed brains, even if they are nicely served with sippets of toast.

One thing I noticed while I was in Mount Barker: it has a high school. My scheming mind has filed away that fact and will quietly work on possibilities for next year ...

The return train journey was much more pleasant, because we were put aboard a first-class carriage filled with officers, which wasn't nearly as crowded. Also, because they were just setting off, the men (and some women) were all spick and span. I wasn't sitting with Heather, who squeezed in next to two nurses, so I was the only one to meet a young soldier called Donald – who had fought with Uncle Brian! Truth really can be stranger than fiction.

As I said, that trip home gave rise to another story. Next instalment soon!

⊶

It was amazing how cold the house still got most nights. Sylvia was scanning an old newspaper prior to screwing it up and setting the fire. Two more US destroyers lost ... Another US carrier sunk ... Big assault on Guadalcanal ... Heavy damage to Japanese ships ... All this blasted war news; no one followed it because everyone knew, after the web of lies and half truths they'd been spun all the year, you couldn't believe a word you read any more. Surely there was a happy story somewhere? Ah yes.

'Look, Heather – here's the winners of the Red Cross baby contest. Isn't this Mrs Patrick O'Rourke your old schoolfriend? Now, what's her name?'

Heather glanced at the newspaper her mother was holding out. 'Oh yes, that's Daphne. She was Violet's friend more than mine.'

'My, she did marry young. You'll be able to enter next year's competition, won't you? Bonniest baby – what fun! Violet won't be able to show her face at things like that though.'

'Have you heard from Violet?' asked Rosemary.

'Yes, I got a letter on Monday. She –'

'You might have told me!'

'Well, if you recall, you slept for about fifteen hours after I got you home from the dentist. Anyway, her only news is that her mother has got her a job in a uniform unpicking factory down the road from their place. Next thing to slave labour, she says.'

After Sylvia had lit the fire, Heather went off to help her with the dishes while Joyce put Bob to bed. Rosemary was left with

Johnny, who was allowed to stay up for an extra half hour, since he had turned nine the previous week. He had seemed a bit edgy and jumpy earlier, after his mother threatened him with the strap if his new cricket ball landed in the vegetable patch once more. But now, as his cousin towelled his hair dry, he sat propped against her legs and relaxed. The two of them were like brother and sister after eight months together.

'Johnny,' said Rosemary, 'When I was on the train on Monday I met a man who knew your daddy.'

# 29

This is the story I told Johnny.

'It was a bit hard for me to talk properly on the way home on the train, because I had a big roll of gauze clamped between my teeth. But Donald, the man sitting next to me, was very friendly and didn't mind that I was spluttering and mumbling, so I told him the names of all the people I know who have gone away to fight – my father, Jim, and your daddy.' (I didn't tell Johnny that I added Kyle's name to that list.)

'Brian Scott!' this man exclaimed. 'But I was in Tobruk with him – bravest bloke I ever knew!'

Johnny asked suspiciously, 'Did he really say that?'

'Yes, cross my heart. So I asked him what Uncle Brian did that was so brave. And he reckoned your father saved six other lives just before he died.'

'How?' Johnny had skewed around now, and was staring hard at me as I spoke. (I prayed that I could make the story sound good, without upsetting him with too many horrible details.)

'Well, first I have to describe where they were fight –'

'I know that. Daddy was in Libya. It's up the top of Africa – Grandpa Jack told me.'

Good old Grandpa Jack … (I never thought I'd write that!)

'That's right. The north. The Australian and British forces were defending the town of Tobruk from the German and Italian forces.

The German General – his name was Rommel – especially wanted to capture the harbour there, because it's a deep sea port, and he needed it to get men and supplies in if he was going to advance over the border into Egypt.'

'Where the pyramids are.'

I nodded as I fished into my pocket and pulled out an old envelope on which Donald had drawn a rough map showing the curved coastline, Tobruk and its port, and Egypt just to the east. Johnny studied it and took it all in. 'So what happened?' he asked.

'The Allies held on to it all the year. And your daddy's battalion was making it safe for supplies to come in by ship. Either a British or an Australian destroyer would arrive every night; they came to be called 'Tobruk Ferries', and they were very daring. They made about six hundred raids in all, arriving under cover of darkness with food and weapons. Letters from home too, so your father would have heard from you. When the ship got as close as it could, rowing boats would go out to it to unload supplies. Then the ship would carry away any wounded soldiers.'

'Did Daddy get wounded?'

'No.' (My stomach cramped, as I thought of what I must tell him.) Some nights he rowed out to the ferry, but more often he waited on the shore in what they called 'no man's land', keeping watch for enemy soldiers who were going to fire at those little boats – especially while the stretchers were being loaded on board. It was very dangerous patrolling there, because the ground was covered in land mines and barbed wire.'

It was so quiet when I paused to sort out the next bit that you could have heard a pin drop in the rest of the house. That's when I became aware that Aunty Joyce was hovering in the doorway; but I took a slow breath and carried on with my story. Too bad if she disapproved.

'Now, the Government needed our Australian men back to fight closer to home and, anyway, they were battered. They needed a break. So most of them left in October last year, except for your daddy's battalion –'

'The 2/13th!'

'Yes. The 2/13th stayed for another month. And in the very last week, on a night when quite a few sick and wounded men were being evacuated, your father, who was crouching behind a rock halfway up a cliff, spotted the dark outline of a man below him, creeping around the cliff face towards the shoreline where the stretchers were lined up. The enemy's right hand was raised. He had something in it.'

'A bomb?' Johnny's eyes were like saucers.

'Soon he could see that it was a hand grenade. If your father had fired and missed, the enemy soldier would have thrown that grenade; and those wounded men and the stretcher-bearers would all have been killed. So he made an instant decision to launch himself on top of the German soldier.'

Johnny was quite still for a minute. 'He died to save those men,' he said softly.'He really was brave, wasn't he?'

My voice was choked up by now. 'I knew you would be proud of him. And do you know how this Donald that I met knew the story?'

'No?'

'He was one of those wounded soldiers.'

Johnny just snuggled up and buried his head in my shoulder. I know that meant, 'Thank you for telling me, Rosie.' Aunty Joyce crept away up the passage.

'Now then, Rosemary,' said Grandpa Jack, ''ow much of that story about Brian did you make up? Joyce's been tellin' me about it.'

Rosemary blushed, but looked him in the eye. 'Only a few little details, like saying that Uncle Brian sometimes rowed out to the ship, and the bit about the German creeping round the bottom of the cliff. But the main story's all true. I've still got the map the soldier drew on the back of a letter. It had his address on the front too. You can write and ask him if you want to.'

'Hmm,' was all Grandpa Jack said, and went off lugging a cream can.

Rosemary had been waiting for Joyce to mention the matter, but now three days had passed, it seemed that wasn't going to happen. She wondered if it was a good sign that her aunt and Grandpa Jack had been talking. Not necessarily!

Grandpa Jack returned with an empty can. After a second's hesitation, he said, 'She's apologised to me. Joyce, I mean. About sayin' that I pushed Brian off to fight. Said she always knew deep down that Brian 'ad Australia an' 'is fellow men at 'eart, an' wasn't just doin' what I wanted. Or off gallivantin' to 'ave an adventure.'

'Hmm,' said Rosemary in turn. 'It's a pity she made you feel so bad about it all this time, isn't it?'

'A whole year, it's been. Hard to fathom, that one. An' jus' between you an' me, she knows somethin' else about Brian that would make young Johnny 'appy as a pig in clover if she'd only tell everyone. She's come to 'er senses at a good moment, anyway. Did you know that it's twelve month to the day since Brian died?'

'No!' A wave of sadness swept over Rosemary. She had been wondering if there was a reason why Norm and Ivy were coming over to tea that night, since it was a Monday. But when she had asked, Joyce just told her in a curt voice that it wasn't any sort of celebration.

Celebration or not, it was the warmest gathering Rosemary had been part of since they had come to the farm. The Scotts seemed to be starting to function as a family again. Joyce was even making an effort to be – yes, charming. And she actually nodded approval when Grandpa Jack poured them all a whisky, sherry or lemonade, then asked them formally to raise their glasses in memory of Brian.

'To Brian!'

The memories about Brian began to pour out.

'Do you remember when …?'

'Then there was the time he …'

'It's 'is sense of 'umour I'll always think of.'

Sylvia listened to their recollections.

*I suppose this is doing them all good. I'll bet you and your friends do lots of reminiscing too, Les.*

It was Johnny who had the best story. 'Do you remember the time Daddy came running in from the long paddock, shouting, "Come and see the elephant!"? And when we asked what elephant, he laughed and told us that one of the cows must have turned into an elephant overnight.'

This had been the highlight of all their lives. Of course the tale was now part of their family folklore. Bob wriggled with pleasure, giggling louder than anyone, even though he had only been two at the time. 'Mummy got cross and told Daddy he must be drunk, and said to stop wasting her time with his nonsense.' He was retelling Joyce's story as if he really remembered it.

'And I said, "I suppose it's a pink elephant, is it?"' Joyce smiled sheepishly.

'But *I* went back with him,' Johnny went on. 'And there *was* an enormous elephant, just standing swinging its trunk in the far paddock – you know, near the Nairne road.'

'What happened then?' asked Rosemary, pretending not to know the story.

Joyce took over. 'After he'd had a look at it close up and seen that it was all alone there, Brian went down to the house that the Gurners have now, to ring the zoo. And of course the man who answered got wild; told him it wasn't April Fools' Day, and they were fed up to the back teeth with pranksters calling them out.'

'Daddy left me to keep watch in case anyone came for it.' It was Johnny again. 'I stayed the other side of the fence, right away from its *enormous* feet! Then about ten minutes later this big truck pulled up – with 'Wirth's Circus' painted on the side. And these men said their first truck had broken an axle in the middle of the night when the whole circus was on its way into Nairne along the back road, so they had unloaded the elephant into our paddock, and towed the truck away.'

'We dropped everything to go and see our trespasser of course,' said Joyce. 'Before they could take it away, a photographer arrived. Someone on a train had spotted the elephant in the distance and told the paper. So Johnny and Brian got their photo on page three along with the story of the Scotts' unusual visitor.'

Grandpa Jack finished the tale while Bob ran to find the photo. 'Brian wasn't backward. Said 'e wouldn't charge an agistment fee if they'd give us a few tickets to the circus. So we all 'ad ringside seats the next afternoon – an' Joyce 'ad to apologise to Brian for disbelievin' 'im, before she got given one.'

They lit the big fire in the sitting room after tea, even though it was hardly cold enough. Somehow it felt good for all of them to be sitting round it together, the men smoking the last of their week's ration of cigarettes, and the women with their fingers busy as always. Heather and Sylvia were knitting of course, though this time Heather's bonnet was for Violet's baby's layette. Ivy was embroidering a handkerchief to put on a CWA stall, while Rosemary had been consigned to help Joyce sew the tapes on pillowcases made from bleached flour and sugar bags. The boys were lying on the hearthrug playing Chinese checkers. Only Ian and Audrey were missing, having agreed to represent the two families at a meeting in the town about produce prices.

It was Joyce who first spoke about Brian again. 'There's one thing that doesn't add up,' she addressed Rosemary. 'If that man was really over there with Brian, why didn't he go on to Malaya with the rest of the battalion? I reckon he makes up stories for every kid he meets, if you ask me.'

Luckily Grandpa Jack came to Rosemary's aid, because she had no idea what to say.

'For goodness sake, woman, that's what 'appens when someone eavesdrops! They 'ear 'alf the story. The man *said* 'e was wounded, didn't 'e? So it's probably taken 'im all this time to get fit again.'

'How do *you* know that bit then?' asked Joyce.

'Well I was listenin' in too from the porch, wasn't I? Always did 'ave excellent 'earin'!'

When they finished laughing, Johnny said he wanted to know more about Tobruk, because his new friend at school had been asking him about it.

'It's a desert,' Norm told him – with a wary eye on Joyce. 'All day it's hot as an oven, then it's freezing at night. Worst thing's lack of water. "Two pints per man, per day, perhaps" is the saying. Then there's sand, dust, flies, fl –'

'But tell me more about the soldiers,' said Johnny.

'– fleas too. Well, the Aussies like Brian hung on in their fortress there for so many months that they put paid to old Rommel's hopes of taking Egypt.'

'Yes,' Grandpa Jack took over. 'There's a story goin' round that Rommel admired their fightin' qualities so much that 'e said to Hitler, "Give me a battalion of Australians an' I'll win the war for you."'

'People are calling them the Rats, aren't they?' said Rosemary.

'You been readin' them papers again! That's right. General Rommel called them the Rats of Tobruk because the Germans thought they 'ad the Allies trapped – holed up like rats. But in fact our men was just bein' brave. Stubborn, maybe – an' refusin' to give in.'

*Not mice-minded,* Rosemary smiled to herself.

'We should be proud of them all,' said Sylvia.

*Les, will you have stories to make us proud of you? Of course you will …*

'Speakin' of pride,' Grandpa Jack went on, 'Joyce 'as got some good news to tell everyone.'

Joyce looked a bit embarrassed. 'Oh that –' She trailed off.

'Have we won some money?' asked Johnny.

Bob looked up from poking the fire. 'Are you going to have a baby like Heather is, Mummy?' he asked – which of course brought howls of laughter.

Then Joyce told them the news she had been hugging close for months. 'Brian's been recommended for a medal for bravery,' she said. 'The Military Medal.'

Their delighted responses came in a jumble, but she put up her hand and stopped them. 'A medal doesn't bring anyone back,' she snapped.

'Maybe not,' Grandpa Jack insisted. 'But 'is sons are goin' to be honoured to wear 'is medals in memory of 'im one day. An MM is pretty damn special.'

And Johnny crowed, 'Wow! Wait till I tell that to my friend Greg.'

# 30

*WEDNESDAY 25 NOVEMBER*
Father is alive!!!

We got a card today – not a proper handwritten postcard, but a typed message. It had his name, rank and number on the top, and then said:

> DEAR FAMILY
> I AM A PRISONER OF WAR AND
> I AM FIT AND WELL
> ALL MY LOVE
> Les

The best bit was that he signed it himself, in a strong hand that convinced us that it was genuine. We all broke down and cried, especially Mother, who kept sobbing, 'Thank God! He's alive! Thank God!'

I feel sorry for Aunty, but she was very gracious about it. I'm glad she began facing up to Uncle Brian's death before this came.

We think Father must be in the Changi prison camp. Let's hope we will hear from him often now. And, of course, we'll write straight away to say we received his message.

Mother can't stop smiling, and I even heard her singing 'The Sunshine of Your Smile' along with Frank Sinatra in the milking shed just now. She is starting to contact Grandma, the aunts and Father's closest friends to tell them the good news. We don't think we need to put a notice in the paper like some families do, as word will soon spread. I'm so excited!

Sylvia was walking on air, her head in the clouds, a smile on her lips, a song in her heart. Now there would be no more weeping when the radio played the tune that had become Les's favourite in the months before he left them.

*TUESDAY 1 DECEMBER*
Isn't it strange how good news is usually followed by something that dampens your mood? I've been dancing through life since hearing from Father. Then today I got a letter from Kyle – written just before he embarked for New Guinea to join the 2/27th battalion ... So he is gone, and I haven't spoken to him.

He says he tried to phone me, but the trunk lines were down, as happens so often. It was a lovely letter, of course, but now I know he won't be able to contact me for ages, maybe even months. (Surely not *years*?) And I'll be thinking all the time of the dangers he will face. At least while he was still training I knew he would be fairly safe.

I feel really off colour and headachy tonight. I thought it must be the result of this depressing news, but Heather seems to be the same way. We both picked at our sausages, and weren't even interested in Mother's bread and butter pudding. So perhaps we are getting colds or something.

A minute ago I felt hot, and now I'm a bit shivery. Think I'll go to bed.

Whoever would have thought that the two girls would come down with a childish malady like German measles? Since no one else in the district seemed to have it, they must have caught it from the soldiers on that troop train a couple of weeks ago.

First Heather came out in a rash on her face, and Sylvia, worried

229

her daughter might have picked up some dreadful foreign disease, immediately rang Doctor Carter. But when he called in on his way home – by which time Rosemary too had a pink rash on the back of her neck and felt very tired – he reassured them all that although they had almost certainly caught it from the troops, it wasn't anything either exotic or serious.

'German measles is just a mild illness. Stay in bed and you'll be right as rain in a day or two,' he told the girls. And ordered Sylvia, 'Give them some Clements Tonic to build them up.'

The boys had been watching. A doctor's visit was rare. 'Is it called German measles because the Germans are nasty?' asked Bob.

'No,' replied the doctor. 'German comes from the word germane, which means related to. The spots look a bit like real measles ones, but it's not the same disease at all.'

Rosemary was reminded of the way Mr Marryat always told you more than you needed to know, because the doctor added, 'Its real name is rubella. That comes from the Latin word for red.'

'Rubies!' Johnny crowed. 'You are both red like rubies.'

Of course, it was possible that Johnny and Bob were already hatching the virus, but that couldn't be helped, even if they missed out on performing in the Christmas concert at school and enjoying the Sunday school breakup. You could add Marjorie to the list too, since she had permission to come home early from boarding school on the pretext she would be needed to help with Norm's harvest. There was not much evidence she had lifted a finger, let alone a single ear of wheat, because she had spent most of the last few days over at Joyce's, bored as usual.

It would have taken more than a couple of spotty children to upset Sylvia these days. Her conversations with Les were taking on a new lease of life since the welcome arrival of that card – even if its message was obviously not a personal one. At least he was strong enough to sign his name …

*Now that we know you are safe and well, Les, and the Japanese don't seem to be too intent on invading us any more, we can go ahead and enjoy life a bit more.*

'Give me your smile, the love-light in your eyes,' she hummed as she pushed the carpet sweeper along Joyce's threadbare hallway runner.

Joyce was writing Christmas letters already, with Beryl in Sydney first on the list, as hers had the furthest to travel. She was making up for last Christmas, when she hadn't sent cards, only formal replies to all the letters of condolence she had received.

Soon Beryl's reply came. 'A shame about the German measles. I hope the boys don't miss their concerts. Lots of schools over this way have closed early because of epidemics, since those soldiers coming back from abroad have brought in every disease known to man. They can't help it, of course – they must have lived among such filth over there.

'As for the Americans – well, they're outwearing their welcome in Sydney. Yes, you have to have sympathy for them, because each and every one of them is someone's precious son, after all. We all know they are missing home and friends, and frightened of what is to come. But some sections of the public are becoming quite hostile towards them. Have you heard this little ditty, Joyce?

*They saved us from the Japs*
*Perhaps;*
*But the place is at present too Yankful*
*For us to be decently thankful.*

Clever, isn't it?'

'Listen to this everyone,' Joyce ordered at the tea table, pulling Beryl's letter from her apron pocket. And for once, her contribution to the night's conversation made them laugh.

CHRISTMAS DAY, 1942

Happy Christmas, Father! And Kyle, and Jim. I just had to write that.

It's only 3 pm, but I'm almost the only person awake round here, except for Johnny and Bob. Even they have been sent to lie down and read the comics from their Christmas stockings before they go outside with their new beach bats and ball. Heather says she will play Snakes and Ladders with them later, and they will be getting more presents from their cousins, so they are having a happy day. We have all stuffed ourselves with turkey, lots of roast vegetables and plum pudding smothered in brandy custard; and now the adults are taking off a couple of well-earned hours. Of course there's been a week's drudgery getting ready for all this. I got the job of cleaning the silver. The boys and I also made Christmas crackers filled with almonds and raisins, which was fun.

Too bad that it's what Grandpa Jack calls 'a real stinker of a day'; the sweat was pouring off us in the kitchen. We had hysterics over the boys singing, 'Dashing through the snow in a one-horse open sleigh'. And the first carol we sang in church began, 'In the deep mid-winter, frosty wind made moan …'

It's time we had some Australian carols, I think. Poems and other songs too. You should have heard the crummy song that Bob's class sang for the Christmas concert. (Yes, we all went; amazingly, neither of my cousins got German measles.) I know this one, because I had to help him learn it. It's from *The Book of the School Concert* and it starts: 'We're merry little children, for we've a holiday, And in the fields and woodlands, we'll dance and sing and play.'

It goes on to talk about weaving bright garlands of buttercups and daisies. Oh dear! Flinging cakes of dried cow dung at each other would be closer to the truth.

Johnny's item was a bit better; it was a poem called 'When I'm a Man', and different verses were about being a shopkeeper, or a teacher, or a doctor. (Too bad about the girls' jobs.) Johnny chose to be in the group of boys acting out the train driver verse, since there wasn't a farmer one. I know it off by heart by now, unfortunately:

*When I'm a man so straight and strong, perhaps I'll be a guard,*
*To wave the flag for starting, and to blow the whistle hard,*
*Maybe I'll drive the engine then, and make her puff and fly,*
*And send the sparks so swiftly up towards the sunny sky;*
*But whether guard or driver though just now I cannot tell,*
*I only know for certain – I'll be sure to do it well.*

Billy would like that one. Which reminds me the Marryats are moving. Mr Marryat has been made head teacher of a country school up north, at a place called Burra; too far away to visit easily. How many more people will move out of my life?

Of course, the American billets, Larry and Glen, have had to go somewhere else. Apparently their last night was also Betty's birthday, so Mrs Marryat made a cake for a double celebration. She was struggling with the icing, and doing a terrible job of it, when suddenly Larry, who had never once lifted a hand to do anything for her in all those months, grabbed the icing bag and said, 'May I help you with this Ma'am?' In no time the cake was looking like something from Balfours' display window: it turns out that in his civilian life he is a pastry cook! Mrs Marryat had to thank him, but in fact she was seething he had waited so long to make himself useful.

Here's one last verse before I try to forget Christmas jingles. It's from the closing item at the Sunday school breakup, and sums up the theme that is in all our minds today:

*Hear our Christmas music*
*Echoing from above,*
*It brings a joyful message*
*Of peace, goodwill and love.*

At lunch we all agreed that Christmas Day is one for families and thankfulness, so I'm not being even remotely glum. Mother is still especially cheerful these days.

I'll let myself muse on deeper matters when the New Year comes. It's time now for me to make a lettuce, tomato and onion salad, to take to Aunty Ivy's for tea. Then it will be home to 'sleep in Heavenly peace'. (That's if we don't all have massive doses of indigestion!)

Oh – I forgot to write down the verse that Grandma put inside the Bible she sent me for Christmas. I'll start with it next time, because I'm needed outside: Bob has just hit his ball on the roof.

*NEW YEAR'S EVE 1942*
In my mind I'm wishing a very happy New Year to all my family and friends, everywhere.

As promised, here is Grandma's verse, which is very well written, and seems a good way to look forward to better things for 1943 (although Johnny thinks it's soppy). She says it's from an old magazine and she doesn't know who wrote it.

> *Hold fast to thoughts that lift the heart*
> *above the crisis and the strain,*
> *There never was a song that failed*
> *to pierce its way through storm and rain.*
> *There never was a tide that failed*
> *at last to reach some golden shore;*
> *There never was a peace that failed*
> *to break above the fields of war.*

I wish I could be as optimistic as Grandma. We're all glad to say goodbye to the year that war came to Australia and took away my father, Kyle and Jim; and separated me from my friends and Grandma too. My only New Year's wish is for the fighting to end and all our men to come home safely.

One thing makes me as contented as one of our jersey cows chewing her cud, though. As I promised, I worked carefully on the idea of going to high school at Mount Barker next year, until finally Mother agreed that I could! Since I got good results from my correspondence lessons, I will be able to do my Intermediate Certificate as long as I get some extra coaching to catch up in French. Grandpa Jack, who is not nearly as disgruntled as he used to be, laughed and said he knew a bit of 'Parley Voo' from his year in France; I thanked him but turned down his offer of help! More usefully, he has pulled some strings, finding out that his friend Ralph the dentist's married daughter teaches at the school, and can give me a lift each day if I ride into Nairne by eight.

Note to myself: must insist on a bike without that cart attached!

It's going to be a very full life for me; long days and not much time for going out, or my own writing. Anyway, this diary Grandma gave me on my birthday is getting full, so I have decided that after today's entry, which promises to be long, I will save the last twenty or so pages just to record any special events.

I will keep filling my scrapbook with cuttings, but there is a sameness about the news these days, with the war dragging on in Europe and Africa and especially our region. One article said it could take another two or three years until the Germans are finally crushed and the Japanese 'isolated and neutralised'. What an appalling thought! Our forces and the American ones are making some progress in New Guinea and the Islands, but the fighting is bitter and there is great loss of life – not to mention ships and planes. The Americans have had terrible losses. This month, after Kokoda was recaptured, the fighting switched to a place called Buna, where the Japanese had made successful new landings. Then just this week the Japanese tried to withdraw, after our forces cut theirs in two. And so it goes on … Victories and defeats. Every day I wonder where Jim and Kyle are.

I know where Kyle's brother Leith is, he got in touch for Christmas. He trained at Woodside, and is very frustrated that his Battalion, the

48th, has been kept there, while the 43rd who have had less training have gone up to Darwin. He says the men are itching to get overseas, but when they complained that they wanted to see some action his unit was told, 'War is no occasion for rejoicing, and nothing to look forward to with any relish.' I have to say I agree. But it doesn't make sense to leave fully trained men just sitting here, does it?

Jim's parents talked to Heather before Christmas too. They are delighted to be having their first grandchild. They wish she would move back to Adelaide after the baby is born. When Heather told them she is half thinking about sharing a couple of rooms with Violet and her baby, if they can get them, they said perhaps they could divide their big bluestone villa into two flats and let them have one! Heather knew I heard all of that, since I couldn't help being nearby at the time, but she begged me not to say anything because she hasn't told Mother of her plans. I asked, 'What's it worth to keep quiet?', so she grinned and said I could keep Angus the bear forever. We had another childish slanging match – just like in the old days – but it was good-humoured one, and Angus is safely stowed away.

Last week we all gathered to listen to Mr Curtin's Christmas message, of course. The bit that I remember is when he said, 'We must make selflessness the guiding factor in everything that comes to pass.' Those last five words left me in a thoughtful mood, because I still have a premonition that something will go horribly wrong in our lives. Perhaps if I was less self-centred I would be more accepting of the hand fate is dealing us, and also not be dwelling so much on tragedy. I tried to talk it over with Mother and Heather the other day, and they just said I was going through a difficult teenage stage. Naturally I was furious. Heather added that I'm letting my imagination run riot since we saw *Wuthering Heights* last Saturday night in the Institute; she caught me wiping my eyes when the lights went up. It was magnificent (it stars Laurence Olivier and Merle

Oberon) but so dark and heart-rending. I got Miss Whyte to send the book too, in my last-ever batch, and have nearly finished it.

I even worry about Heather – something I could never have imagined a year ago! With Jim absent, we are all clucking over her, and I have to admit I already love that tiny baby; the doctor told Heather this week when she went for another check-up that it is about eight inches long now. She thinks she felt it move yesterday!

However, the doctor is puzzled that the baby seems rather small. He asked Heather if she might have got her dates wrong, and be only four months pregnant, instead of nearly five. But of course that's impossible, as she explained. What's more, the little heartbeat that can now be heard through a sort of trumpet is slightly irregular. The doctor tried to reassure Heather, saying that perhaps it was to do with the baby's position. He also ordered her to get more exercise, as she has put on quite a bit of weight. That tonic must have been too effective in increasing her appetite. I said I thought perhaps some farm work wouldn't hurt her, like taking over the care of the chooks, but she thinks gentle walks are what he meant.

Too much to write about: I should have mentioned that Violet had a little boy a few days ago. He's strong and healthy and looks just like her, apparently. Heather says that's a relief! She has called him Tony. She is determined to keep him and give him a good life. She told Heather she would never forgive herself if he went to a home where he didn't get lots of love.

I sent her a card and asked if I could come and see her when I go to town. Because this is my last bit of news: I'm going to be off the leash for a whole two weeks, having a holiday at Janet's house by the beach. What bliss! (Even if you have to walk around the barbed wire on the sand.) We'll swim and sun-bake, and go for walks eating double-coned ice creams. Janet will be checking out all the boys, and I'll be imagining that a certain special one is walking next to me, with his arm round my waist. I leave on the fourteenth.

# 3I

*MONDAY 15 FEBRUARY 1943*

This is my fifteenth birthday, but I've just lived through one of the worst moments of my life. Oh, what have I done??

I have been jolted back into that state of dread I was trying to overcome by the latest letter from Beryl in Sydney – which of course Aunty *had* to read to us all. I knew that Beryl's husband was a leading doctor at a big hospital, the Royal Alexandra. Now Beryl tells us that one of his colleagues, an eminent eye surgeon called Dr Norman Greig, made a link last year between a mother having rubella during pregnancy and an unusual number of cataracts in babies. When she wrote at Christmas Beryl didn't let us know that. But she's decided she should get in touch because, as if it wouldn't be bad enough for a baby to have damaged eyesight, this specialist has worked out the virus may be responsible for other physical defects in babies as well.

I felt the blood draining from my face: what if the German measles we caught on that troop train has affected Heather's baby?

Heather asked abruptly, 'What other defects?'

'She doesn't say,' said Aunty. As usual, once she has inflicted some mischief, she backs off and won't talk more about a subject. Mother glared at her and declared there is nothing to be gained by worrying unnecessarily about something as vague as that information, when there is every chance that all will be well.

That was probably sound advice; but it came too late. Heather turned to me and said, 'If there's something wrong with my baby, it will be your fault, Rosemary. You dragged me along on that train trip.' For once I had no reply. I ran off here to my bedroom, where I have been just lying on the bed in a state of shock.

I'll never forgive myself if something really is wrong with the baby. But it won't be, will it? As Mother has just come in and told me, I'm over-reacting and I must put the whole thing out of my mind. After all, there are a hundred things that can go wrong when you are pregnant, and you'd be a nervous wreck if you fretted about even a tenth of them. She says Beryl and Joyce have always been two of a kind – melodramatic to say the least.

*LATER*
Mother is right of course, and I've calmed down a bit. Audrey has crept in and had a friendly chat with me, which makes me feel better. Father wouldn't be proud of me if I go on being as difficult as I was a year ago when he went missing. So, whatever my private feelings, I won't say another word about this storm cloud hanging over us. And I hereby vow not to retaliate even if Heather taunts me.

Easter had come round again. That letter of Beryl's a couple of months ago had given the family a bit of a jolt, but they had soon put their worries aside, especially since Heather was keeping so well. Sylvia could see that her two daughters were still rather cool towards each other, but of course that was nothing new.

The prospective grandmother was in a reflective mood as she dressed for the Easter service, watching Heather in the full bloom of pregnancy calmly adjusting the hem of her best maternity smock at her mirror. They had all plodded through these uneventful months until today when, with Easter Day falling on its latest possible date and coinciding with Anzac Day, the adults at least were pondering gratefully on life and rather more solemnly on death.

'Time to go! Aren't you all ready yet?' came Joyce's managerial voice. Sylvia rounded up the young ones and made her way to the car, resuming her reverie. It amounted to a bi-annual report card for Les, taking her past the ride into town, through an uninspiring sermon and on to the end of the service.

*Why haven't we heard from you again, Les?*

She and the girls had sent Les half-a-dozen letters over the summer, detailing the small but important events in their lives, but goodness knew if he was getting them. To their great disappointment there had been no follow-up yet to that first postcard from Singapore. Since the gossip grapevine was heavy with fruit, Sylvia knew of several wives who had received another card. That nice woman at the Mothers' Union who had helped transport the wedding food to town got one that said, 'Mail received. Glad all well. Health and spirits good. Hope to see you all soon. Keep smiling. Fondest love to everyone. William.' Sylvia felt a sharp pang of envy when she saw it being passed around.

*I know you would be writing if you could; you were always a great letter writer. Or perhaps your cards are just not getting through. We'll just have to imagine that you are sending your fondest love, won't we? Anyway, we must count our blessings that we even know you are alive, because some poor souls haven't heard a word yet.*

Rosemary, the cunning little monkey, had got her own way about returning to school, and wasn't much use to them on the farm any more. At least Heather had taken on feeding the poultry, even making them warm mash in the mornings now the season had turned. Sometimes when Sylvia filled the sink with boiling water from the big black kettle to wash those blasted separator parts she felt a bit resentful. Still, she told Les, she knew he would have made sure his younger daughter went on with her studies. And even Sylvia realised, after reading that glowing report from the correspondence teachers, that it would have been unfair to stop the child. The English teacher had gone as far as to say that Rosemary was a highly intelligent and thoughtful pupil, with an exceptional command of language and a fine appreciation of literature for someone of her age.

Sylvia looked across at Joyce, who was at least paying lip service to the hymns these days. She wouldn't have been singing 'Now thank we all our God' a year ago. She was softening a little with each passing month, to the point of organising the loan of a crib and high chair for Heather's baby, scrubbing up the old wicker pram, and making sure she always had petrol to spare for the coming trip to the hospital. She and Grandpa Jack still had their regular scraps, but then leopards didn't change their spots, did they?

The boys were happy, especially Johnny. Sylvia thought he must have taken Joyce's good advice about standing up to bullies, because he wasn't being harassed any more, and had made friends with that tough little nut named Greg, who turned out to be a good kid when you got to know him. Johnny was growing up fast, and was responsible now for herding all the younger children along their road to school. Little Bob? Well, he was just a lovely, uncomplicated child. As for the wider family, she recapitulated for Les, the biggest event in Norm and Ivy's life had been the purchase of a new buckboard. Ian was still in love, while Valerie had apparently gone into the highly valued and very hush-hush field of code breaking (though they were not supposed to know that). Marjorie seemed to have settled into boarding school life at last – winning several Sports' Day ribbons – and even Grandpa Jack now admitted that Audrey, who was almost family, was a real treasure.

Staring absent-mindedly at a shimmering stained-glass window that featured Jesus the Shepherd with his flock, she itemised the state of the farm and the nation next. More work to do in the dairy since spring, with a new batch of young cows in milk after their first calving; so on with the business of supplying the troops. Mr Curtin was still not admitting openly that Australia was now unlikely to be invaded. He was, however, switching his exhortations to promoting the idea that the country must become the food bowl for the Army, its allies and even the people of Britain. Disgruntled that so many were treating the war as just an inconvenience, not a tragedy, he had asked how Australians could complain about being rationed to half a pound of butter a week, when Britons survived on a quarter of that amount.

The triumphant strains of 'Let all the world in every corner sing' brought Sylvia back to earth. Well, they had better belt out the last hymn extra loud to make up for the half of the world not singing. A few days later Sylvia updated Les.

*The Easter break did us all good.*

Heather had even had Violet's company for a day, and they had all made a fuss over her absolutely beautiful baby boy. Poor little Violet, she had such sad eyes. This was the first real outing she had had with Tony, and it had taken her a week to organise it.

*It's a real shame; he's a bonny infant, with bouncy black curls like Violet's.*

It was good that Violet had been there for the customary party over at Norm and Ivy's, where she and Heather had spent an age after lunch in animated conversation, making up for their time apart.

But you could never quite get inside the heads of these young ones, could you? When she asked the two of them if they were recalling the good old days, Heather had told her, 'No, we're making plans. I'm a big, grown-up married woman now, remember?'

'What plans?' she asked, and they shrugged. Neither girl would give even a hint. The incident had left her feeling a little irritated.

*I hope Violet isn't influencing her too much, and that she's not going to do something silly like moving back to town without consulting me, Les. Doesn't she know what a good wicket she's on up here?*

*SUNDAY 16 MAY*

'The child that is born on the Sabbath day is bonny and blithe and –' Well, I'm not sure how the old rhyme ends, but this is the birthday of my niece, Helen Lesley Smith, who arrived early this morning. At 7.23 to be precise. Heather went to hospital after tea last night, complaining the lamb's fry and jam roly-poly I cooked must be giving her the gripes, and pretending the pains she had been having on and off all day were really nothing. Then as she started to get in the car, I saw her gasp and double over (as far as she could with her bulky overhang); and when she straightened up again she looked really frightened. I'll bet she was wishing Jim was there to give her some sympathy – not that men are allowed to stick around when it comes to the hard part. Apparently most of them head for the pub.

Heather wouldn't share any details of what has been going on over the past months with me. And she never bothered to read anything about childbirth, just listened to all the old wives' tales directed at her. One day, I'll want to know all about the whole process. When I said this to Heather she laughed then jeered at me: 'Poor little sister! Don't you know how babies are made?' Which left me scarlet faced. She hasn't been very nice to me since Beryl – but I forgot, I'm not talking about that.

I haven't seen the baby yet, but Mother says Heather will be in hospital for a fortnight, so there's no need to rush. Anyway, it's always next of kin only for the first few days, because the mother is usually very dopy from all the ether for a while. She needs to rest and get her strength back too. Heather won't even be allowed out of bed for days yet, with the baby only being brought in for four-hourly feeds.

Grandpa Jack says (with his usual lopsided grin) that this fuss over birthing is all a load of nonsense, because peasant women often squat down and have their baby in the field, and then get back to work an hour or two later. You can imagine Heather's horrified reaction to that! But I think he has a point; after all, cows don't have two weeks off after dropping their calves. It's definitely a case of 'on with the job' for them!

About the baby's name: Helen is Jim's mother's first name and also Grandma's middle name; while Lesley is the more common female version of Father's name, Leslie. Unusual but pretty, I think.

Of course, Mother is busy telling everyone the good news. This baby has already received lots of presents, the best one by far being a big, lacy shawl crocheted by Grandma. Did I knit a little garment? No, I did not. Instead I have bought a book of nursery rhymes and folk tales. I am going to get Helen a book for every birthday. Mrs Marryat has already sent us a letter with a silver pusher and spoon set. She is very happy in her new town, where the other women are giving her the sort of support she always seems to need. Country people are like that. Which is just as well: all the children have come down with scarlet fever over the last two weeks.

Some general chitchat before I finish. Speaking of books reminds me of library books. I'm missing the ones I used to get sent from the Public Library, but I scrounge around and can usually find something to read. Luckily I have made a couple of friends who like reading too. When I sent Miss Whyte a final thankyou letter, she wished me luck with my future career (which made me feel very grown up already) and had typed up some new Australian poems for me, including one more by Dame Mary Gilmore. I have pasted that on the last page of this diary, because it is about looking back after a war finishes. It mentions bread again, like that other one

I recited to Aunty Joyce. I wonder if that's because the Bible uses bread as a symbol for life.

Father has been imprisoned for fifteen months now. Jim has been gone for about seven, and Kyle for nearly five. We don't know which of the skirmishes we hear about involve those two. Nobody gets letters from troops. The Allies are slowly inching back into the territories the Japanese overran so easily. The best news for the world as a whole is that the German and Italian forces in Africa were defeated and surrendered three days ago; the war on that continent has been won. Major progress! But the Germans still have a strong hold over Europe. So this time it seems to be 'Lose a few, win more'.

Closer to home, there's more sorrow. Uncle Norm has heard that Verna – the nurse from down the road, who just got back from overseas recently, was on the hospital ship the *Centaur* which has been sunk by the Japanese twenty-four miles off the coast of Brisbane. That's so cruel! Apparently the ship was fully lit, and had its red cross showing clearly. Today's paper says that 268 people died – medical staff and crew – of 333 on board. Some of the survivors drowned or were attacked by sharks, and only one nurse was pulled from the water alive. If only it could have been Verna …

It occurs to me that in ancient wars there were rules to stick to, like in a gentlemen's game of polo. But the Japanese don't play our games. I don't think I'll ever come to terms with the need to make war, even though I'm grateful to those who are keeping us safe. Whatever career I choose, I want to be doing something that makes my little bit of the world a better, more peaceful place – for children like baby Helen. What a sentimental mood I'm in!

That's my quota of pages, I think. Must leave a few to make progress reports on my new niece; and of course the last ten or so to tell about the end of this war and the return of all our men. That will round off my story well, won't it?

Eventually.

# 32

*FRIDAY 2 JULY*

I don't want to write, but I must.

Heather went for her six-week check-up with Helen today. Of course we all dote on that baby – so pretty, dainty and placid. She hardly ever cries. Heather, who is a very good mother, has read all of Dr Truby King's advice on caring for babies, because naturally she has a copy of his *Baby and Childcare*. So she knows you mustn't spoil them with cuddles, and have to be very firm about not feeding a baby more frequently than four hourly, even if it is screaming. But in fact, half the time she has to wake Helen to feed her. And that's rubbish about spoiling!

I can't put off saying this. The doctor thinks the baby is not very robust because her heart is weak. Its beat is still irregular, and sometimes Helen's face seems to turn a bit blue, especially round her mouth. Aunty Joyce said that is just a sign of wind, but she is probably wrong. Heather has to take Helen to see a specialist at the Children's Hospital in town in a couple of weeks.

Too upset to write more.


*MONDAY 19 JULY*

My worst fears have come true. My darling niece may not only have a hole in the heart, but she is probably deaf. This is what we have found out.

Heather saw a Dr Charles Swan, whose research in this field has gone much further than the Sydney doctor's. The statistics he has been keeping through the epidemics of rubella over the last two years are suggesting that the disease, if caught by a pregnant woman in her first three or four months, may cause heart abnormalities, sight problems, other physical defects – and especially deafness. Any of them, or all of them. Dr Swan's research is not accepted overseas yet, but he has no doubt his discovery is correct, and a world first.

As for little Helen, it's too early to know if her heart condition is operable, or how poor her eyesight and hearing are. If she hasn't been seeing much, or hearing practically anything, and if her circulation is bad, it's no wonder she is such a quiet, fragile little mite …

Dr Swan has put Heather in touch with two or three other mothers who have had the same misfortune, as they will be able to support each other. They have either had family members returning ill from other countries, especially Africa, or have caught rubella from their older children while pregnant. So Helen is the latest admission to an elite group – known as rubella children. It's not a club you'd queue up to join.

My heart is broken, but chiefly I feel numb. I've had a couple of weeks to prepare for this news, so I can face writing about it. I have a double burden though; I not only share the sorrow that all our family feels, I'm also weighed down by guilt.

My mind keeps playing 'What if?' What if I'd gone to a dentist in Adelaide before my toothache got so bad, so that I didn't have to go on that train? What if I hadn't eaten so many sticky lollies as a child to give me a rotten tooth in the first place? What if the haystack didn't burn down and leave the buckboard gutted? Should I blame God for sending lightning? You could go on doing this all day. But you can't ignore the obvious one: if only I hadn't been such a scaredy cat about catching that train alone.

Oh, I wish you could be here, Kyle. I need you so much.

They were all devastated about the baby's handicaps, but were putting on brave faces in front of Heather. With family members closed up like rosebuds, Sylvia found herself confiding in Mrs Gurner, who turned out to be wise beyond her years.

'That little pet is not a handicapped child; she's a *person* first – just one who has some problems. She'll bring you more love than you could ever imagine, and that will make you all strong.'

'But then there's Rosemary.' Sylvia's voice was choked up. 'She tries to hide how upset she is, but I haven't seen many worse actresses. She blames herself, you see.' She explained to Joyce's neighbour the new theory about the effects of German measles.

'I've already got poor Heather clamming up, and now Rosemary won't talk to me,' Sylvia finished, tears running down her face.

'Why don't you get Audrey to have a quiet word with her?'

Sylvia nodded and blew her nose. Their Land Army girl was, as Grandpa Jack put it, part of the furniture now.

Audrey listened patiently to Rosemary's litany of self-recrimination, finally stopping her in mid sentence. 'Look,' she said, 'even if Heather hadn't gone with you, she would probably have caught German measles from you a few weeks later anyway.'

'Johnny and Bob and Marjorie didn't catch it. And anyway – '

'The boys must have just been lucky that you didn't sneeze or cough in their faces. Their mother kept them away from you. And you know that as it turns out Marjorie had already had the disease.'

'None of that matters. *You just don't understand.* If Heather had caught it from me at home weeks later, she wouldn't have come out in spots until the middle of December. And by then she would have been over four months pregnant. Past the danger stage. So don't try to tell me I'm not to blame. *Everything* points back to me.'

The family got just one more card from Les that year. It brought as much frustration as joy, for it gave no hint he knew about Heather's wedding or the baby, even though they had posed for a family photo to send him as soon as Heather came home from hospital. If they hadn't learnt from others that most of the cards said standard things about having a fine time putting on plays and concerts, or 'working healthily', they would have been very puzzled. It said, 'We have joyfully received a present of some milk, tea, margarine and cigarettes from the Japanese authorities'.

*But Les, you don't smoke!*

Never mind, the signature proved again that he was alive.

The days and months dragged on. As rationing became more stringent they had to make do with whatever goods they could get, especially in the clothing area. Sylvia reported to Les that she had even made Rosemary a housedress out of a checked tablecloth, with enough over for a little sunsuit for Helen. Pity it was brown. While Joyce had produced a winter dressing gown for Grandpa Jack made out of a reject Army blanket from the Military Disposals shop in town. It had some red cord round the collar and cuffs, and looked quite smart. Over next door Ivy specialised in unpicking and re-knitting old woollies into smart jumpers for children.

They had done a lot for families round the district who were really struggling too. For instance, when Johnny said Greg always stayed home from school on the day his mother did the washing because he only had one pair of pants, Joyce had some made for him in no time out of a pair of Brian's trousers.

Most families got very little butter, and there were new strict rules that even stopped retailers selling cream to individuals. Ice cream factories were suffering, as all available dairy output was supposed to go to feeding the troops and Australia's allies. But since the farm could always quietly keep some butter back after filling its quota, Sylvia had been making fruit cakes for the Red Cross to send to troops serving overseas.

*I don't have to use fat or oil like most of the ladies do. It's such a pity I can't get one through to you in Singapore though, Les. But I'll make a beauty when you get home. I'm learning cake decoration from one of the neighbours – gradually buying up bits and pieces like nozzles and a revolving stand.*

By November, though, all her attention was focussed on helping Heather get ready to move back to town. Already Sylvia felt a void that even Les's absence had not produced, for, as Mrs Gurner had predicted, that precious, frail baby was at the centre of all their lives. Sylvia couldn't express these sentiments, instead only querying whether the two girls could provide for their babies adequately. And was assured that they would do very nicely when they pooled their extra coupons for baby food. Each baby was entitled to an egg, an orange and half a pint of milk a day, plus a small jar of Vegemite for the week. Moreover, as they would be sharing the care of the babies, Violet would be able to return to work part time. She was hoping to tee up a job at some classy restaurant called the Covent Garden.

Violet's mother had let her down again, reneging at the last minute on minding Tony, the very day that Violet had a job interview with Mr Ellis, manager of the Covent Garden. 'I forgot that I'm playing bridge this afternoon,' she said, 'and I can't back out because I would be letting down the team.' Anyway, the event was to raise money for limbless soldiers, so it wasn't just an indulgence, it was a part of the war effort.

'I can't wait to get out of here!' Violet exploded. After checking her clothes and makeup were flawless, she dressed Tony in the navy rompers and cream shirt with blue feather stitching on the collar that Heather's lovely Grandma had just sent, and angrily set about gathering everything she needed for a trip to town with him. Her heart was pounding: how was she ever going to get the sort of job she wanted with a baby in tow?

But her natural resilience had come to the fore by the time she got off her bus in town. Looking frazzled wasn't going to help, was it? And this wouldn't be the first time she had managed to fool others. She crossed the road to the Covent Garden.

Luckily little Tony was in a sunny mood, babbling to himself in his pusher. Violet took a deep breath as she headed up the centre aisle of the shop with its modern glass cabinets on each side displaying all manner of wonderful cakes, pies and pastries.

'May I help you?' called an over-zealous assistant, one of ten lined up. Head up, she kept going, back through the café section, and on to the door marked 'Manager'. She couldn't help glancing up the stairs: only a position as waitress in the best restaurant in town would satisfy her. She knew exactly how to do that job, and it would give her a perverse pleasure to watch society at play again; even if from the outside.

She carefully positioned the pusher to the side of the manager's door where it would not be instantly visible. Just as she raised her hand to knock, a voice behind her called out, 'Miss Violet!'

It was the same American officer who had broken the news of Chuck's departure, rising from his lunch table. When he saw Tony, he looked confused, and changed his 'Miss Violet' to 'Ma'am! Forgive me for approaching you, but – '

She charmed him with her most dazzling smile. 'That's all right. I always wished I could see you again, and thank you for … Well, you know.'

Apparently encouraged by her warmth, the officer overcame his embarrassment to blunder on. 'Did you hear about Chuck at all?'

'Never another word,' she told him wryly.

'Well then, I'm real sorry, I have to tell you this, Ma'am. He died at Morotai – some five or six weeks ago.'

Violet felt no grief at all. The paralysis creeping through her body made it seem as if she was observing the scene from a great distance. She managed to ask, 'Do you have any details – um, I mean, how did it happen?' And the officer told her that Chuck had simply been in the wrong place at the wrong time. He had been shot in the stomach by sniper fire when he was heading out to the latrines early one morning.

*Well,* thought Violet. *I'll think up a better story than that for Tony when he's bigger.* Every child's daddy should be a hero.

The manager's door opened, mercifully putting an end to their conversation, at which the officer bowed deeply to her, assuring her of the condolences of all the men. Throwing back her shoulders and forcing her mind to focus on the task in hand, she turned to face Mr Ellis, back at his desk. He was motioning her to wheel in the pusher.

She apologised first for having to bring Tony, saying that a friend would be minding him at night if she got the waitress position in the restaurant. When Mr Ellis asked her why she wanted this particular position, she explained that as she had been a frequent diner at the Covent Garden in better times, she knew exactly what customers expected: it was all about making them feel special.

'And if I just offer you a shop or café job in the day time?' asked Mr Ellis.

'I would turn it down,' said Violet. 'My child needs me too much while he is small.' She leant over to scoop up a sock that Tony had kicked off.

Right on cue, the baby smiled at Mr Ellis, who promptly turned into a doting grandfather, grinning a foolish grin right back. He picked Tony up, playing 'This little piggy went to market' with the now giggling baby's toes, before placing him on Violet's lap.

'You probably know our good reputation for looking after our employees' needs,' said Mr Ellis. 'We're a family business. Staff picnics, reasonable hours – and we try to be flexible with rosters. I've already noted your pleasant manner with one of our valued customers; does he know your husband?'

'The baby's father –' Violet buried her face in Tony's tight black ringlets – 'died recently in New Guinea. At Morotai.'

She got the job.

## SUNDAY 28 NOVEMBER

I'll take a break to pen my next update since I'm sick of studying for exams.

This time I'm writing because Heather is leaving us next week, and going to live with her parents-in-law at Prospect. Violet will be sharing the flat too. They are really lucky to get it; Heather says some girls have been looking for suitable accommodation for nearly two years. I've been quietly waiting for this to happen, and even Mother didn't seem too surprised, just resigned to the fact. Heather's excuse is that she needs to be closer to the Children's Hospital. I think she must be looking forward to not having me around each day to remind her of how Helen's condition came about.

Actually that's probably not fair, as she never shows any sign she blames me. I'm the one with the problem. As Grandpa Jack said to me last week, while rocking the baby in her pram, everyone else has forgiven me – if there is anything to forgive – but I must forgive myself. I haven't been able to do that.

Yes, I did say Grandpa Jack was rocking the pram! In fact, I suspect he will miss little Helen the most. Although he still flies off the handle at times, he has mellowed. He is very good at calming her when she gets going with the high-pitched squeal that she has developed lately. When she does get agitated, and her little limbs flail frantically, it's not a normal cry at all. The other day he took over when she was fussing while Heather was having a bath, and next thing he was cradling her and singing. Not a lullaby: it was that old music hall song, 'Don't sit under the apple tree with anyone else but me', which Father likes! The baby was watching his face intently, and next thing she dozed off. 'First time in decades anyone's liked my singin'!' Grandpa Jack exclaimed. 'Or starin' at my ugly mug.'

So Helen's sight doesn't seem to be too bad. However, I don't think she is hearing much. She doesn't startle when one of the boys slams a door or shouts suddenly, and doesn't seem to respond to people babbling nonsense words to her. It's too early to get a hearing test done, but none of us has any doubt she is deaf.

That's another reason why Heather is going back to town. One of the mothers Dr Swan introduced her to, Elizabeth Forwood, is moving heaven and earth to get the best treatment and education for her little girl Tiffany. At the moment she is ordering work sheets and information from America and teaching Tiffany at home, but she hopes the mothers can start a special school for the deaf. She says the last thing in the world that she would do is to put her child away in the Institution for the Blind, Deaf and Dumb, where even the youngest pupils have to live in. It's right down at Brighton.

Mrs Forward's husband is a POW like our father.

Anyway, the latest research shows that deaf children can learn to speak, especially if they get lots of help early, so she and Heather don't want their children taught sign language. Tiffany, who is two, already says a few words.

Not much more to report. The battles continue in various parts of New Guinea, the latest being Lae, and occasionally now soldiers are getting a week or so of leave before they move on somewhere new. That's one thing Heather and I agree on: we live in hope of seeing our men (if I can call Kyle my man – it's been so long). We heard of a father who wangled a bit of leave when he received news about the birth of his child, so Heather is disappointed that Jim hasn't got back. It doesn't surprise me at all; can you imagine the commander of a unit saying, 'You look a bit run down, Smith. Why don't you take a week or two off? Go and see the family.'

As for me, I daydream about Kyle, only sometimes I feel as if I just imagined how close we were. I go out with other boys, as he expects me to do, though mostly as part of a group. So far I haven't come close to falling in love with any of them, even when I get a goodnight kiss. But will Kyle and I ever be together? Will he still have time for me? He'll have a broader view of the world now.

This bit is for you, Father, in case you want to catch up with news one day. When I started this diary I wrote about the time you have lost. Well, now it's the lost years – I reckon stolen is a better word. Anyway, the US has invaded the Philippines, with General MacArthur going back there to supervise. There seems to be some disenchantment with the American involvement now, despite the amount that country has done to help us. I've been reading protestations of loyalty to Great Britain again (which will please Mrs Gurner!), and apparently Mr Curtin is becoming worried about the intentions of our 'American saviours' on the Pacific region. They have certainly lost favour with the public too: you hear people recite, 'Overpaid, oversexed and over here'.

Oh yes – Mr Curtin has just had an overwhelming election victory. Not surprising, considering the way he has held this country together. His colleagues are worried about his health though, and have warned him he may break down if he doesn't take things a bit easier.

So 1943's nearly gone, and a few more pages filled. I start my Intermediate exams next week, but am not worried since I have found the work quite easy. In fact I came top of my class and will be getting the senior Literature Prize at Speech Night. (It's not that great an achievement, as at least half the school's pupils – i.e. all the boys – seem to think that English is a useless subject for anyone who lives on a farm.) I've quite enjoyed school; it hasn't been all work. Sometimes the grey blanket of depression that hovers over me lifts and I even forget that my sweet niece is so damaged because of my selfishness. Then I join in mucking around with the girls in my class, whom our history teacher calls 'Giggling Gerts'.

Next year will be my last one at school before I can start university or get a job in 1945. Let's hope we will be back in our own home by then. If not, I'll board in town – but I'll be giving Mrs Jones's place a wide berth.

# 33

When Heather walked into the flat, back from an appointment at the hospital with Helen, Violet was standing stock still in the middle of the kitchen with an envelope in her hand.

'What is it? Have you got bad news?' Heather asked.

Violet's hand was shaking. 'No, it's a telegram – for you.'

There was no help for it. Her hand shaking too, Heather tore open the envelope. 'Oh – *oh*!' she shrieked, 'Jim's got a week's leave! He's coming home!'

Their squeals and hysterical laughter woke both babies of course, but that didn't matter. Heather swept up Helen and swung her in an arc. 'You're going to meet your daddy,' she crooned. Then realised that Violet, nestling Tony, had gone quiet.

*SATURDAY 18 MARCH 1944*

Jim has been home on leave, thank goodness. I was beginning to think that if he didn't get back soon, he might never see his little daughter. At ten months Helen is a delicate baby, hardly ever well enough to smile or play. Her crying is mostly a soft, monotonous wail. Mother says she looks as if a puff of wind would blow her away. We're all afraid that one serious illness could do the same.

Once again, Heather and Jim have only had a few days together, as travel takes so long. Apart from the rest of his journey down from Brisbane, It took him twenty hours on the train just to get back from Melbourne. No wonder people are calling the Overland the Overdue! Still, he's lucky even to get a week's leave. At first it wasn't granted. On returning from Milne Bay, where Australians lost so many men in their first victory against the Japanese, he was supposed to be sent straight out again to Borneo, but he was so desperate to get home that he was thinking seriously of going AWOL. The penalty for being absent without leave is a fortnight's detention, plus the loss of pay and other benefits. Not a good idea when you have a family to support. But in the nick of time one of Jim's superiors took up his cause, and got him a few days at home.

We all met at his parents' house the day after he got back. We had quite a party! I'd love to have seen Jim getting his first look at his little daughter though. Heather said it was just beautiful to see her in his arms. Jim, who was very thin, looked rather ill. He seemed to go off into daydreams sometimes, before shaking his head a bit and trying hard to be sociable. Who knows what he has been through? It must be strange for him to be part of the normal world again; imagine what it will be like for Father.

Imagining is all I can do too. I've given up hoping to hear from Kyle. Hardly anyone gets letters from troops, no matter where they are.

While we were in town that day Mother and I went to see Miss Browning, because she wrote us a note a few weeks ago in a shaky hand asking if we could call in before the end of the month if possible. We were quite upset to find she has had a couple of small strokes, so she has sold her house to a great-nephew (who can't believe his luck). Now she has begun clearing out all her belongings, ready to go into a nursing home. She had two parcels, one large and bulky, one very neat and tiny, ready for us 'lovely girls'. Heather's was the pretty tea set with the daffodils on it that mother and I admired, and mine is – the Maltese lace!

All the family came up here on Sunday for Helen's christening, which was just perfect. Violet and I are the baby's godmothers, and with no young man around to be godfather, Jim's father has taken on that responsibility. Grandma sent a smocked christening gown edged with fine lace down from Whyalla, and guess what it was made of? Parachute silk! Everyone joked that it will never wear out, however many babies we both have. I forgot to say months ago that mother has had Heather's wedding dress dyed pink and has re-made it as a cocktail dress. My sister (who, I must admit, is now far from ordinary) looked very stylish in it.

Of course we had another party afternoon tea, with the top layer of Heather's wedding cake used as the christening cake. It was still moist and tasty, since Mother makes excellent cakes. I decided to make another wish, like I did with the wedding cake. It turned into three wishes; I couldn't choose between wishing good health to Helen and wanting Father and Kyle to come home safely and soon.

Now Jim has gone again, Violet, who moved out with Tony for those few days, has gone back to their flat. The babies are like twins. Come to think of it, Heather and Violet are as close as sisters too. I confess I've been so childish in my criticisms of Violet; she's been more help to Heather in every way than I could ever be. I have a feeling that both of them will always be stronger because of the circumstances forced on them by this war. In fact I reckon it is good they don't have the luxury of simply sitting around waiting for their husbands to bring home the wages and make all the decisions and handle their affairs for them. I'm sure that's what Heather always expected of married life.

Only one cloud always hovers: our concern for Helen. Heather didn't tell us till after Jim left that the baby's heart condition is worsening. When she is a bit bigger and stronger, a decision must be made on whether she should undergo a heart operation.

In 1945 the family and the nation were trudging through that last dreary year of the war. For most wives and mothers, news of their loved ones overseas was so rare that it was no longer expected, and when a letter did come it usually had only a patchwork of uncensored snippets left. There had been widespread dismay when Mr Curtin suffered a severe heart attack in November 1944; it seemed unlikely he would be able to resume his duties.

Gradually though, inspiring stories of the D-Day rescues in France and other victories fed the feeling that the fighting was near its end. The phrase 'when the war is over' was increasingly on people's lips these days.

That's how it was for Sylvia, who looked forward to moving back to her old home when Les returned.

> *With Heather and Mum gone, and Rosemary off to board too, I might take up my cake icing more seriously, Les. I think I could earn us a bit of money by making and icing wedding and birthday cakes. I've done quite a few, and they looked lovely, if I say so myself.*

As once again months had turned into years, Sylvia was still composing regular family chronicles in her head for a husband who was by now a shadowy figure in her mind.

> *All of us are so very different, Les, yet our lives are intertwined.*

Liking that image she added another comment.

> *Some just with a twig or two, the rest of us completely entangled.*

Nothing was likely to change for Joyce and Grandpa Jack, she mused. Bound by their love-hate relationship, they would doubtless continue to hold their family together while running a very successful business. The young ones were all maturing, especially Rosemary, now she had moved to town to start her Arts degree. Ian was engaged to Wendy, and Marjorie was turning into a reasonably pleasant young lady. She even liked school now! Valerie, on the other hand, as abrasively assertive and self-reliant as ever, had announced she wouldn't be coming back to live. These days Johnny listened endlessly to the crystal set Grandpa Jack had rigged up for him, with an aerial heading out of his bedroom window and up to the tank stand; while Bob had an equal fascination for anything small that breathed and had fur, feathers or – especially – scales.

*Of course our Heather, Les, treads the roughest road. You know, I totally misjudged that girl.*

Their daughter's whole life revolved around little Helen's welfare. Thank goodness for Violet, generous, spirited, uncomplaining despite her own situation. Violet kept Heather in touch with the world and even got her laughing once in a while. She would obligingly swap shifts at work to be home when Helen was ailing or Heather needed to go to yet another appointment or Mothers' meeting.

You had to admire these rubella families who were spending untold hours fundraising to start an Oral Kindergarten for deaf children. Sylvia and Joyce, in tandem with Jim's parents, had organised a barn dance at Nairne, assisted by half the district of course. The city visitors all dossed down on the property for the night, voting it the best outing they'd had for years. Then every Monday Joyce sent dozens of rabbits, which Ian had shot, down to a shop at Norwood. By the end of the year they hoped to have enough funds to rent a building and hire a teacher.

But by April Helen's condition had deteriorated so badly that Heather was faced with an agonising decision. If her precious toddler had an operation to repair her damaged heart, the risks were grave. If she didn't, her chances of living a normal life were almost nil.

At the end of the month, when Helen convulsed and turned blue one night, Heather chose the operation.

*TUESDAY 8 MAY 1945*

It's over a year since I last opened this diary.

This should have been a very happy day, for the news broke this morning that the war in Europe ended yesterday, with Germany formally capitulating.

But VE Day has not brought rejoicing for my family. Today we held a funeral service for little Helen, who was buried beside my great-grandparents in our family plot at the North Road Cemetery. She didn't regain consciousness after her operation. And it was just a week before her second birthday.

Heather, Mother, Grandpa Jack with Aunty Joyce, Jim's parents, Violet and I were at the service. Grandma couldn't make the trip because her rheumatism is very bad. (Anyway, she still follows the old custom that decrees women should not attend burials.) Only two things saved it from being just the greyest day of my life. One was the minister's lovely talk in the little chapel, in which he asked us to recall something about Helen's life that had given us joy. (I thought of the night she laughed aloud for the first time; it was when I wiggled Angus the teddy bear over her cot.) And the other nice touch was the mass of colourful flowers from our gardens, spread like a pretty rug on her little coffin.

I'm dripping tears all over this page.

When I had a quiet moment with my sister, I just said to her, 'Heather, I'm so sorry.' I tried to go on, but I couldn't.

She knew what I was referring to. She gave me one of her familiar chilly looks for a split second, but then her face softened. She sighed and said, 'There's only one thing to blame, and that's the evil in the world. If we hadn't had this war – '

She floundered too then, so I finished for her. 'This damned war.' We nodded at each other, and she turned away.

That's all. We didn't cry or hug, or kiss and make up. We're not like that. But I will make it up to Helen one day, indirectly. Because tonight I have decided that after I graduate I want to work with children like my lovely niece, who are deprived of the chance to hear and speak. After all, these are two of life's greatest gifts, and words are what I use best.

# 34

*WEDNESDAY 15 AUGUST 1945*

THE WAR IS OVER!! This is VP Day – Victory in the Pacific. An historic occasion.

This morning I was taking an account payment into a business in Rundle Street for my landlady before my first lecture, and when I got there I found the office door shut. Then suddenly it opened and all the staff came pouring out – laughing, crying and shouting. They had all been listening to the broadcast. Of course any thought of work was abandoned for the day, there and everywhere else.

Crowds were jamming the streets, truckloads of cheering workmen were weaving their way through, and most of the shops closed their doors. But Allen's music store pushed a piano out on to the footpath, where everyone started dancing and singing. I stayed for a while, then went to Beilby's grocery store to see if I could get something special to take round to Heather's and Violet's for a celebration. All I managed to buy was an ancient bottle of cider. We drank it, and it was awful! But who cared.

Neither Heather nor Violet has a great deal to celebrate, but they were glad for everyone else. And at least Heather and I can look forward to seeing Father again. Then there's Kyle. I feel I hardly remember him, and don't dare expect that we will pick up where we left off. I can't help hoping we'll make contact again though. His sister did write a while back out of the blue to say he's all right, but added their brother Leith, who finally got as far as the Northern

Territory, came down with tuberculosis, and had to be discharged.

Why haven't I mentioned Jim? Well, it's because he got back to Australia a week ago, from a battlefield called Gona, and is in hospital in Sydney recovering from a bullet wound; as if Heather hasn't had enough worry. Jim is incredibly lucky to be alive, because that bullet went straight into his heart. But he had a pouch above his chest made of heavy webbing, which deflected the force of the bullet. The doctor in Gona who operated on him said he had to pull strands of the fibre out of the hole in the aorta! He is getting stronger and will be home in a few days.

Violet has been called in to work tonight, as the whole city will be flooded with merrymakers, and the Covent Garden is already booked out for two shifts. So I left Heather alone with Tony. He is like her own child, now that Helen is gone, and gives her a lot of comfort and pleasure.

At teatime the children of the family where I board were excited too. They told stories of the planes that kept flying low overhead at their school (East Adelaide) this morning. A couple of bombers even had their doors open, and airmen sitting with their feet hanging out, waving at everyone below. One of the children shouted, 'That's my father's plane! He's a fighter pilot.' Another said, 'No, it's *my* daddy.' And so on, as the little ones started copying them. Lots of them decided it was their brother, cousin or uncle, but it's highly unlikely that anyone was right!

I have just phoned Mother at the farm, where there is the same story of enormous relief. The boys had just helped them tear down all the blackout curtains. Aunty Joyce is waiting to hear from Beryl, our Sydney correspondent, because they said on the news tonight that the whole city is in chaos, with Martin Place, in the centre, a cauldron. Revellers are dancing in the streets, singing 'Waltzing Matilda' almost non-stop and throwing down torn-up paper from the tops of buildings. What fun!

Wonderful times are ahead.

One unfortunate event that I must record so that I'll remember to tell you, Father, and since I have mentioned him so often, is that our Prime Minister died just six weeks ago. It seems so wrong that he did not live to see the victory he gave his heart and soul for.

Enough of that. None of us wants to think about those atomic bombs dropped on Japanese cities either. We all need to believe that such a terrible event can only result in good for the world. Surely no country will ever go to war again after this?

# 35

FRIDAY 24 SEPTEMBER 1945

Just nine days ago I wrote 'Wonderful times are ahead'. How naive I still was to think that everyone has a quota of happiness and sorrow – and that we've had our share of the latter. The event I have to report is so tragic that I haven't got my own words for it. This is simply a factual account of how Violet died. Most of it comes straight from the newspaper reports that will be the last ones I will ever paste into my scrapbook.

Last Monday Violet went off to her job at the Covent Garden Restaurant, leaving Tony with Heather as usual. She normally didn't work on Mondays, but she was making up a shift she had swapped with a friend the night before because Heather had needed help in cooking a welcome home dinner for Jim and his family. Violet would have headed up to the second floor on arrival, to set tables, arrange flowers, put out menus and fold serviettes.

'At 6.25 pm flames from an overheated griller on the ground floor spread up a flue to the next storey, causing a refrigerator to explode. Within seconds the fire had spread outwards and further upwards, trapping ten young women on the first and second floors. Five of them died, and the other five were injured.'

(Violet must have jumped from the second-floor balcony.)

'The building was gutted within an hour. Adelaide is deeply shocked by this catastrophe, and it is said that it has nearly killed the owner, Mr Ellis, who was almost like a father to his "girls".'

Poor, beautiful Violet. To me she is the last victim of our war, for if her American lover hadn't got her pregnant and then dumped her so heartlessly, she wouldn't have had to keep working as a waitress. Violet would have made something of herself.

I'm forcing myself to write one more thing, because, as Grandma has just said on the telephone, a little ray of light always comes out of the blackest night. (Sounds like the poem she sent.) That ray is the joint decision of my sister, my mother and Violet's parents that Heather will adopt Tony and bring him up as her own son, with all of their support. Not that he will replace sweet Helen.

That's all I can bear to say. We must look to the future, and for my family that means Father coming home and a new start.

Now that prisoners of war were starting to trickle back into the country, Sylvia knew she would soon have to stop talking to Les in her head all the time; but it was a habit that would be hard to break.

*When am I going to see your name, Les? I've been reading those lists of POWs about to be released for weeks now, and we're into October. I know, they can't get everyone out at once.*

She was edgy, of course. Many of the former prisoners, they were told, needed to put on condition before they could return. That was why they were coming slowly by ship, and not being hurried home by air. Stories abounded of wives who were told their men were on the way, only to find they had been too weak to survive the voyage. Not to mention hundreds of prisoners being transported to work camps and the coal mines in Japan, whose ships, it was now known, had been torpedoed by American submarines.

Appalling tales that were beginning to circulate, about what the prisoners had been through, were even more disturbing. Many of the men were like corpses, just bone and sallow, parchment-like skin. Some, it was rumoured, weren't quite right in the head after all they had suffered.

*But not you, Les, surely? When I get you home, you'll have*
*all the care in the world. You'll be right in no time.*

All this anxiety was such a letdown after the jubilant mass hysteria that accompanied the sudden release of pent-up emotions when the bombing of Hiroshima and Nagasaki had brought the war to an end. Beryl's first letter from Sydney contained a newspaper cutting (which Rosemary pinched on her next visit) of a young man dancing in delirious joy and throwing his hat into the air during the victory celebrations. But Beryl was now doing charity work among families in distress or need, and in her most recent phone call she recounted stories of their feelings of futility, grief and disillusionment. Guilt too, in those who felt they had let their country down in Singapore.

In a moment of unusual clarity it occurred to Sylvia that some families who had been split for so long, or who had suffered bereavement, would never recover. And for some servicemen who carried memories they could not share, perhaps the war would never end. This was wisdom which, for once, she had no wish to share with Les.

*FRIDAY 19 OCTOBER 1945*
Today, at last, we have received word that Father is on his way home, and should be with us before Christmas. Mother, who has an ear-to-ear grin in spite of the strain of the last month, has come to town to give the tenants in our Dulwich house two months' notice to move out, and to share the good news with Heather, the aunts and her friends. So we will have Christmas there, and next year we will be a real family again.

Aunty Joyce will have the farm to herself. Well, she'll manage. Grandpa Jack has re-ordered that milking machine at last, and I expect he will hire a couple of 'good strong men' to boss around, as there will be plenty of them looking for work. The boys are happy, active little fellows these days, and at present are excited that they (and all schoolchildren) have been given silver victory medallions with red, white and blue striped ribbons. It's nice to make people feel appreciated.

And so I have reached the last page of my diary. This is where I will stop my story unless anything exceptional happens, in which case I can paste in an epilogue. Not that my saga has come to an end, of course. Life never divides itself into neat chapters, with all the strands tidied up, does it? It's especially deficient in the happy endings department.

I was a carefree child of eleven before the war began, and an apprehensive, self-centred fourteen-year-old when I started writing this. Now that I'm going on for eighteen I'm a different person. Sadder and wiser, as they say. Here are my latest thoughts:

What my family and I have gone through is nothing compared with the sufferings of millions of others; our troubles are three or four raindrops in a global thunderstorm. The world has changed forever. As for our own story, although we will all try to get our lives back to normal, I wonder if we will ever completely cast off our burdens. We certainly won't be glorifying war, as Aunty Joyce once put it. I already felt this years ago when I decided to let Dame Mary Gilmore write the last lines for me. Here is her poem; it is called 'Life':

> How shall I,
> Who have eaten the dry
> And unsalted bread of grief,
> Eat the sweet loaf of another day?

*Though it were in my mouth,*
*I should remember*
*That other bread –*
*Alway!*

# *Epilogue!!!*

*MONDAY 19 NOVEMBER 1945*

What a bleak finish that would have been! Let's try this one, which is the happy ending every writer wishes for.

Heather, little Tony and I went up to the farm for the weekend, chiefly because Audrey, who will always be my friend, was about to go home to Sydney. Of course I enjoyed catching up with Mother, Aunty Joyce, Grandpa Jack, Johnny and Bob. I admit I even gave old Bluebell a fond pat in the milking shed, and she butted my arm a bit cheekily. Then there were Uncle Norm's family, Wendy, the Gurners and others. We have a strong sense that we have all been in this together – sharing the hard work, the sorrows, the hardships, and some good laughs. We made plans for good times to come: when Ian marries Wendy, when Grandma comes to live at the farm for a while and, best of all, when Father comes home – which will be any day now. Audrey says she won't just be a shop assistant in her next job. I think she'd make a perfect farmer's wife! Heather has spoken tentatively of the new start she and Jim will soon make. Everyone had plans; but there was still a vacuum in my life. Until the phone in the passage rang just on teatime, that is.

Luckily I was the one to answer it. 'Is a Miss Rosemary Lister there?'

'That's me,' I said. Did this stranger have bad news for me? That all too familiar sinking feeling grabbed me again.

The voice went on. 'This is Nairne Station. There's a message that says there will be a newspaper to collect at Scott's siding a bit after six. Does that make sense?'

Kyle must be back!! I quickly thanked the stationmaster, slammed down the receiver and looked at my watch: a quarter to six.

Then I went into a dither. Was Kyle getting someone to drop off a letter, or would he be on the train? What if I didn't recognise him? What if the train went by so fast I didn't spot him?

'Pull yourself together, Rosemary,' I ordered. 'Be strong.' A minute later I sauntered out to the kitchen, hauling on my cardigan, and said in a casual voice, 'Think I'll just go for a bit of a stroll.' Bob pestered me to let him come too, but luckily Aunty told him tersely to stop being a nuisance. I left the house under the questioning gazes of my family.

I dared not wish for more than a note or a wave. (Surely not just a newspaper?) Yet I did wish. I could hear the train approaching for minutes before it appeared, of course; and hardly took a breath as it came tooting and clanging out of the cutting, enveloping me in that familiar cloud of smoke that turned from a grey mass to white wisps when it rose into the late afternoon sun. The platform, a-swirl with steam, shook under my feet as the engine rumbled by, hauling an assortment of carriages. Once again it was a troop train and inside, as always, were indistinct shapes. But with the last carriage passing, nothing had happened. A chill started to creep through me, from the head down.

Suddenly a kitbag, launched from the train's back platform, thumped down by the shelter. I gasped as the hurtling body that followed bowled me right over!

When Kyle and I had picked ourselves up we clung to each other, laughing and sobbing. I needn't have worried: the real Kyle was still there, his cheeky, lively expression blending into his now mature, gaunt countenance. And if I'd had any doubts about recognising him, there was that snowy hair. Not to mention those green, green eyes.

In between kisses I gasped, 'I can't believe you've done this!'

'And I can't believe you would doubt me,' he replied. 'I said the next time I saw you I would jump right off one of these trains and into your arms. So here I am.'

When we finally drew apart, we sat down on the siding's wobbly bench, just like when we first met. I couldn't take my eyes off his face. I told him it was pure luck I was at the farm, and couldn't help saying rather petulantly that he'd taken so long to get back that I hadn't expected to see him again. (I didn't add that it's just as well I'm not in love with someone else by now.)

He explained that since the war ended he had been stuck on a beach in Borneo for months. Not the sort of place where you could post letters. First the sick and then the married men were sent home, followed by the 'five and tuppennies'. The latter were troops who had served for five years, including at least two years' overseas service. Then, when another ship arrived weeks later, and he was about to board it, it was suddenly blown up in the harbour by a mine! He finally embarked on the *River Clarence*, enduring a dreadful trip in the holds, as only officers could sleep on deck. The ordinary soldiers were just brought up for meals of bully beef stew, curried sausages or the like.

'Anyway,' Kyle grinned his heart-melting grin, 'speaking of food, what's your Aunty Joyce cooking for tea?'

A day later, I'm still in a state of shock. So, have we started our 'happily ever after' life? I can only use the cliché: time will tell.

# Acknowledgements

The first version of this work of fiction was written in the early 2000s. Learning about the so-called rubella babies born during World War Two while I was researching a school history led me to delve further into stories of Australians at home in those years.

I have no regrets that the internet was not yet widely available for research. I read war histories and watched films; but it was trawling through many pages of 1942–1945 newspapers in the State Library of South Australia (just before they were digitised) that gave me a real sense of how life changed for families, especially the women.

I thank Wakefield Press for deeming this the right time for my refurbished *Troop Train* to steam off into the world. Working with its dedicated staff is a dream come true.

My author and illustrator colleagues, the Ekidnas – sharing a journey with me since 1994 – also deserve thanks for their continued support; as do a trainload of reading and travel friends and the May Gibbs Children's Literature Trust team.

I want to honour the dozens of interviewees, many of them now deceased, who added colour to my research. They generously gave me threads to weave into my story, ranging from slivers of memory and enjoyable yarns to comprehensive oral histories. Just a few contributors can be mentioned here. This rich tapestry helped me establish a sense of place, enrich my story, bring my characters to life and imagine how it *felt* to live in a country on the brink of invasion.

I am deeply indebted to the late Mrs Joyce Shephard, whose story was the catalyst for this novel.

The late Mrs Cora Barclay, another founding parent and then Principal of the South Australian Oral School, sustained me with her enthusiasm for my project.

The late Mrs Heather Powell, my much-loved cousin, who worked in a munitions factory and married in 1942, wrote me a memoir. She described everything she could recall about the wedding, suburban life in the ensuing years and the jubilation on the day the war ended.

Mr Collis (Col) Rogers was a retired Nairne dairy farmer. He and his wife Rita gave me a thorough insight into 1940s dairy farming, and he also had pertinent memories of his war service.

The late Professor Alex Castles had wide knowledge about and great enthusiasm for trains and the railway system. His information, shared with me over cups of coffee, was invaluable.

Lieutenant-Colonel Sven Kuusk helpfully read my manuscript to check details of military operations, ranks and service medals.

The late Major Len Opie had a seemingly endless supply of troop train anecdotes. I was unaware of his important status when he was introduced to me simply as Len on my visit to the impressive Rats of Tobruk exhibition at the Keswick Barracks Museum.

On that afternoon I also met the late Private Bill Schmitt. The next morning I received a letter in the post containing photocopies of the postcard that he sent to his mother when a POW in Singapore, and the official letter she received announcing that he was missing.

Wakefield Press is an independent publishing and
distribution company based in Adelaide, South Australia.
We love good stories and publish beautiful books.
To see our full range of books, please visit our website at
www.wakefieldpress.com.au
where all titles are available for purchase.
To keep up with our latest releases, news and events,
subscribe to our monthly newsletter.

Find us!

Facebook: www.facebook.com/wakefield.press
Twitter: www.twitter.com/wakefieldpress
Instagram: www.instagram.com/wakefieldpress